Praise for Boris Vian

"Vian has been canonized by a whole generation of revolutionary young people. . . . This fantasy of perishing purity is an affirmation of youth and innocence, laced with the biting humor of Jacques Prévert and Ionesco."
—*Newsweek*

"Vian often writes with great physical vividness, and his determined irresponsibility is underpinned by a real verbal talent."
—*London Observer*

"Boris Vian's early death robbed French literature of a novelist who was coherent while still modern. *Heartsnatcher* is an esoteric, surrealistic comedy about guilt, set in a deceptively familiar, almost ordinary locale."
—*New Statesman*

"The sheer linguistic virtuosity of the original French, in its Queneau-like brilliance, adds another dimension to the experience of Timortis."
—*Times Literary Supplement*

Other Works by Boris Vian in English Translation

Novels
Autumn in Peking
I Spit on Your Graves
Mood Indigo★

Short Stories
Blues for a Black Cat and Other Stories

Plays
The Empire Builders
The Generals' Tea Party
The Knacker's ABC

Poetry
Barnum's Digest

★also translated as *Froth on the Daydream* and *Foam of the Daze*

Heartsnatcher,

BORIS VIAN

Introduction by
John Sturrock

Foreword by
Raymond Queneau

Translated from the French by Stanley Chapman

THE SPRINGER COLLECTION
OF MODERN LITERATURE

HONORING

Norman & Mary Doyle Springer
Professors Emeriti

FOR OVER 75 YEARS OF SERVICE AND DEDICATION

SAINT MARY'S COLLEGE
of California

Originally published in French as *L'Arrache-cœur* by Éditions Pro-Francia Vrille, 1953
Copyright © 1962 by Éditions Jean-Jacques Pauvert
Foreword copyright © 1953 by Raymond Queneau
Translation copyright © 1968 by Stanley Chapman
Introduction copyright © 1989 by John Sturrock

First U.S. edition, 2003

Library of Congress Cataloging-in-Publication Data

Vian, Boris, 1920-1959.
 [Arrache-coeur. English]
 Heartsnatcher / Boris Vian ; introduction by John Sturrock ; foreword by Raymond
Queneau ; translated from the French by Stanley Chapman.— 1st U.S. ed.
  p. cm.
 ISBN 1-56478-299-9 (alk. paper)
  I. Chapman, Stanley. II. Title.

PQ2643.I152A8613 2003
843'.914—dc21

                                                    2003055446

Partially funded by a grant from the Illinois Arts Council, a state agency.

Dalkey Archive Press books are published by the Center for Book Culture, a nonprofit organization.

www.centerforbookculture.org

Printed on permanent/durable acid-free paper and bound in the United States of America.

INTRODUCTION

Boris Vian is a delight twice over: he is a delight to read and a delight to read about, because he lived his much-too-short life with the same openness, levity and cheerful insolence as you will find everywhere in his writing. The French as we know look up to Writers, who in Paris can be heroes; but Boris Vian refused to be looked up to, or to be stintingly typecast as a writer. Be a specialist in everything, that was what he advised, and he had himself the zest and variety of mind to be a specialist in extraordinarily many things. As a student at the end of the thirties he was meant for an engineer, and he eventually had two jobs as such, but they bored him definitively; his was an anarchic spirit, not cut out for work in offices or for regularity of any kind. Engineering turned from a profession for him into an amusement; he kept it up as a lover of old cars, as an inspired DIY man, and as the inventor of technological whimsies such as an elastic wheel. Work was all right only so long as it was not like work, when it was not too serious and not all the time.

Once he had become an ex-engineer Vian led any number of lives, as journalist, as writer, as jazz musician and publicist, as man about St Germain-des-Prés – as the prime mover indeed of that epically stirring quarter of left-bank Paris in the years immediately after the Second World War. The Liberation of France in 1944–5 brought with it the happy liberation of Boris Vian. He was twenty-four years old when the German occupiers were removed from Paris and how the sudden euphoria of that longed-for moment suited him. He already had strong American tastes, in movies, in crime writing, in SF, and in jazz, which now took off in France on a postwar wave of philo-Americanism. Vian was a fine trumpet player, in a style modelled on that of Bix Beiderbecke, and the groups he played with, amateur though they stayed, were the traddest and hottest in France. He played jazz and he promoted it. When its giants came across to Paris – Miles Davis, Duke Ellington, Charlie Parker – Boris Vian was their host and their friend on the left bank. But there was more than jazz to postwar St Germain, because its charismatic *caves* or underground nightclubs were where new ideas too got aired, the new doctrine of Existentialism first and foremost, with whose twin popes, Albert Camus and Jean-Paul Sartre, Vian also mixed. Camus, he found, could be stuffy and Vian preferred the boisterously convivial Sartre, but only as a fellow *cave*-dweller, never as a thinker – Existentialism was too abstract and overblown a philosophy for his materialistic tastes; indeed, Sartre's crushing masterwork, *L'Etre et le néant* (*Being and Nothingness*, no less) is cut punningly down to size in one of Vian's novels as *La Lettre et le néon*, a treatise no longer concerned with life, death and the universe, but with illuminated street-signs.

Vian's own writings were intended to amuse, not to browbeat. Their manner is that of the 'surprise-parties' (they were known in France by the English term) which he loved giving and loved going to when others gave them, unscripted gatherings where convention gave way hilariously to invention, and the more wayward the invention the better. He wrote a lot: journalism – he even had a column in Sartre's earnest philosophical monthly, *Les Temps Modernes*, under the byline of 'The Liar' – poems, stories, scenarios for films and for operas, translations from English, six novels, and three and a half plays (one was very short), not to mention his songs, anything up to four hundred of them his bibliographers reckon, written often to order and in a few minutes only, with a wit and facility that were the wonder of the trade. Vian couldn't sing but he went on stage just the same and sang them himself; one in particular got him into trouble, 'The Deserter', an angry make-love-not-war song which he performed during the emotional days of France's war in Algeria, when there was a good chance of his being beaten up or even killed by colonialist bullies.

Yet when he died, in 1959, Boris Vian's diverse and delectable works seemed to have died with him, the novels especially, which had been published by small, commercially pinched houses in the late forties and early fifties and had flopped, selling mere hundreds of copies. If he was known at all as a writer, ironically, it was for something which he had written under an assumed name, and not even an assumed French name; disguised as the 'translator' of a new American writer called Vernon Sullivan he had published four outrageously tough, full-frontal crime stories. The first of them, *J'irai cracher sur vos tombes* (*anglice* 'I'll go spit on your graves'), took him a fortnight to write, sold by the tens of thousands and was found to be too tough and too full-frontal by some: Vernon Sullivan was sued for indecency. The case went on for six years, there were fines, a ban, and then at the end an amnesty. Out of it Vian got a certain fame and full opportunity to establish his credentials in public as the most amusing, waspish and convinced of the new libertarians. *J'irai cracher* served him well but it may also, grotesquely, have helped to bring about his death. He died suddenly on a June morning, in a Paris cinema, watching the preview of a screen version of the book, a version he had refused to help with and which he did not expect to like. The heart weakness that he had lived with since early adolescence had finally killed him, at the age of thirty-nine.

A year or two later, Boris Vian began to be truly famous, when his friends got his novels published for a second time in new, and this time visible editions, and they were taken up in a huge way by the young. Vian had written the books when he was himself very young, all but one of them before he was thirty, and they are the purest celebrations of youthfulness, presented by him as an age of caprice, of imagination, of honest friendship and of an easy carnality. His new young readers found them irresistible, not least because they are beautifully literate without being literary, full of small verbal jokes and surprises, and in their casualness just the sort of reading-matter we need to work our release from the solemnities of a literary education. By the mid-1960s, Vian was a bestseller and was being translated in other countries; his most endearing and accomplished novel, *L'Ecume des jours*, was racing towards a sale of a million copies, and actually appeared twice in English, translated once by Stanley Chapman as *Froth on the Daydream* and simultaneously, less well I have to admit, by myself, as *Mood Indigo*. And of course when May 1968 arrived, with its benign if hopeless insistence that Imagination take power in France, Vian did better still, he was the very prophet the gallantly fantasizing students needed.

As a novelist he is funny, but not altogether funny, because sad things too happen in his books. In *L'Ecume des jours* young love is horribly blighted, by a strange, encroaching disease which smothers the innocent girl. And in the same novel there is another macabre invention, an *arrache-coeur* or 'heartsnatcher', an implement with which that traditional seat of our emotions can be gorily extracted – one victim of it is a philosopher named Jean-Sol Partre. Whence the title for this, Boris Vian's last book, published when he was thirty-three and starting to take himself more seriously as a writer. *Heartsnatcher* is unlike his earlier novels; it is equally as inventive as they are, being set in a by no means natural landscape, it has some charming absurdities in it, but the mood is more sombre. Vian knew all his adult life that he might die at any moment, and though he lived with a splendid, indeed a famous insouciance, the thought of his early death could also oppress him. The very title of what is his most reflective novel incriminates that organ whose debility threatened him, and the themes which darken the story have to do with cruelty, with solitariness and with the curbing of our vitality by those who have power over us. The obsessive young mother, Clementine, is a worrying character and the effects of her obsession are bleak. This, then, is the most thought-out of Boris Vian's fantasies, a deeper book than the others, strange in the psychopathology into which it delves. Its translator, Stanley Chapman once again, has made what is called a 'free' translation, and very rightly so, for once; because it is no good merely reproducing French like Vian's as best you can, you have to try and do a Vian in English, to make words up, to invent. Mr Chapman has done a supremely good Vian here.

John Sturrock

IN

THE

BEGINNING

WAS THE FOREWORD

*

*

*

Boris Vian
has had a fine upbringing
and a fine education
he went to the Poly
which isn't to be sneezed at
although it's
far from being the whole story

*

Boris Vian
has tootled
on his tin trumpet
like no one else ever could
and was a master-rebuilder
of the jazz dive in France
he fought for Dixieland
although that's
far from being the whole story

*

Boris Vian
also helped
young Rock'n'Roll to come out of the West
although that's still
far from being the whole story

*

Boria Vian
has been caught
in the cogs
of the machinery of the laws
constructed by his fellow men
and has appeared
before their practitioners
because he wrote
I'll Go Spit On Your Graves
under the name of
Vernon Sullivan
although even that's
far from being the whole story

*

Boris Vian
has pseudonymbly
and nomdepluminously
aliassisted
this fictional author in composing
explosive spirals
of nitroglycerincognitro
and advocating
a further devil's trilogy
although that's still
far from being the whole story

*

Boris Vian
has translated
absolutely authentic
genuine American writings
crammed with grammatical complexities
before they could dare to petrify
the boggled mind and the ham-clenched fist
although such incredible skill
is still
far from being the whole story

*

Boris Vian
jumping on to the platform

catching the buskin
and conducting his overture
as if born on the boards
without being left busking on the pavement
has written a play
The Knacker's ABC
which has been performed
by real live actors
on a real live stage
and even this is still
far from being the whole story

*

Boris Vian
is a foundation stone
a rolling farawayfarer
an olympiadventurer
among the great mines
of the think-al-hikers
a sagent
of that peak of Parisian secret societies
The Algebraingels
and yet this is still
far from being the whole story

*

Boris Vian
has written
fine beautiful books
strange and pathetic books
Froth on the Daydream
the most heartbreakingly poignant
modern love story
ever written
Autumn in Peking
an obscure
forgotten
and unjustly neglected work
Pins and Needles in the Anthill
the most clandestine termitarium
of short stories
written about the war

but even all these are still
far from being the terminus of the tale
and are hardly even
anything
yet

*

*

for
Boris Vian
is just setting out
on
the
road to
becoming
Boris Vian

R
A
19 Y 53
M
O
QUENEAU
D

Heartsnatcher

FIRST PART

I

THE PATH dawdled round the top of the cliff. On each side of
it a border of blossoming calamines mingled with clumps of
overblown scarlet nightwort whose withering petals strewed
the surrounding earth. Sharp narrow insects had burrowed
thousands of minute holes into the earth; it was like walking
on frostbitten sponge.

Timortis sauntered along, looking at the deep bloodred
centres of the calamines throbbing in the flat sunshine. At each
beat a cloud of pollen rose and, soon afterwards, settled on the
dreamily trembling leaves. The bees had all disappeared on
holiday.

The soft yet curiously harsh and raucous sound of the
waves could be heard coming up from the bottom of the cliff
below. Timortis stopped and leaned over the narrow edge that
was separating him from space. Everything fell sharply away
beneath him, and spindrift hovered in the hollows of the rocks
like a jelly of jissom in July. There was a smell of barbecued
seaweed. Suddenly feeling giddy, Timortis knelt down on the
limp summer grass and reached out for the earth with his
hands. His fingertips met some nanny-goat droppings whose
strangely irregular shapes led him to conclude that somewhere
in the vicinity there must be one of those sodomite goats he
had thought long extinct.

Recovered and reassured, he once again felt strong enough
to continue his ascent of the cliff. Great lumps of red rock shot
down vertically into the shallow water, springing back almost

3

immediately to form part of the red cliff at the top of which Timortis had been peering over.

Black reefs emerged here and there, lubricated by the surf, with haloes of mist crowning them. The sun corroded the surface of the sea and then garnished it with a spice of obscene graffiti.

Timortis got up and started walking again. The path took a sharp turn. On his left autumnal bracken was mingling with budding briars. Salty crystals glistened on the bare rocks, left behind by the stacked coaster. Further inland, the earth rose sharply upwards. The path meandered round menacingly brutal masses of black granite, punctuated here and there with more nanny-goat's droppings. Yet there was not a nanny-goat in sight. The Customs and Excise men exterminated them because of their droppings.

He began to walk faster, and suddenly found he was in deep shadow because the sun's rays could not keep up with him. Refreshed by the cool shade he walked even faster. And the rows of calamines ran constantly before his eyes like undulating threads of flame.

Unmistakable signs indicated that he was approaching civilisation again, so he combed his straggling red beard. Then he strode off again lightly. Suddenly he saw The House between two crags of granite, eroded into gigantic lollies by the elements, that framed the path like the gate-posts of some mysterious and expensive masonic lodge. The road took another sharp turn and the house completely disappeared from sight. It was still quite a distance from the cliff, and right at the very top of it. As he passed between the two sombre blocks of stone it appeared again, an icy white, and completely surrounded by gaunt gesticulating trees. A white line broke away from the door, wriggled lazily down the hill and, at the end of its journey, joined the path. Timortis stepped on to it. When he had almost reached the hilltop he began to run because he could hear somebody screaming.

A red silk ribbon had been thoughtfully stretched from the

4

wide open gate to the steps leading up to the front door of the house. The ribbon ran up the stairs inside and ended in the bedroom. Timortis hastily followed it. The mother was lying on the bed, suffering the hundred and thirteen pangs of child-birth. Timortis dropped his leather bag, rolled up his sleeves and lathered his hands in a crude pumice trough.

II

ALONE IN his room, Angel was surprised that he was feeling so little. He could hear his wife moaning and groaning in the next room, but couldn't go in to hold her hand because she had threatened him with her revolver. She preferred to suffer and scream alone because she hated her swollen belly and wanted nobody to see her in that condition. For two months Angel had been locked up alone waiting for it all to be over; he meditated on the most mean, most minute things. Like a melancholy merrygoround he continually went round and round the room, having read somewhere that prisoners walked up and down like caged animals, although he couldn't remember which. He slept too, and when he slept tried to think of his wife in a callipygian kind of way, for the memory of her bulging belly when he closed his eyes made him automatically turn her over and only think of her from the back. Every other night he would wake up with a start. The damage, in most cases, had been done by then and there was nothing in the least satisfying about it.

Timortis's steps echoed on the staircase. At the same time the woman's screaming ceased and Angel stopped too, stupefied by the sudden silence. He crept to the door and tried to see through the keyhole, but the foot of the bed hid everything but itself from him and he painfully dislocated his right retina for no appreciable benefit. He stood up again and lent his ear to nothing and nobody in particular.

III

TIMORTIS PUT the soap back on the edge of the trough and picked up the soft towel. He wiped his hands and opened his bag. Water was sizzling close at hand in an electric cauldron. Timortis sterilised his fingerstall, stalled his finger like an expert and pulled back the bedclothes to see what was happening to the woman underneath.

Once he had seen what was happening he pulled them up again and said, rather superciliously, 'There are three of them.'

'Three...' murmured the mother-to-be with incredulous astonishment.

Then she got back to her howling because her belly suddenly reminded her that she was forgetting that it was hurting her very much.

Timortis took a handful of pep pills from his bag and swallowed them, knowing that he would shortly be needing them. Then, taking an antique bedwarmer from its hook, he banged it very hard on the floor to summon all the servants. He could hear the sound of running footsteps below, followed by a thunderously escalating attack on the staircase. The nurse appeared, dressed in white as if she were going to a Chinese funeral.

'Get the instruments ready,' said Timortis. 'What's your name?'

'I'm called Whitarse, Sir,' she replied with a strong country accent.

'In that case I don't think I'll be calling you,' groaned Timortis.

The girl said nothing and began to sandpaper the chromium plates, knives, forks, scissors, scalpels, tongs, etc. She went over to the bed. Its occupant suddenly froze into silence. Pain was raping her.

Timortis grabbed an implement from his toolbag and shaved the pudenda as if he had been doing it all his life. Then, with a brushful of paint, he drew a white Caucasian halo round the operational target. The nurse watched him as he did this, her mouth half-open with wonder, because her knowledge of obstetrics did not go beyond calving.

'Have you got an *Enquire Within?*' enquired Timortis, putting his brush away.

Having said this and done that, he bent down over his work and breathed on the paint to make it dry more quickly.

'Only got the B.S.A. Catalogue of Middle Eastern Arms and Tibetan Tandems,' the nurse replied.

'Damn!' said Timortis. 'It might have been able to tell us what to do next.'

Without listening to her answer, he let his eyes wander at will round the room until they stopped at the door behind which Angel was boring the pants off himself.

'Whose pants are being bored off behind that door?' he asked.

'It's the Master . . .' replied the nurse. 'He's locked in.'

At this moment the mother torpedoed out of her torpescence with an accelerating series of superanguished screams. She clenched and unclenched her fists . . . Timortis looked at the nurse.

'Is there a bowl anywhere?' he asked.

'I'll go and look for one,' the nurse answered.

'Get a move on then, you stupid creature,' said Timortis. 'D'you want her to spoil the sheets for us?'

She dashed out like a whirlwind and Timortis rubbed his hands with glee as he heard her go reaping down the stairs whitarse over blacktip.

He went over to the woman. Tenderly he stroked her fright-

8

ened face. She grabbed his wrist tightly in her two clenched hands.

'Do you want to see your husband?' he asked.

'Do I?' she replied. 'Yes. But first of all give me my revolver out of the cupboard . . .'

Timortis shook his head. The nurse came back, armed with an oval tub that was used for plucking dogs.

'It's all we've got,' she said. 'You'll have to make the best of it.'

'Help me to slip it under her hips,' said Timortis.

'The edges are very sharp,' remarked the nurse.

'So I see. I should imagine,' stated Timortis, 'that they're made like that especially to punish them.'

'That doesn't make sense,' mumbled the nurse. 'She's done nothing bad.'

'And has she done anything good?'

The mother's overloaded back rested on the edges of the flat tub.

'Now,' sighed Timortis, 'what comes next? This sort of thing isn't at all the right kind of job for a psychiatrist . . .'

IV

UNSURE ABOUT what to do next, he tried to rack his brains. The woman was quiet and the servant, her face completely vacant, stood and looked at him for instructions.

'Her waters have got to break,' she said.

Timortis agreed, although he did nothing about it. Then a thought struck him and he raised his head. The light was fading.

'Is the sun hiding?' he asked.

The maid went to look. The daylight was flying away behind the cliff and a silent wind had just started to rise. She came back looking worried.

'I don't know what's happening . . .' she murmured.

The only thing that could be seen in the bedroom was a phosphorescent glow round the mirror over the mantelpiece.

'We'll just have to sit and wait,' suggested Timortis, his voice soft and tender.

A smell of bitter grass and dry dust wafted in from the window. The daylight had totally disappeared. In a hollow of the concave shadow filling the bedroom, the mother began to speak.

'I'll never have any more,' she said. 'I don't ever want to have any more.'

Timortis put his hands over his ears. Her voice was thumb-nails filing through the green patina of copper. The terrorised nurse was sobbing. The voice battered its way into Timortis's head and beat a tattoo on his brainbox.

'They'll soon be here,' said the mother with a steely laugh.

'They're going to come out and they're going to hurt me. And that will only be the beginning.'

The bed began to squeak like an aviary. The only other sound that could be heard in the silence was the mother's heavy breathing.

Then her voice went on, 'This will take years and years . . . Every hour, every minute, may be the one I have been waiting for . . . And all this pain will have been only for that, so that it might hurt me for the rest of time.'

'That's enough of that,' snapped Timortis.

The mother was now screaming again, loudly enough to split her windpipe. The psychiatrist's eyes were growing used to the glow coming from the mirror and he could see the woman lying there, her body arched upwards, making an overwhelming effort with every limb and member. She gave out long successive cries, and her voice pierced Timortis's ears and echoed inside his head like a lost ship's hooter bouncing through a clinging veil of sharp fog. Then suddenly, between the angle of her raised legs, one after the other appeared two lighter patches. He could imagine what the nurse was doing. She had wrenched herself from her terror in order to catch the two babies and wrap them in linen.

'And one more still to come,' he said for his own benefit, under his breath.

The tortured mother seemed just about ready to give up. Timortis got to his feet. As the third baby arrived, he quickly seized it and helped the mother. She fell back, limp and exhausted. Silently the night split open and craftily the light crept back into the room. At last the mother was resting, her head turned to one side. Large dark blotches camouflaged the features of her labour-ravaged face. Timortis wiped his neck and forehead. He was surprised to hear sounds coming from the garden outside. The nurse was finishing wrapping the last baby, which she then placed alongside the others on the bed. Then she went over to the cupboard from which she took a sheet and began to fold it lengthwise.

II

'I'm going to bind her belly,' she said. 'And she's got to get some sleep, so you'd better go.'

'Have you cut the cords?' asked Timortis. 'You have to tie them very tight.'

'I tied them into bows,' said the nurse. 'They're prettier than grannies and they hold much better.'

He nodded an exhausted agreement.

'Go and fetch their father now,' suggested the nurse.

Timortis went to the door behind which Angel was waiting. He turned the key and went in.

V

ANGEL WAS sitting round-shouldered on a chair, every fibre of his body still ringing with Clementine's screams. Hearing the key turn in the lock, he raised his head. The psychiatrist's red beard gave him a shock.

'May I introduce myself? My name's Timortis,' he explained. 'I was just going by and I heard the screams.'

'That was Clementine,' said Angel. 'Did everything go all right? Is it all over? Tell me.'

'You're a father, three times over,' said Timortis.

Angel was visibly shaken.

'Tricklets?'

'A pair of twins, and one on his own,' Timortis rectified. 'He arrived very definitely a moment or two after the others. It's the sign of a strong personality.'

'How is she?' asked Angel.

'Fine,' said Timortis. 'You'll be able to see her presently.'

'She's got it in for me,' said Angel. 'She locked me in.'

Then, remembering the conventions of his forgotten manners, he added, 'Would you like a drink?'

He tried to get up, but found it hard to stand.

'No thanks,' said Timortis. 'Not for the moment.'

'What were you doing on the cliffs?' asked Angel. 'On holiday?'

'Yes,' said Timortis. 'And I think I'll be very comfortable here, since you've been kind enough to ask me.'

'We were lucky you happened to be near,' said Angel.

'Haven't you got a doctor?' asked Timortis.

'I was locked in,' said Angel, 'so I couldn't see to all these things. The girl from the farm had to do everything. She's a very faithful servant.'

'Ah! . . .' said Timortis.

They said no more. With his five spread fingers Timortis combed his red beard. His blue eyes sparkled in the sunshine that was filling the room. Angel watched every one of his movements and looked him over in great detail. The psychiatrist was wearing a black sharkskin suit with tight trousers that fastened under the instep and a long flared jacket with high buttons that made him look very slim. On his feet he had black patent leather Roman sandals, while a lilac satin shirt frothed and bubbled between his pointed lapels. It was all madly simple.

'I'm pleased you're going to stay,' said Angel.

'Good. So am I. Come and see your wife now.'

VI

CLEMENTINE DID not stir. She was resting on her back, her eyes looking straight up at the ceiling. Two of the little rascals were on her right, and the third on her left. The nurse had tidied up the room again. Silent sunshine glowed all round the frame of the open window.

'They'll have to be weaned tomorrow,' said Timortis. 'She can't be expected to feed those two, *and* the other one. It will be quicker too, and three, she'll be able to hang on to her pretty bust.'

Clementine moved slightly, turning her head towards them. She opened two stern eyes and spoke.

'I'll feed them all myself,' she said. 'All three. And it won't spoil my bustline. But all the better if it does. I'm not interested in pleasing anybody any more.'

Angel went up to her and went to stroke her hand. She moved it away.

'Don't do that,' she said. 'I don't feel like starting all over again now.'

'Just a minute . . .' murmured Angel.

'Go away,' she said, with a tired weary voice. 'I don't want to see you yet. It hurt me too much.'

'Don't you feel better?' asked Angel. 'Look . . . That tummy that disgusted you so much—it's all gone now.'

'And with the sheet that's binding you,' said Timortis, 'there won't be any signs of it left when you get up again.'

Using all her strength, Clementine raised herself up on her elbows. She spoke breathlessly and huskily.

'So I should be feeling better, should I? . . . just like that

. . . straight away . . . with my belly ripped to ribbons . . . and my back broken . . . and my pelvis twisted and tortured . . . and my eyes all bloodshot . . . I should take it easy, do as I'm told; be a good girl; get myself a nice trim figure back again; a pair of nice firm breasts . . . just so that you, or any other fellow who happpens to be around, can hold me down and inject me with your filthy junk; so that we can start all over again; so that I can go through all that agony again, swell up, put on weight, bleed and burst . . .'

With a wild movement she thrust her arm under the blankets and tore away the sheet that was binding her. Angel went to stop her.

'Don't you dare come near me!' she said, with a voice so full of hatred that her husband immediately stopped moving, dumbstruck.

'Clear off!' she said. 'Both of you! You—because you did it to me . . . And you—because you saw me as I was. Go on! . . . Clear off!'

Timortis went to the door, followed by Angel. As Angel stepped into the passage he was hit on the back of the neck by a football made of the rolled sheet that his wife had flung after him. He stumbled forward and hit his forehead on the frame of the door. The door itself slammed hard behind him.

VII

THE STURDY red tiled staircase felt slightly rickety as they both went down it together. The house was firmly constructed with broad black beams and thick whitewashed walls. Timortis tried to think of something to say.

'Things'll soon be back to normal . . .' he began.

'Mmm . . .' replied Angel, without much conviction.

'Got a lot of things to get sorted out?' queried the psychiatrist.

'No,' said Angel. 'It's just that I've been locked up for a couple of months. That's all.'

He tried to force some kind of a smile.

'It feels funny to be free again.'

'What did you do all that time?' asked Timortis.

'Nothing,' said Angel.

They went into a large room, tiled with red quarries like the staircase. There was very little furniture in it; a massive whitewood table, a low sideboard of similar wood and, on the walls, two or three paintings, very white, very calm and very serene. Matching chairs. Angel stopped by the sideboard.

'You'll have that drink now?' he said.

'Willingly,' said Timortis.

Angel poured out two glasses of home-made hop-scotch.

'Terrific!' gasped Timortis, showing his appreciation.

As his host didn't answer, he added, 'Tell me now. How d'you like being a father?'

'It's not much of a joke,' said Angel.

VIII

CLEMENTINE WAS alone. Not a sound in the bedroom. Only the occasional lapping of the sunshine against the bottoms of the curtains.

Thankful that it was all over, completely exhausted but relaxed, she passed her hands over her flat tender stomach. She felt regret, remorse, shame for her body—and forgot the sheet that she had rejected the day before. Her fingers tracked around the lines of her neck, across her shoulders and over her abnormally swollen breasts. She felt rather too warm— feverish, probably.

An indistinct sound, a distant rumble from the village, came in through the window. It was time for work to start in the fields. The snarls and yelps of animals doing penance in the darkness of their sheds could be heard too, but they were less angry at being left behind than they pretended.

By her side the rapscallions were asleep. Rather reluctantly she picked one up and held him above her at arm's-length with a delicate and dainty disgust. He was all pink, with a little wet mouth like an octopus, and eyes of raw wrinkled meat. She turned away her head, uncovered one of her breasts and brought the scoundrel down on to it. The tip of the breast had to be forced into his mouth; then he clenched his fists and drew in his cheeks. He swallowed down his draught mouthful in a single gulp, with an ugly noise like a guzzling gully-pipe. It wasn't very pleasant. It brought a certain relief, but it also brought a certain amount of mutilation too. When the scamp had had his two-thirds of a breast, he showed his

18

thanks by unclenching his fists and snoring like a pig. Clementine put him down beside her. Snoring, sucking and sleeping all at the same time, he went through the appropriate motions for each, a great gurgling sound coming from his swivelling mouth. He had some scruffy fluff on the top of his skull, and his soft spot was palpitating in such a frightening way that Clementine wanted to press on the middle of it to make it stop.

A dull thud shook the house. The heavy front door had just closed. Timortis and Angel had gone out. Clementine had complete rights over the life and death of the three objects which were sleeping beside her. They were hers. She caressed her heavy aching breast. There were gallons there to feed all three of them.

The second one pounced greedily on to the brown nipple that his brother had just abandoned. He sucked automatically while his mother stretched out. The gravel in the yard crackled under the footsteps of Timortis and Angel. The baby guzzled. The third one turned in his sleep. She picked him up and gave him the other breast.

IX

SECTIONS OF the Babylonian garden hung far over the cliff, and certain species of plants clung to the most perilous spots. Although it was possible to tend them there, the majority were left to grow wild in their natural state, like the amizaltzes whose violetindigo foliage is tender greygreen on the underside and patterned with coolly exuberant cartographical white veins more splendid than baroque tendrils; like the wild powaroses, with last year's marienbuds still clinging as umbrella-like skeletons of black straw to the straphanging yellowplush, occasionally bursting into monstrous nodes which thrust out dry tripartite flowers as unappetizing as meringues of blood; like the tufts of lustrous pearlgrey dreamrape; the long clusters of paletipped creamy ginger fenellacas, hanging to the lower branches of the monkeypuzzle trees; the ninastangas with more nests than leaves among their winglike clumps of jewelled astrakhan and tailfeathered collars of fossilised seagulls; every variety of becabunga whose thick green carpet sheltered frisky baby frogs; dark bristling marazardins with stiff corrugated leaves like the peaks of little crimson corduroy caps; hedges of seacrocus and green cormorant shag; bruinzozos and barbed bazabobos, finned and polished with petaleaves like the fringed palmy gamboge rays of drunken African cotton suns—five hundred petulant and five hundred modest flowers making a thousand varieties seeding in the dry recesses of the rocks, drawn like the scarred curtains of a cruel theatre along the massive crumbling garden walls, clambering out of the earth like ferocious forms of flowering seaweed, sprang up everywhere or slyly wheedled their way round the bold metal bars of the great gates. Higher up, the horizontal part of the garden was divided into lush cool lawns, separated by gritty gravel paths. Numerous trees cracked the earth, breaking through it with their varicose roots and their knotty gnarled trunks.

This is the spot that Angel and Timortis had chosen for their walk, still weary after a restless night without much sleep. A crystal tablecloth of fresh sea air hovered just above the whole of the cliff and, above that, where the sun should have been, there was a hollow flame burning in a square.

'You've got a pretty garden,' said Timortis, without attempting to add any more or go into greater detail. 'Have you lived here long?'

'Mmm,' said Angel. 'Two years. I needed to get away from everything. I'd become a failure at quite a number of things.'

'You had plenty of scope,' said Timortis. 'All isn't lost yet.'

'True enough,' said Angel. 'But it took me longer than you to find that out.'

Timortis nodded his head.

'People tell me everything,' he remarked. 'I end up by knowing what's inside most people. And while we're on the subject, could you suggest anybody I might psychoanalyse while I'm here?'

'You've got plenty of choice,' said Angel. 'You can have the nurse any time you like. And the village people won't say No. They're a bit coarse, but they're interesting—and they're rich.'

Timortis rubbed his hands.

'I'll need loads,' he said. 'I've got an enormous appetite when it comes to turns of mind.'

'How's that?' asked Angel.

'I can see I'll have to explain to you why I came here,' said Timortis. 'I was looking for somewhere quiet to carry out an experiment. Try to imagine a young Timortis as a completely empty vessel.'

'Such as a barrel?' proposed Angel. 'You were feeling thirsty?'

'Not at all,' said Timortis. 'I'm just empty. The only things I have are movements, reactions, habits. I'm looking for something to fill myself up with. That's why I psychoanalyse people. If I am a barrel, as you suggest, then I'm the one the Danaides never had a hope in hell of filling. Nothing sticks to me. I take people's thoughts from them, their complexes, their fears, their doubts—and none of it sticks. I just can't assimilate any of it; or I assimilate it all only too well... It comes to the same thing. Of course I don't lose the words, and I keep the vessels, the jars and bottles, that they come in, along with their labels. I know the right headings to file all these passions and emotions under. But I feel none of them.'

'And so you're making this experiment,' said Angel. 'All the same, are you really sure that you want to go through with it?'

'Of course I do,' said Timortis. 'This experiment is the only thing I do want to do. But when we come down to it, what exactly is this experiment that I'm talking about? That's the problem. What I really want to do is to make an *integral* psychoanalysis. I've been inspired to do it.'

Angel shrugged his shoulders.

'Has it ever been done before?' he asked.

'No,' said Timortis. 'The person that I psychoanalyse in that way will have to tell me everything. And I mean *everything*. His most intimate thoughts. His most terrible, heart-rending secrets; his hidden ambitions and desires; the things he dares not even admit to himself; everything; *everything*—and then everything that lies beyond that everything. So far no analyst has ever done it. I want to find out how far it's possible to go. I want to have envies and desires of my own—and I shall take them from other people. I can only suppose that if I haven't retained any so far, then it's because I've never gone far enough. I want to bring about some kind of transference of identity. It's horrible to realise that passions exist yet not be able to feel them.'

'Well, I can assure you,' said Angel, 'that you do at least have *that* desire—and that should be enough to prove that you're not quite as empty as you think you are.'

'But I have no reasons for doing one thing any more than another,' said Timortis. 'What I principally want to take from other people is the reasons they have for doing and feeling these things.'

They had nearly reached the back wall of the garden. Symmetrical with the gates through which Timortis had come into the garden the day before, but on the opposite side of the house, rose another pair of gilded wrought-iron gates, their high austerity breaking the monotonous pattern of the regularly laid stone walls.

'My dear chap,' said Angel, 'let me repeat to you that wanting to want something is quite enough proof of passion as far as I'm concerned. That's what made you set out on this adventure in the first place.'

The psychiatrist stroked his ginger beard and began to laugh.

'At the same time it also proves that there was something missing,' he said.

'No . . .,' said Angel. 'If you weren't going to have any desires, any prejudices, you'd have had to have gone through a thorough social brainwashing first. In that way you'd be scotfree of all influence, nothing would affect you, and you'd have no personal memories.'

'You've stated my case exactly,' said Timortis. 'I was born last year, just as you see me standing before you. Here's my birth certificate.'

He gave it to Angel who took it and read it carefully.

'That's what it says,' said Angel as he gave it back to him. 'But it must be just a mistake.'

'Of course you would know better than me! . . .' protested Timortis indignantly.

23

'They fill these forms in far too quickly,' said Angel. 'It's true that that's what it says—but what it says is wrong.'

'Yet there was a notice beside me,' said Timortis, 'saying *"Psychiatrist. Vacant. To be filled."* A notice! You can't argue with that. There it was in black and white.'

'So?' said Angel.

'So you should be able to see perfectly clearly that the desire to be filled didn't come from me,' said Timortis. 'It had all been worked out in advance. And I wasn't free.'

'But you were,' replied Angel. 'You want to do something —therefore you are free.'

'But suppose I had no desires at all? Not even that one?'

'Then you'd be dead.'

'Oh, damn you!' shouted Timortis. 'I'm not going to talk about it with you any more. You scare me.'

They had gone through the gates and were walking along the road leading into the village. The path was white and dusty. Cylindrical grass was growing on both sides, dark green and spongy like pencils made of gelatine.

'Anyway,' protested Timortis, 'it's just the opposite. We're only free when we don't want to do anything—and somebody perfectly free would have no urge to do anything at all. And it's precisely because I simply don't want to do anything that I've concluded that I must be free.'

'No, no, no,' said Angel. 'Since you want to want something, then you do *in fact* want something and all the things you've been saying are wrong.'

'Oh! oh! oh!' exclaimed Timortis, each ejaculation sounding a deeper note of outrage. 'Anyway, wanting something means being chained to that desire.'

'Not at all,' said Angel. 'Freedom is something that comes from inside ourselves. Anyway . . .'

He stopped.

'Anyway,' said Timortis, 'you're pulling my leg, and that's all there is to it. I'll psychoanalyse whoever I can and take their real desires from them, their wishes, the way they make their minds up, every little thing. And you're just trying to get at me.'

'Just a minute,' said Angel, after a moment's reflection. 'Let's try another experiment. Try for one whole moment—and be absolutely sincere about it—to completely stop wanting other people's desires, and see what happens. Try. But don't cheat.'

'O.K.,' said Timortis.

They stopped by the side of the road. The psychiatrist closed his eyes, seemed to take a deep breath and then relax. Angel watched him closely.

Something like a kind of coloured crack crept across Timortis's complexion and features. Slyly a paler shade of transparency seemed to absorb and take over the visible parts of his body—his hands, his throat, his face.

'Look at your fingers . . .' murmured Angel.

Timortis opened his almost colourless eyes. Through the back of his right hand he could see a black flint glinting on the road. Then, as he pulled himself together again, the transparency was washed away like the tide and his melting flesh grew solid again.

'There, you see,' said Angel. 'When you're completely relaxed, you just don't exist any more. There's nothing left of you. That's when you really look vacant.'

'Ah,' said Timortis, 'you're in a real tangle now. If you think that one conjuring trick is going to convince me . . . All the same, tell me how you did it . . .'

'All right,' said Angel. 'I'm delighted to see that you don't believe me and that the evidence of your own eyes means nothing to you. It's perfectly natural. A psychiatrist must have a lot on his rotten conscience.'

They had reached the outskirts of the village by this time and, with perfect unconscious agreement, they started to turn back.

'Your wife is looking forward to seeing you,' said Timortis.

25

'How do you know?' said Angel.

'I can just feel it,' said Timortis. 'I'm an idealist.'

Once they were back at the house they went straight up the stairs. The carved oak handrail flattened itself out obsequiously under Timortis's sturdy grip. Angel went into Clementine's bedroom first.

X

HE STOPPED on the threshold. Timortis waited behind him. 'Do you really want to see me?' asked Angel.

'Come in,' said Clementine.

She looked at him dispassionately, neither as a friend nor as a foe. He just stood there, not daring to sit on the edge of the bed for fear of disarranging it.

'I can't trust you any more,' she said. 'A woman can't trust men any more once one of them has given her children. And least of all the one that did it.'

'Poor Clementine,' said Angel. 'You've been through a lot . . .'

She shook her head. Being felt sorry for was not what she wanted.

'I'll be up tomorrow,' she said. 'In six months they've got to know how to walk. And in a year they'll be reading.'

'I can see you're getting better.' said Angel. 'You're your old self again.'

'I wasn't ill,' she said. 'And it's all over now. And it's not going to start again. They're going to be christened on Sunday. And their names are going to be Noel, Joel, and Alfa Romeo. It's all settled.'

'I don't think much of Noel and Joel,' said Angel. 'You could have chosen Sam, Ham and Honeylamb—or even Spam. Or Sabena, Subpoena and Ribena. Or even Ronnie, Johnny and Dubonnet.'

'You're not going to change their names now,' said Clementine in a business-like voice. 'It's Noel and Joel for the twins, and Alfa Romeo for the third one.'

27

And then, in a low voice, for her own benefit, she said 'I've got to get the upper-hand over him from the start. It'll be hard—but he's soft.'

'And tomorrow,' she went on aloud, 'they'll be needing beds.'

'If there's any shopping to be done,' Timortis offered, 'don't forget that I'm here. Don't be afraid to ask me.'

'Good idea,' said Clementine. 'Like that you won't be standing about idle and getting yourself into mischief.'

'That's not what I usually do,' said Timortis.

'But you might easily make a start here,' she replied. 'Run along now. Run along both of you. Order three beds from the carpenter. Two little ones, and another one slightly larger. And tell him to make them properly so that they'll last. And send in Tarse on your way down.'

'Yes, sugarloaf,' said Angel.

He bent down to kiss her and then stood up. Timortis moved out of the way as he went to the door. Then the psychiatrist closed it and followed him.

'Where's Tarse?' he asked.

'Downstairs . . .' said Angel. 'In the wash-house. Doing the washing. Let's have lunch. There'll be plenty of time to think about the errands later.'

'No, I'll go now,' said Timortis. 'You can stay here. I don't want to get involved in another discussion like the one we had before. They're very exhausting. And I've not been trained for that kind of trade. After all, it's pretty clear what a psychiatrist's job is supposed to be. He's supposed to psychiatrise.'

XI

TIMORTIS WENT out through the back gates for the second
time that day and took the road to the village. On his right
was the garden wall, then the face of the cliff, and, in the far,
far distance, the sea. On his left there were fields filled with
crops, sparsely sprinkled with trees, and divided by hedges
into irregular shapes. A well that he hadn't noticed in the
morning surprised him with its little stone coronet and its
patina of mossy ermine at the top of its two tall stone columns
between which a rough and rusty chain hung from a strong
ash axle. In the depths of the well, water was boiling, rising
to the rim in a froth that was immediately whisked away like
a daydream by the blue evaporation of the sky. The first
houses came into sight from a distance, and he was struck
by the crudity of their construction. They were U-shaped
farms, with the legs of the U facing the road. At first there
were only one or two of them on the right. Their yards were
laid out in the normal way. They were square, with a large
pond of black water—swarming with shrinkels and whimps—
in the middle; on the left-hand side was the wing where the
farmer and his wife lived; and on the right and at the back
were the cowsheds and stables on two levels, the animals
reaching the first floor by going up a steep thirty-degree slope.
The upper storey was supported on strong pillars whose bases
were decorated with crappy barrels into which the pschittr
littred above was shot and collected through the grace of
gravity. Any vacant cowsheds were used for keeping the
straw dry, the seed secure and the silage safely stored. And in
the cosiest corner, abundantly garnished with sweet-smelling

29

haybags, was the spot where the milkmaids were tumbled. The yard itself was paved with grey granite setts, their shapes sharply defined by the rubbery rods of the same spongy cylindrical grass which bordered the roadway.

Timortis went on his way without seeing any signs of life. The farms slowly became more numerous. There were some on the left too, now, and the road, which was growing wider, began to slope down on this side. Suddenly it was shadowed by a red stream whose flat meniscus rose almost as high as the surface of the road. Not a ripple, not a wrinkle ruffled the smooth water on which all kinds of unidentifiable and apparently indigestible scum, filth and rubbish was floating. Occasional odd sounds could now be heard coming from the empty houses, although they were far from filling them. Timortis tried to tabulate mentally the various complex smells that assailed him from the right of each set of buildings.

The brook intrigued and fascinated him. At first there had been nothing at all, and then, suddenly, there it was, running full and wide, flowing to the brim as if it were under a taut membrane. The colour of dribble or spit mixed with blood, pale red and opaque. Like posterpaint. Timortis picked up a pebble and threw it in. Without a splash it went straight to the bottom as if it were being swallowed down into a stream of soft pubic hair.

The road widened out into a raised rectangular green, shaded by tall rows of trees. The road split into two in order to go round the green. Something was happening on the right, so this was the side that Timortis took.

When he got there he saw that it was only the Old Folks Fair. There was a wooden bench, right out in the sun, with the latest arrivals sitting on large boulders at the sides of it. The old folks were lined up on the bench, and three of the stones were already occupied. He counted seven men and five women. Gerry Mander, the municipal knacketeer, was gesticulating in front of the bench with his moleskin logbook tucked under his arm. He was wearing an old chestnut corduroy suit with hu   ed boots and, in spite of the heat, most of his head was buried deep inside a greasy moleskin cap. The smell he gave off was bad enough, but the old folks were even worse. Most of them sat there like waxworks, their hands crossed on their shiny worn sticks, dressed in dirty old rags, unshaven and with their wrinkles deep with dirt. Their eyelids were squeezed tight together through having worked for so long in the glaring sun, and their toothless gums chewed a stinking cud of snuffy tobacco.

'Come along,' mandered Gerry in a voice like a cracked horsechestnut, 'this one's going cheap and there's plenty of work still left in him. Come on, Ezekiel, wouldn't you like him for your kids?'

'And he's got plenty to show them!' said one of the other men.

'Yes, he has. I'd nearly forgotten,' agreed the knacketeer municipally. 'Come over here, you old whatsit, and let's see it!'

He made him stand up. The old man, doubled in two, took a step forward.

'Show them then. Let 'em see what you've got tucked away inside your breeches!' gerried Mander.

With trembling rheumaticky fingers the old man began to undo his flies. Their edges were all greasy with wear. The people curled up with laughter.

'Well, just look at that!' said Ezekiel. 'It's true that he still has got something left in him!'

Shaking with laughter, he reached out to the old man and flicked the motheaten tassel.

'All right. I'll take him,' he said to the knacketeer. 'I'll give you a fiver for him.'

'Sold!' cried Gerry Mander in a voice full of merry danger.

Timortis knew that such things took place in the country, but it was the first time he had ever seen an Old Folks Fair and it more than surprised him.

The old man did up his buttons and waited.

31

'Get along, you old hound!' said Ezekiel, kicking him so that he went sprawling. 'Here you are, kids. Have fun with him.'

The old man trotted off, taking tiny steps. Two children stepped out from the crowd. One of them began to slash at his back with a whip, and the other clung round his neck, trying to make him tumble over. The men didn't look. Only Timortis, unable to take his eyes away, went on watching the children. The old man was down on his knees, the skin was off his nose and it was bleeding, and he spat something out of his mouth. Timortis turned away and went back to the main group. This time Gerry Mander was offering the charms of a short stout old woman of about seventy whose sparse greasy hair made a nibbled fringe for the old black shawl that was wound round her head.

'Come along, this one's in fine form,' he said. 'Who wants her? She's got no teeth left. Could come in handy.'

Timortis began to feel slightly sick. He studied the faces of the people around him carefully. They were mostly men between thirty-five and forty, tough and hard, with caps pulled down straight over their heads. The tribe was hardy and fit for survival. Several of them had thick moustaches. What further proof was necessary?

'Fifty shillings for Martha!' mandered on the gerryteer. 'And you won't be paying for even the stump of a tooth. She's a real bargain. How about it, Christian? Or you, Jonah?'

He gave the old woman a crashing wallop on the hump on her back.

'Get up, you old mare, so they can see you in all your glory! Come on, she's a bargain!'

The old woman stood up.

'Turn round,' yelled the knacketeer. 'Show the nice people your great fat arse. Just take a look at that, folks!'

Timortis forced himself not to look. The old woman had such a terrible smell that he thought he was going to faint.

But he still caught a glimpse of a horrible heap of fat tied together with varicose veins.

'I'll give you forty for her . . .' said a shrill piercing voice. 'She's yours then. Take her away!' manderknacked Gerry.

Before the old lady had even had time to pull down her coarse sacking skirt, he gave her another punch that sent her over. Timortis was standing near an enormous darkskinned giant who was laughing away wholeheartedly. He put a firm hand on his muscular arm.

'Why are you laughing like that?' he asked him. 'Doesn't it make you feel ashamed?'

The man suddenly stopped.

'Make me feel what? What did you say?'

'Make you feel ashamed?' Timortis softly repeated. 'They're all so terribly old.'

The punch landed before he even had time to realise that it was coming. His lip split open on a tooth. Blood gushed into his mouth. He stumbled and slipped from the green on to the road. Nobody paid the slightest attention to him. The auction went on.

He got up and brushed down his trousers with the palm of his hand. He was now on the outside of a semicircle of dark hostile backs.

'How about that one!' yapped the voice of the barker. 'He's got a wooden leg. That's the sort of thing people really go for. I'll start at seven ten. Seven pounds ten!'

Timortis slowly went away. At the end of the green a street ran across in the opposite direction, looking as if it had several shops in it. He went over to them, and a few minutes later went into the carpenter's shop. He felt uneasy and worried. The door closed behind him and he waited.

XII

THE BOSS wasn't in that particular room which was just a
kind of grubby little office. The floor was pine planks worn
black, the table was made of equally black wood, and an old
out-of-date calendar hung on the wall. One corner was even
blacker than the others where a stove had been. Two chairs
with frayed straw seats completed all the furnishings contained
in the room. Stud partitions with tongued and grooved boarding. At the back there was a door from which came sounds of
the workshop. One set of irregular hammering was being
superimposed on another, but the simultaneous sounds never
mixed.

Timortis went over to the workshop.

'Anybody there?' he asked quietly.

As the hammering did not stop, he went through into the
workshop. All its daylight came from above. It was a long and
fairly wide shed, filled with planks, beams, trusses and gibbets.
There were three or four work-benches, one small band-saw, a
drill and a lathe whose base seemed to be broken. On the walls
there were various tools, but not in very great number. On the
right, near the door which Timortis had just come through,
there was an enormous pile of sawdust and shavings. The air
reeked strongly of glue. The glue pot containing it was cooling
over a little fire of sawn-off pieces at the far end of the shed
beside another door which led out to the garden. From the
overloaded and sagging roof timbers hung various objects such
as old saw blades, dislocated jack planes of all trades, damaged
tools, broken vices, chipped chisels and a whole load of junk.

Immediately on the left an enormous oak trunk was being
held down, kept just a few inches above the floor by a pair of

strong wooden wedges. Straddling it, a tiny young apprentice was hacking away at it in an attempt to carve out a square beam with a heavy hatchet. He whacked away as hard as he could, although his skinny arms, sticking out of his rags, found it hard to manipulate his man-sized weapon. Further in the shed, his boss was tacking a leather embellishment over the edges of a bizarre construction of light oak—a sort of square niche in which a man could stand upright. This box—or cubicle—had shutters on all its walls. They were all standing open and their hinges gave discreetly pained little squeaks of surprise every time the hammer came down.

The man nailed and the child laboured. Neither of them looked up at Timortis and he stood on the threshold without being too sure what to do. In the end he spoke.

'Good morning!' he said, as loudly as he could.

The boss stopped his hammering and lifted his nose from the timber grindstone. He had a great open dangling mouth and a nose like a saucepan handle, but his hands were thick and veiny, with a coating of thick red fur.

'What d'*you* want?' he asked.

'I'd like some childrens' beds,' said Timortis. 'They're for the house on the cliff down there. We want two. One double, and a bigger single one.'

'I'm only going to make one,' said the carpenter, 'and it'll have to do for the three of them. Two can face the street.'

'And a larger one . . .' said Timortis.

'A larger one . . . We'll have to see,' said the carpenter. 'D'you want 'em made by hand or on the machine?'

Timortis looked at the little apprentice who was hammering away as if in a trance; a wretched automaton riveted to his interminable toil.

'It's cheaper if you have 'em done by hand,' said the carpenter. 'Machines are expensive, but trash like him comes thirteen to the dozen.'

'You bring them up the hard way here,' remarked Timortis.

'By hand or by machine, then?' repeated the carpenter.

35

'By machine,' said Timortis.

'You would . . .' grumbled the carpenter. 'I suppose you want me to wear out my equipment.'

'And have them ready by tomorrow,' said Timortis.

Then, trying to pour oil on the troubled waters that he had churned up, he pretended to show some interest in the man's work.

'What are you making there?' he asked.

'It's for the church,' said the carpenter. 'It's a pulpit.'

He seemed proud, yet embarrassed at the same time. When he spoke his enormous mouth let out a gob of drizzle that dangled for a moment and then fell.

'A pulpit?' said Timortis.

He went closer to see better. It was in fact a pulpit. A covered pulpit. A strange kind which Timortis had never come across before.

'This is the first time I've ever been in the country,' he said. 'In town, you know, we don't make them quite like that, so naturally it's interesting for me to see.'

'In town,' said the carpenter, 'you don't believe in God any more.'

He looked at Timortis as viciously as a walrus. Just then the little apprentice let his hatchet drop and fell prostrate, face forward, on to the oak trunk that he had been knackering. Timortis was alarmed by the sudden silence. He turned round and rushed over to the child. Meanwhile the carpenter had taken a few steps in the other direction and came back with an old tin can filled with water which he tipped brutally over the back of the child's neck. Then, seeing that the boy didn't get up, he sent the can after the water. The apprentice gave a sad sigh and, horrified, Timortis went over to him to help him. But the dirty little fist had already begun to swing itself up and down again, attacking the timber trunk with its feeble monotonous strokes.

'You're too rough with him,' said Timortis to the carpenter. 'A kid of his age! You ought to be ashamed!'

The punch that landed on his chin all but sent him sprawling, and he took two steps backwards in order to regain his equilibrium. With the tips of his fingers he felt his jaw. His bushy beard had deadened the shock.

The carpenter was getting on with his work again as if nothing abnormal had taken place. Between two whacks of the hammer he stopped.

'Come and see it Sunday,' he said. 'It'll be up then. It's a grand pulpit.'

He proudly felt the smooth wood. The white polished oak seemed to thrill under his fingers.

'And your beds'll be ready tomorrow,' he added. 'Come and pick 'em up about five.'

'O.K. . . .' answered Timortis.

The contrapuntal banging had started up again. The smell of strong glue was growing denser. Timortis took a last look at the apprentice, then shrugged his shoulders and went out.

The street was quiet. He took the road back to the cliff. As he went past the houses the curtains trembled at the windows. A little girl came out of one of them singing. She was carrying a gigantic jug as big as herself. She would not be singing like that when she went back in again.

XIII

ANGEL AND TIMORTIS were sitting in the big cool downstairs room of the house. The maid was toing and froing. She set out the jug and glasses on a tray in front of Angel. The windows and the door were wide open on to the garden. Now and again an insect would come zooming in and its wings bombarded every corner of the high room. All else was at peace.

Timortis opened his mouth.

'The beds should be ready today at five o'clock,' he said.

'Then they're ready now,' said Angel. 'Because he most certainly meant five o'clock this morning.'

'D'you really think so?' asked Timortis. 'In that case, then, they're bound to be.'

They said no more and drank in silence. Timortis waited for a moment or two and then opened his mouth again.

'I don't want to talk to you about things that you know about already and which will probaby bore you,' he said, 'but some of the things I saw in the village yesterday gave me quite a shock. People are strange round here.'

'You find them strange?' queried Angel.

His manner was polite, but his tone showed that his opinion in the matter was not completely unbiased. Timortis noticed it and quickly cut in again.

'Yes,' he said, 'I do find them strange. But I suppose that their mentality will become clearer to me when I get to know them better. After all, I'd be equally surprised wherever I went. I'm just new, that's all.'

'Obviously,' agreed Angel, whose mind was already elsewhere.

A bird shot past the windows like an arrow. Timortis followed it with his eyes.

'Naturally,' he said, sharply changing the subject, 'you wouldn't like to let yourself be psychoanalysed.'

'No,' said Angel, 'I certainly wouldn't like to. Anyway, I'm not in the least bit interesting. But I am interest*ed*. That's different.'

'What in?' asked Timortis, making a tremendous effort to keep the conversation going.

'In everything—and in nothing,' said Angel. 'In life. I like being alive.'

'You're lucky,' murmured Timortis.

In a single gulp he drunk down what was left in his glass.

'This stuff is good,' he remarked. 'Can I help myself?'

'Make yourself at home,' said Angel. 'Don't be shy.'

Silence again.

'I'm going to have a word with your wife,' said Timortis, standing up. 'She must be bored stiff all alone.'

'Of course,' said Angel. 'By all means. Come down and pick me up, then I'll get the car out and we can go and get the beds.'

'See you,' said Timortis, crossing the room to the door and then going up the stairs.

He tapped gently at Clementine's door, and she answered by saying 'Come in.' Which he did.

In Clementine's bed were Clementine and Clementine's three babies. Two on the right of her and one on the left.

'It's me,' said Timortis. 'I came to see if you wanted anything.'

'No,' she said. 'Nothing. Will the beds be ready soon?'

'They must be ready now,' said Timortis.

'What are they like?' she asked.

'Er . . .' replied the psychiatrist. 'I think he's made them more or less according to his own ideas. Two to sleep facing the road, and the other one crosswise.'

'But larger?' insisted Clementine.

'That's what I told him.' Timortis contended himself with being prudently precise.

'Have you got yourself settled in comfortably?' asked Clementine after thinking for a moment.

'I'm extremely comfortable,' Timortis assured her.

'Nothing *you* need?'

'Nothing at all . . .'

One of the rascals began to move and carry on as if something were annoying him. There was a noise in his stomach like steel girders careering down a helterskelter, and for a moment the wrinkles in his little monkey's face ironed themselves out. Clementine smiled and tapped him on his tummy.

'There . . . there . . . there . . .' she said. 'Has my little man got a nasty tummy-ache?'

Then the second one began to groan. Clementine lifted her eyelids to look at the clock and then looked at Timortis.

'It's time for their feed,' she said.

'Then I'll leave you alone with them,' murmured Timortis. And he went out without making a sound.

Clementine picked up the hungry baby and looked at him. It was Noel. His mouth was pursed up at the corners while the gums below were gnashing and grinding to help his grimacing expression. Quickly she put him down and unbuttoned one of her breasts. Then, picking up the child again, she brought him down on to it. He began to suck so hard that he almost lost his breath. Then, with a sharp jerk, she wrenched him away from the nipple. A little squirt of milk rose in the air in a parabola and fell back in a dribble on to the firm globe. Infuriated by Clementine's cruel behaviour, Noel screamed. She brought him back and he started drinking again, madly eager but still whimpering. Once again she lifted him off.

He cried still louder. Clementine was having fun. She began

all over again. Four times in all. Mad with rage, Noel's face turned puce. Then suddenly he seemed to suffocate. His face was horribly swollen, paralysed into a silent cry, and bitter tears gushed down his cheeks that were black with fury. Clementine had a terrible shock and was suddenly fearfully afraid. She shook him.

'Noel . . . Noel . . . Come back . . .'

She was going mad. She was just going to call out when, suddenly, Noel got his breath back again ready for a new bout of shouting. Very swiftly, with trembling hands, she gave him back the breast.

Immediately calmed down again, he got back to his greedy guzzling.

She put her hand across her damp forehead. She wouldn't try that trick again in a hurry.

Finally satisfied, Noel stopped a few minutes later. He went on swallowing the air, burped a little, and fell almost immediately into a still sleep broken only by deep sighs.

When she picked up the last of the three, she noticed that he was looking back at her. With his thick curly hair and his eyes wide open, he had the profoundly enigmatic and worrying gaze of a little oriental god. He gave a funny little conniving smile.

He drank his share. Now and again he would stop and look at her, and then, still staring, keep the tip of the breast in his mouth without swallowing anything.

When he had finished, she put him down on her left and turned her back on him. The room hummed palely with the frail irregularity of their breathing.

Still perturbed, she stretched out and let herself fade away into another trip into the vagueness of space. An acrid smell of young sweat rose delicately from the three vests. She had a bad dream.

XIV

ANGEL HAD just got the car out of the garage and was waiting for Timortis to join him. The psychiatrist lingered, contemplating the marvellous panorama, the violet sea and the brilliant hazy sky, the trees and the flowers bursting out of the garden, and the house, white and firm as an ancient rock in the midst of the swirling orgy of colours.

Timortis plucked a little yellow flower and hopped in beside Angel. It was a tough old Pata-Morgana-Lafayette convertible moke-truck, not very comfortable, but still thoroughly reliable. The back was kept open by a pair of chains, and fresh air circulated freely throughout the framework.

'What an incredible landscape!' said Timortis. 'And all these flowers! They're breathtakingly beautiful! It's . . .'

'Yes, isn't it?' said Angel.

He accelerated along the powdery road. A cloud of dust rose up behind the car and fell back on to the spongy grass to which Timortis was already growing accustomed.

A goat, by the side of the road, made a sign with its horns and Angel stopped.

'Jump in,' he said to it.

The goat jumped into the car and sat in the truck behind them.

'The animals all hitch lifts,' explained Angel. 'And as I don't want to get on bad terms with the local people . . .'

His sentence remained incomplete.

'I see,' said Timortis.

A little further on they picked up a pig. The two animals

got off on the outskirts of the village and each trotted off towards its own farm.

'When they behave themselves,' Angel went on, 'they're allowed a day off. If they don't, then they're punished and beaten. And sometimes they're locked in. And eaten raw.'

'Yes . . .' said Timortis, numbly.

Angel's car stopped outside the carpenter's shop. The two men got out. This time there was a rectangular box in the little office. The body of the young apprentice, who had been busy the day before in adzing away at the oak beam, was lying in it, half-covered by an old sack.

'Anyone home?' called Angel, banging on the desk.

The carpenter came out. From the workshop sounds similar to those of the day before could be heard. Doubtless it was a new apprentice. The carpenter wiped his nose with the back of his cuff.

'Come to fetch your beds?' he asked Angel.

'Yes,' said Angel.

'All right. You can take 'em,' said the carpenter. 'There they are.'

He pointed inside the workshop.

'Give me a hand,' said Angel.

They both disappeared inside. Timortis brushed away a bluebottle which was buzzing in circles round the colourless head of the dead child.

The carpenter and Angel put the beds in the van. They were built in demountable sections.

'Will you take this for me too?' said the carpenter, pointing to the box with the apprentice lying in it.

'O.K.,' said Angel. 'Shove it on the back.'

The carpenter picked up the box and put it on the back of the van. They set off and, after a few moments, drove alongside the red stream. Angel stopped, got out, and lifted off the box. It was light and not very large. Without much extra effort he picked it up and carried it down to the stream. Then he tipped it into the water. The wooden box sank straight

43

down to the bottom. But the child's body floated, carried along by the stream's slow current, as if on a magic carpet of frozen wax.

The bed-boards jostled and banged together in the van, unable to keep their balance on the cakewalk created by the jolting tyres over the groove-engrained road.

XV

TIMORTIS'S ROOM overlooked the sea. It was at the very end of the long tiled corridor on the first floor. The bristly beard of a dragon-tree plant made a fringe round the frames of the lower panes. Rising above the green blades was the sea. The low walls of the square room were all finished in narrow pine boarding, polished and smelling strongly of resin. On the ceiling, long deep rafters, varnished too, created the skeleton of the roof with all its varying pitches, propped up at the corners with clumsily adzed oblique oakre struts. The furniture consisted of a low lemonwood bed, an imposing looking desk with an orange morocco top, a matching pear-shaped armchair, and a wardrobe whose glass reflected the view from the window. The floor was tiled like the rest of the house, but with little light buff hexagons, half-hidden by a thick black woollen rug. There was nothing on the walls, neither prints nor photos. A low door led to the bathroom.

Timortis finished washing and got dressed ready to go out. He had given up his professional psychiatrist's uniform and now wore a pair of tight-fitting suede trousers, a purple silk shirt and a flared jacket of chestnut velvet to match the colour of his trousers. He tied the thonged laces of his purple sandals and went out of his room. He had to go to the village to make arrangements with the vicar about the service on Sunday and he dressed himself simply to suit the occasion.

In the corridor he caught a glimpse of Clementine just going back into her room. She had been up for the first time and had just taken a stroll in the garden. She waved to him with her hand before closing her door.

He went downstairs. Angel was still asleep. Without waiting for breakfast, Timortis walked straight into the garden. The leaves of the wild dewberries were creaking in the fresh breeze of the early morning.

The earth was dry, like asbestos. As it had been the day before, the well-water was boiling, and the sky, transparent down to the very bone, was obviously hiding not even a single drop of rain up its sleeve. Timortis took the path to the village, which the contempt of familiarity had already made seem less lengthy.

He hadn't yet been to the church whose top rose only slightly higher than the surrounding houses and farms. To get there he had to follow the scarlet stream for a good way further than he had previously been. He stared at the expanse of water and the hairs of his imagination stood on end when he thought of all that was hidden below its taut surface.

The path turned and the stream with it. The grey buildings edging it on the left masked from Timortis what lay beyond the bend.

Another fifty yards and, still a fair distance ahead of him, the church began to rise. And, on the scarlet stream, a static barge began to rise too. Its oars dangled on each side. Behind the prow which jutted out at him diagonally, he could distinguish a sombre moving shape in silhouette, and he went closer to find out what it was doing.

When he was by the side of the boat, he saw the man clutch its edge and try to get on it again. The water from the scarlet stream splashed on to his clothes in quicksilver drops without making them damp. His head appeared above the deck. The boat wobbled, moving with his efforts to get on board. Timortis could finally pick out the man's features as, in one last attempt, he managed to get an arm and a leg over and fell prostrate at the bottom of the boat. He was getting on. His features were sunken, and his distant blue eyes were the colour of a circular horizon. He was completely clean-shaven, and his long white hair made him look both dignified and distinguished. But his mouth, when he was not speaking, was lined with bitterness. At that moment he held an object which Timortis could not identify between his teeth.

Timortis hailed him.

'Having trouble?' he asked.

The man scrambled up and managed to sit down. He dropped whatever he had just picked up in his jaws.

'What's that?' he asked.

He bent over the oars and brought his barge close to the bank. With a few strokes he reached the shore. Thus Timortis understood that the bank plunged vertically under the water like the edge of a canal.

'Do you need any help?' asked Timortis.

The man looked at him. He was dressed in old rags and sacking.

'You a stranger round here?' he said.

'Yes,' answered Timortis.

'Thought so. Otherwise you wouldn't have spoken to me like that,' the man mumbled, almost to himself.

'You could have drowned yourself,' said Timortis.

'Not in this water,' said the man. 'You never know where you are with it. Sometimes even wood sinks in it, and at other times stones float on the top. But bodies never go under—not even once.'

'What had happened just now?' asked Timortis. 'Had you fallen out of your boat?'

'I was getting on with my job,' said the man. 'They throw dead things into this water for me to fish out again. With my teeth. That's what I'm paid to do.'

'But couldn't you do it better with a net?' said Timortis.

He felt awkward and uncertain, as if he were trying to talk to somebody from another planet. A feeling that we all know only too well, of course.

'I *have* to fish them out again with my teeth,' said the man.

47

'Dead things or rotten things. That's why they throw them in. Often they let them go bad specially, just so that they can throw them in. And I have to fish them out again with my teeth. So that when they give up the ghost, kick the bursting bucket and croak between my jaws, all the pus and the filth will splash into my face.'

'Do you get much money for doing it?' asked Timortis.

'I get the barge,' said the man. 'And they pay me out in shame and in gold.'

At the sound of the word *shame* Timortis took a step back —and then felt ashamed of himself for having done so.

'I've got a home,' said the man who, having noticed Timortis's movement, gave a sour little smile. 'I get my food. And they give me gold. Loads of it. But I haven't got the right to spend it. Nobody wants to—and nobody will—sell me anything. I've got a house and I've got loads of gold—but I have to swallow the shame of the whole village for them. They pay me to feel their remorse for them. Remorse for everything wicked and evil that they do. For every one of their vices. And every one of their crimes. For the Old Folks Fair. For the tortured animals. For the apprentices. And for all the filth and scum.'

He stopped for a moment.

'But all this can't be very interesting for you,' he went on again. 'You don't mean to stay here, do you?'

There was a long pause.

And then, 'Yes. I do,' said Timortis, decisively. 'I *do* mean to stay here.'

'Then you'll grow like all the others,' said the man. 'You'll learn to live with a clear conscience and you'll load the weight of your shame on to me. And you'll give me gold. And sell me nothing for it in return.'

'What's your name?' asked Timortis.

'Glory Hallelujah,' said the man. 'At least, *they* call me Glory Hallelujah. It's really the name of the boat. I haven't got one any more.'

'Well, I'll be seeing you . . .' said Timortis.

'You'll grow to be just the same as them,' said the man. 'You won't talk to me again. You'll just pay me. And you'll throw all the skeletons out of your cupboard at me. And *all* your shame.'

'But why do you do it?' asked Timortis.

The man shrugged his shoulders.

'Somebody else did it before me,'

'Well then, how did you take over?' insisted Timortis.

'The first person to be more ashamed than I am takes my place,' said the man. 'That's the village tradition. They're very religious here. They've got their consciences for themselves. But never any remorse. And the man who weakens . . . The man who revolts . . .'

'They put him on to Glory Hallelujah . . .' Timortis completed the sentence for him.

'So you went into revolt,' he said.

'Oh! It doesn't happen very often nowadays . . .' said the man. 'Maybe I'll be the last. My mother wasn't a local girl.'

He got back into position and bent over the sculls.

'I've got to get on with my work,' he said. 'Good-bye.'

'See you,' said Timortis.

He watched him slowly disappear over the red ripplefree sheen of the water and then began to walk away himself. The church, a buckminster hen's egg perched on top of a fuller's nest that was like a crown of thorns, was only a stone's throw away. When he reached it, he rapidly went up the seven steps and stepped inside. But before having a word with the vicar he wanted to have a look round.

XVI

A COMPLEX web of beams and lattice girders held up the blanket of fine black crystalline slate over the oval nave. In front of Timortis stood the sombre granite altar with its condimentary turquoise and emerald equipment—sectarian symbols of the denomination. On the right, between a pair of soaring beams, the wide open shutters of the brand-new pulpit rose upwards with a jagged white outline.

It was the first time that Timortis had seen a church built in the shape of an egg, without heavy stone columns for arches and vaults to fly from, without chancel and aisles, without clerestory and crossing, without drums, trumpets and battle-ripped banners, and without the everlasting and threatening presence of the life to come. Long lengths of curiously jointed timber curved sinuously along the invincible walls, constituting their geodesic armature. The dark recesses were crammed with sculptures in high relief. They appeared to be polychromatic, although the eyes of these saints, serpents and satanic monsters gleamed and glittered in the darkness. The whole of the central space of the church was completely free. An oval stained-glass window, placed immediately above it, bathed the altar with an unflinching ultramarine glow. Without this window it would have been pitch dark inside the church. Multiple candelabras stood on each side of the altar, throwing little flickering lights haphazardly into the depths of the random shadows edging the expanding circumferences of their graduated ripples.

The floor was thickly strewn with rushes, from the entrance right up to the altar. Timortis took a step inside. After his eyes had grown used to the darkness he noticed the grey rectangle of an open door on the right, behind the altar, and he walked towards it, imagining that it would lead to the sacristy and presbytery.

He went through the door and came into a little room filled with sharp corners, cupboards and all kinds and sorts of objects. At the back of it there was another door. And from this there came a murmur of voices. Timortis rapped his knuckles three times on one of the upper panels.

'May I come in?' he asked gently.

The sound of conversation stopped.

'Come in!' Timortis heard.

He accepted the invitation and went through the second door.

The vicar was there, talking to his curate. They both stood up when they saw Timortis.

'Goodmorning,' he said. 'The vicar, I presume?'

'Goodmorning, sir,' said the vicar.

He was a wiry man, his face gimletted with two black eyes thatched with heavy thick black brows. He had long dry hands which he held crossed while he spoke. When he moved, Timortis noticed that he suffered from a slight limp.

'I'd like to have a word with you,' said Timortis.

'Take two . . .' replied the vicar.

'It's about a christening,' explained Timortis. 'Could you manage Sunday?'

'It's my job to,' said the priest. 'Each man has his trade . . .'

'There were three twins born up in the house on the cliff,' said Timortis. 'Joel, Noel and Alfa Romeo. Everything's got to be done by Sunday evening.'

'Come to the Sunday morning service,' said the vicar, 'and I'll tell you the time then.'

'But I never go to church . . .' protested Timortis.

'All the more reason to come this Sunday,' said the vicar. 'It'll make a change for you. And at least there'll be one member of my congregation to find something new in what I'm saying.'

'I'm against religion,' said Timortis. 'Although I do realise that the country can often find good uses for it.'

The vicar snorted.

'Good uses! . . . Religion is a luxury,' he said. 'It's all these brutes who want to turn it into something useful.'

He stood up proudly and began hobbling up and down excitedly.

'But I refuse!' he said abrasively. 'My religion always has been—and always will be—a luxury!'

'What I meant to stress,' explained Timortis, 'is that in the country a vicar's word still carries some weight. He can direct the rough and ready spirits of the peasants, put his finger on the mistakes they make and show them how to rub them out, open their eyes to the dangers of leading too earthly a life, put a brake on their baser instincts . . . I don't know whether you're aware of something that's going on in the village. I . . . er . . . I've only just got here and I don't mean to set myself up as a judge, or shock you by the way I react to something which may possibly seem natural to you since it's always been going on . . . er . . . A vicar can blight theft from the top of his pulpit, condemn hasty or sudden sexual intercourse between teenagers in order to prevent disorder dominating his diocese —or vice violating his . . . vicarage.'

'His parish . . .' rectified the curate.

'His parish . . .' said Timortis. 'Er . . . now, where was I?'

'I haven't got the foggiest,' cut in the vicar.

'To cut things short,' said Timortis, making up his mind to come out with what he had to say, 'I mean this Old Folks Fair. It's just crazy!'

'You want to live with the times!' explained the vicar. 'This Old Folks Fair? The Old Folks Fair means nothing—Nothing, do you hear me?—to me, sir! These men suffer . . . and those who suffer on earth will earn their reward in Paradise. Anyway, suffering in itself is not useless—although I'm only interested in the results of this suffering. I'm worried because of the fact that they don't suffer in God, sir. They're wild brutes. As I was telling you just now, religion is no more than a means to an end for them. They're just materialistic brutes . . .'

He grew more and more excited as he spoke and his eyes almost caught fire from the flashes they sent out.

'They come into my church as if they own the place. In flesh and blood. And do you know what they ask me to do? To make their fields of fodder fertile. And they don't give a damn about the peace of their souls, sir! That's all looked after for them! They've got their Glory Hallelujah! I'll fight to the end and I'll never yield to them. I won't make their fields of fodder flourish. Thank God I've still got a few faithful friends left. There aren't many of them, but they manage to keep me going.'

He snorted once again.

'Come on Sunday and you'll see . . . You'll see how I attack their materialism with an even more materialistic materialism. I'll rub the noses of these brutes in their own messes . . . Their apathy will find itself striking against an even greater apathy . . . And a worrying anxiety will grow from this collision which will lead them back to religion . . . the religion of luxury! . . . To that luxury to which God in all his divine meekness has given them the birthright.'

'Fine,' said Timortis. 'And now, how about this christening? Will Sunday be all right?'

'I'll confirm the time with you at the end of the service,' repeated the vicar.

'Oh, all right,' said Timortis. 'Goodbye then. I was admiring your church just now. It's an unusual building.'

'Unusual, yes . . .' agreed the vicar, his mind already elsewhere.

He sat down again while Timortis went out the same way that he had come in. He began to feel slightly tired.

'Clementine's getting on my nerves with all her errands,' he thought aloud. 'I'll be glad when her three kids are able to do things for themselves. And then having to go to church on a Sunday! ...'

The evening fell.

'Having to go to church—that's a horrible cheek!'

'A horrible cheek!' agreed a fat black cat sitting on the top of a wall.

Timortis looked at it. The cat began to purr and split its eyes with vertical yellow slits.

'Horrible!' concluded Timortis, plucking a leaf of the soft, round, cylindrical grass.

A little further on he looked back. He watched the cat for a moment, thought for another, and then took the road again.

XVII

Sunday, 2 September

ALL READY to go, Timortis was pacing up and down the corridor. He had put on his serious Sunday suit and felt as nervous and embarrassed as an actor in full costume on a naked stage. At last the nurse appeared.

'What a time you take,' said Timortis.

'I had to make myself look respectable,' she explained.

She too was wearing a regulation Sunday dress in ruled white gingham, with black shoes, a black hat and white nylon lace gloves. She was carrying a frayed leather prayer-book. Her face was gleaming, and her messily applied lipstick gave a blurred outline to her lips. Her ample breasts stretched the checks on the pattern of the top of her dress to their limit, and the broad curves of her hips dutifully filled out the remainder of the dress.

'Let's go,' said Timortis.

They went out. She seemed shy and scared and, out of deference, tried not to make any kind of sound as she breathed.

'Well,' asked Timortis, a hundred yards further on, 'when am I going to psychoanalyse you?'

She blushed and looked at him under her eyelids. They were going past a tall thick hedge.

'We can't do it now, before we go to church . . .' said she, full of hope.

The psychiatrist felt his russet beard tremble and then ` begin to bristle when it understood what she had understood, and his firm hand gently guided her to the side of the road. They disappeared behind the hedge through a narrow prickly gap. It was edged with brambles, thorns and briars on which Timortis ripped and tore his elegant suit.

They were now in an isolated screened-off meadow. The maid took off her black hat and put it down carefully.

'Mustn't spoil that,' she said. 'Oh, and I'll get all green stains on me if I get down on the grass . . .'

'Go down on your knees then,' said Timortis.

'I'm going to,' she said, as if she had assumed naturally that this was the only way there was.

As the psychiatrist worked on her, he saw the girl's short nape rise and fall in quick succession. As her hair was only loosely done, several blond strands shook loose in the breeze. She had quite a strong smell, but Timortis hadn't performed since he had been there, and this faintly animal odour did not displease him. Through a very understandable concern for the future of the human race, he avoided giving her a child.

They arrived at the church door with only about ten minutes to go before the beginning of the service. To judge by the numbers of cars and wagons parked outside, the oval nave must have been overflowing with people. Before going up the steps, Timortis looked quickly at the girl who was still flushed and slightly shamefaced.

'Shall I come to your room tonight?' she murmured.

'Yes. Do,' he said. 'Then you can tell me the story of your life.'

She stared at him in bewilderment, realised that he wasn't joking and, still not understanding, agreed. They went inside and mixed with the well-scrubbed crowd that was still rushing in. Timortis was pressed tight against her and his nostrils were filled with her animal odour. Under her arms her perspiration appeared in ever-widening circles.

The vicar concluded his preamble and prepared to climb up into the pulpit by picking up the hem of his skirts. The stifling heat grabbed the congregation by the throat, and the women began to loosen the laces of their corsets under their stiff dresses. The men, however, undid none of the buttons of their black jackets and their stiff starched collars stayed standing upright, tight under their chins. Timortis looked around him. All the faces looked as if their owners were strong, prosperous and well-nourished, tanned by the sun and air, and possessed of some strange certainty. The vicar climbed the steps leading up to the white pulpit whose shutters were wide open. A most unusual type of pulpit. Timortis remembered the carpenter, then thought of the little apprentice, and shuddered. When he thought of the apprentice, the smell of the little maid began to disgust him.

As soon as the vicar appeared between the two light oak piers, one of the men stood up on his pew and, in a powerful voice, bellowed for silence. The mumbling slowly subsided. An attentive calm now reigned over all the nave. Timortis's eyes noticed the myriad lights dangling below the dome which now revealed the jumble of overlapping bodies carved even on to the enormous structure of the church, and the blue stained-glass behind the altar.

'We want rain, vicar!' bawled the man.

With a single voice the crowd took up the chorus.

'Rain! . . .'

'Our fodder-fields are dry!' the man went on.

'Rain!' screamed the crowd.

Timortis, completely deafened, saw the vicar hold out his arms, appealing for his right to speak. The angry noise gradually ceased. The morning sun blazed behind the blue stained glass. It was difficult to breathe.

'Vulgar, vulturous, vulpine villagers!' said the vicar.

His tremendous voice seemed to boom out from every segment of the structure's spherical surface, and Timortis assumed that he attained this incredible volume through some hidden system of amplification. All heads were turned to the dome, to the concave walls. But no signs of any apparatus were visible anywhere.

'Vulgar, vulturous, vulpine villagers!' said the vicar. 'You ask me for rain. But you shall have none! You have come here today, arrogant in your pride like troops of turkeys, like crowing cockerels, swollen with self, inflated with flesh, confident in the over-riding power of your earthly passions. You have come here insolently asking for things you do not deserve. It will not rain! God has no concern for your filthy fodder! Bow your bodies, bend your knees, lower your heads, humble your souls—and I will give you the word of God. But do not count on one single drop of water. This is a church that you are gathered in today—not a shower!'

There was a murmur of discontent amongst the congregation. Timortis found himself considering that the vicar was really quite a good speaker.

'Rain!' repeated the man standing on the pew.

After the sonorous tempest of the vicar's voice, his appeal sounded feebly amateur and derisory, and the congregation, conscious of a temporary lapse in quality, remained silent and did not echo him.

'You pretend you believe in God!' thundered the vicar. 'Just because you come to church on Sundays, because you treat your neighbours harshly, because you do not know what it is to feel shame, and because your consciences do not torment you . . .'

When the vicar pronounced the word *Shame*, cries of protest rose at various points from the floor, swelled with their own echoes, and burst into a single great howl from the whole assembly. The men stamped or leapt on to their pews with their fists clenched. The women, silent, pursed their lips and stared at the vicar with malicious, evil eyes. Timortis felt he was losing his psychological balance. Then the tumult died, and the vicar resumed his speech again.

'What do your fields matter to me? What do your cattle—

58

or your children—matter to me?' He was shrieking now. 'You live sordid, materialistic lives. You don't know what luxury is! ... I am offering you a real, genuine, luxury: I am offering you God ... G, O, D, for whom this geodesic jewel, this ritual in architecture, was invented. But God is not interested in rain. God does not hanker after fodder. Why should he fertilise the fallow furrows of your fields? He couldn't care less about your foul fodder-beds and the boring things you do in them. God is a tasselled cushion made of beaten gold. A blessed jewel set within the golden circle of the sun. A precious scene carved in high relief into the fabric of Love. God is Knightsbridge, Prince's Street, Queen's Gate, King's Road. Checkmate—and the Ace of Diamonds. God is cassocks woven from silken thread. Socks of brocade with embroidered clocks. Necklaces and rings. All things that are useless. All things prized and wonderful. Electric splendour. A third channel in colour ... There shall be *no* rain!'

'Make it rain!' yelled the people's orator, backed up this time by the crowd which was beginning to sound like thunder in a stormy sky.

'Go back to your farms!' lowed the vicar's multiple voice. 'Get back to your dung-heaps! God is the voluptuousness of everything that is superfluous. And all you can think about is essentials. As far as God is concerned, you are lost men.'

The man standing next to Timortis pushed him roughly aside and, taking careful aim, heaved a heavy stone at the pulpit. But the oaken shutters had already slammed together and been bolted on the inside where the vicar's voice rumbled on as the heavy block of stone landed against the massive panels of joinery with a dull but deafening thud.

'It will not rain! God is not a utilitarian. God is a birthday present. A free gift. A luncheon voucher. An ingot of platinum. A priceless picture. A French pastry. God is something extra. And he is neither for nor against. God is eleven thousand buckshee trading stamps!'

59

A hailstorm of stones crashed on the lid of the pulpit.

'Rain! Rain! Rain!' The crowd's yells had now organised themselves into a steady beat and a regular rhythm.

And Timortis, carried away by the passion generated from these men, was astonished to find himself chanting with them.

Before him, to his right and to his left, the peasants were marking time, and the earth-shaking noise of their hobnailed shoes filled the church like troops tramping over an iron bridge. One push sent the group of men nearest the pulpit plunging forward, and they began to shake the four massive pillars that held it up above the ground.

'It will not rain!' repeated the vicar, now seeming to be in a total state of trance behind the shutters. 'It may rain angels' wings! It may rain emerald feathers. Alabaster vases. Works of art . . . But not water! God cares nothing for fodder. Nor for corn, wheat, barley, oats. Nor sesame, clover, alfalfa, rape, stonecrop, yarrow, cow parsley, rosemary, or sage . . .'

Timortis could not help admiring the vicar's erudition, although the snapping of the four oaken pillars laid greater claim to his attention, the ear-splitting wrench reverberating in the scattered loudspeakers. But even this was drowned by the fearful oath let out by the vicar inside the construction as his head banged against its solid timbers.

'All right! All right! That's enough! I give in!' he cried. 'You'll get your rain! Here it comes! Here it comes!'

In a flash the crowd streamed to the back of the church and burst open the doors. The sky had suddenly turned black and the first raindrops slapped on to the steps like soft squashy frogs. Then came a veritable downpour which beat a tattoo with tambourine accompaniment on the black crystalline slates of the roof. Somehow or other they had managed to get the pulpit back on its legs again, and the vicar dared to peep out of the shutters once more.

'Service is over,' he said quite simply.

The people all crossed themselves, the men put on their

caps once again, the women stood up and then everybody went out.

Timortis wanted to go to the vestry, but had to cling tightly to one of the wooden pews in order not to be dragged out in the opposite direction by the crowd.

He felt the carpenter jolt against him, recognising him by his wide drooling mouth and his stubby nose. The man gave him a wicked wink.

'See it?' he said. 'We really believe in God here. And the vicar's not going to be the one to stop us. He doesn't even know what God's for.'

Then he shrugged his shoulders.

'Still,' he concluded, 'we let him get on with it. Doesn't do any harm. And it makes a bit of a laugh once a week. We enjoy our services here. With or without the vicar. And you saw my shutters showed they could take it.'

He made his way out. Timortis didn't know where the nurse had gone, but he decided not to worry about her any more. The force of the tide abated and he managed to find his way to the vestry door. He went in and, without knocking, went through to the second room.

The vicar was pacing up and down, still limping, but forgetting his impediment and his bruises as he blossomed under the compliments being showered on him by his curate, a little insignificant ruddy man that Timortis had to force himself to remember having seen when he had been there earlier during the week.

'You were terrific!' said the curate. 'You were perfect! What a creation! It was the finest thing you've ever done!'

'Ah!' said the vicar. 'I think I got them.'

There was an enormous lump on his forehead.

'You were sensational!' said the curate. 'What breath control! What inspiration! What timing! And what scientific rhetoric! Honest to God, I've got to take off my hat to you!'

'All the same,' said the vicar, 'you're exaggerating a bit . . .

61

I might have been all right . . . But really, I wasn't as good as all that, was I?'

'Allow me,' said Timortis, 'to add my own sincere compliments to those of your assistant.'

'Ah! . . .' sighed the curate. 'What talent! . . . You were . . . You were sublime!'

'Oh, be quiet,' said the vicar. 'Really, you're overdoing it and flattering me too much.'

He swaggered for a few more steps, smiling amiably at Timortis.

'Do take a seat, sir.'

Timortis took one.

'Ah! . . .' panted the curate. 'When you said to them "This is a church and not a shower! . . ." I passed out. Honest. What talent you've got, vicar, what talent! And "God feels no affection for fodder." That's real art!'

'And of course it's so very true!' commented the vicar. 'But don't let's keep the gentleman waiting.'

'Hm. I've come about the christening,' explained the psychiatrist.

'Oh yes, I remember. I remember,' said the voluble vicar. 'Now . . . We can do it for you this afternoon. Get them all here by four o'clock. I'll start all the bells ringing at twenty to four. All right? Don't be late.'

'Thank you, vicar,' said Timortis, standing up. 'And, once again, all my compliments and congratulations. The service was . . . epic!'

'Ah!' said the curate. 'Epic! That's the very word I was looking for. Epic! Ah, vicar, vicar!'

The vicar, overcome with delight, held out his hand to Timortis and vigorously shook the one he received in exchange.

'I'm sorry you've got to go so soon,' he said. 'I'd have liked to have kept you for lunch . . . But I mustn't waste your precious time . . .'

'I am in rather a hurry,' said Timortis. 'Another time, perhaps. Thank you. And bravo!'

He set off, taking large steps. The empty church was dark and quiet again. The rain had almost stopped. The sun was creeping back again outside. And a warm mist was beginning to rise from the land.

XVIII

'WELL, THAT'LL be my lot,' thought Timortis. 'Twice in church in a day—and perhaps I won't step inside another one again for another ten years. Or not for another nine and a half, at any rate!'

He was sitting waiting in the hall. The sound of the nurse's scurrying, scuttling footsteps was reinforced by the shuttle-cocking echoes of those of Angel and Clementine coming down from the first floor, slightly muffled by the thickness of the ceiling with its plaster below and its clay tiles above. Now and again a sharp squeal from one of the pair of terrible twins effortlessly pierced through the whole construction and shot down to reverberate with all its force on Timortis's eardrums. It must have been Noel or Joel. Alfa Romeo never cried.

Katherine Whitarse was wearing a pink taffeta baptismal robe trimmed with long lilac ribbons, and black slippers and another big black hat. She hardly dared to move. She picked everything up with the tips of her fingers. And she'd already broken three vases.

Angel was in his everyday clothes. Clementine in a pair of tight black-and-white slacks and a matching jacket. The three brats were resplendant in little capsules of embroidered cellophane.

Angel hurried down to get out the car.

Clementine carried Noel and Joel, leaving the nurse in charge of Alfa Romeo. Now and again he looked for his mother and his delicate little lips began to tremble. But he did not cry. Alfa Romeo never cried. Sometimes Clementine looked back at him teasingly, pretending to kiss Noel and Joel.

The car pulled up in front of the steps and everyone tumbled down them. Timortis was last. He carried the paper bags of silver spoons, brass bangles, baby baubles and Adam beads to hand round to the animals and children of the village after the christening service.

The sky, as usual, was permanent blue and the garden gleaming in purple and gold.

The boneshaker started off. Angel drove slowly and was specially careful because of the children inside.

Every time the nurse moved a landslide of noise could be heard coming like an earthquake from her taffeta dress. It was an extremely lovely dress. But Timortis preferred the gingham one which clung more accurately to her figure. In this one she looked simply like a beautiful bouncing bumpkin.

XIX

THE DARKNESS around Timortis grew deeper. He was at his desk, meditating. A streak of procrastinating laziness kept him from putting on the light. It had been a tiring day, the last of a tiring week, and he was trying to get back some of the calm that had gone out of his soul. During all these feverish agitated days he had hardly felt the need to psychoanalyse anybody, but now that he was alone and relaxed in his room again, he felt the emptiness and absence of passion—that had been temporarily masked by a glut of sights and sounds—surge back with a sharp and clear anguish. Devoid of desires, uncertain of what was going to happen next, he sat and waited for the maid to knock on his door.

It was warm in the panelled room with its varnished timber, and the smell of the wood was good; the neighbouring sea softened the burning breath of the air and made it calm and delicious. Outside, a few odd birdcalls and the rasping clatter of revelling insects could be heard.

And then somebody scratched at the door. Timortis stood up and went to open it. The young country girl came in and stood there, paralysed by timidity. Timortis smiled; he switched on the light and then carefully closed the door again.

'What's the matter?' he asked. 'Got cold feet?'

Then he immediately felt guilty about using such a vulgar expression, but forgave himself a moment or two later when he reflected that it wouldn't have shocked such a vulgar person as the maid.

'Sit down . . .' he suggested. 'There . . . On the bed.'

66

'Daren't . . .' she said.

'Come on, come on,' said Timortis. 'There's no need to be scared or shy with me. Lie down and relax. Take it easy.'

'Do I take my clothes off?' she asked.

'Do exactly as you like,' said Timortis. 'Undress yourself if you feel like it. If you don't, don't. Make yourself comfortable . . . That's all I ask of you.'

'Are you going to undress yourself too?' she asked, a little bolder.

'Look here,' protested Timortis, 'did you come to see me for psychoanalysis—or for fornication?'

She lowered her head, ashamed at not understanding, and Timortis felt himself becoming mildly aroused by such extensive ignorance.

'I don't understand your big words,' she said. 'I only want to do what you tell me.'

'And I only want to tell you to do what you want to do,' insisted Timortis.

'I like to be told what I've got to do . . . After all, I'm not the mistress . . .'

'Look here, just lie down as you are,' said Timortis.

He went back and sat down behind his desk. She watched him from her low position and then, making a sudden decision, took off her dress in one swift movement. It was one of her everyday dresses—a completely nondescript flowered cotton—that she had put on when she came back from the christening.

Timortis made a detailed inventory of her: a little on the fat side, but well-built; plump round breasts; a stomach so far undeformed by the stresses of labour. She stretched out on the bed and the thought ran through his mind that later, after she had gone, the smell of this girl would remain on his sheets to disturb his sleep.

She moved rather clumsily, like an animal, but this was probably the remaining relics of some kind of rural modesty.

'How old are you?' asked Timortis.

67

'Twenty,' she said.

'Where d'you come from?'

'The village.'

'Who brought you up? What's the first thing you can remember?'

He chatted lightly, trying to gain her confidence.

'Can you remember your grandparents?'

She thought for a minute.

'Is this why you wanted me to come?' she asked. 'To ask me things like that?'

'For that—among other things,' answered Timortis, being cautious.

'You ought to mind your own business,' she said.

She got up and sat with her legs dangling over the edge of the bed.

'You going to cover me or not?' she asked. 'That's what I came for, and you know it perfectly well. I know I can't talk like you, but I'm not stupid enough to let you poke fun at me.'

'Oh, run along then,' said Timortis. 'You're too depraved. You'll be back again tomorrow in a better mood.'

She got up. As she walked past the psychiatrist, he found himself suddenly moved by the curving silhouetted contours of her young breasts.

'All right,' he said. 'Stay on the bed. I'm coming.'

She quickly jumped back to the spot she had just left, panting a little. When Timortis was beside her, she turned round and offered herself to him from the back. He took her in this position, exactly as he had that same morning behind the hedge.

XX

ANGEL WAS lying beside Clementine. In the triple bed the three children's dreamless sleep was punctuated by little anguished snuffles. She was not asleep. He knew that. They had been there for an hour—side by side in the darkness.

He moved a little, trying to find a cooler spot. As he did this, his leg touched Clementine's. She jumped, and swiftly switched on the light. Angel, half-asleep, raised himself on his elbows on the pillow to look at her.

'What's the matter?' he asked. 'Don't you feel well?'

She sat up and shook her head.

'I can't go on,' she said.

'Can't go on with what?'

'I can't go on putting up with you. I can't go on sleeping with you. I'll never be able to sleep again if every moment I feel that you're going to touch me. Or even try to get near me. It drives me mad to feel the hairs on your legs brushing against mine. It makes me want to scream.'

Her voice was strained and trembling, the echo of screams deep inside her.

'Go and sleep somewhere else,' she begged. 'Take pity on me. Leave me alone.'

'Don't you love me any more?' asked Angel, with a simplicity that made him feel stupid.

She looked at him.

'I can't bear to touch you any more,' she said. 'And yet . . . Yes, I suppose I could . . . But I can't bear the thought of you touching me, not even for a second. It's horrible.'

'You must be crazy!' said Angel, reluctantly suggesting this reason.

'I'm not crazy. It's just that any physical contact with you horrifies me. I still like you. I mean, I want you to be happy ... But not in that way ... It costs me too much ... The price is too heavy.'

'But I didn't want to do anything,' said Angel. 'I was only moving and I just brushed against you. Don't get so worked up.'

'I'm not worked up,' she said. 'I'm always like this nowadays. Go and sleep in your own room! ... Please, Angel. Take pity on me.'

'You're not well,' he murmured, shaking his head.

He put his hand on her shoulder. She shuddered, but did not move away. He kissed her gently on the forehead and got out of bed.

'I'm going to my own room then, darling,' he said. 'Don't worry ...'

'Angel,' she said again, 'Angel, I ... I don't want ... Oh, I don't know how to say it to you ... I don't want to ... any more ... and I don't think I'll ever want to start again ... Try to find yourself another wife. I won't be jealous.'

'You don't love me any more ...' said Angel, sadly.

'Not in that way,' she answered.

He went out. She sat still in the bed and looked at the place beside her where Angel's head had been at the bottom of the pillow.

One of the children moved in its sleep. She listened carefully. Then the baby went off to sleep again. She raised her hand to put out the light. Now she had the whole bed to herself—and never again would a man touch her.

XXI

IN HIS room Timortis had also just put out the light. In another part of the house the chirruping mechanical birds of the exhausted nurse's bedsprings slowly sank behind their lockgates into the silent cages of sleep. For a few moments he stayed flat on his back. The events of the last few days danced before his eyes until they reached boiling point and his heart beat violently. Little by little he let himself go and slid into unconsciousness, closing his tired lids on pupils lacerated by the vicious brutality of so many unaccustomed sights.

SECOND PART

I

ON THE cliff, high above the garden, far beyond the bay which
the sea garlanded—night and day—with a beard of dirty off-
white cottonwool, a high mass, a shapeless irregular mush-
room of solid menacing stone rose up, sharpened by the razor
of the wind, and frequented only by goats and ferns. From
the house it was quite invisible. It was known as The Old
Man Of The Mountains as a counterpart to its brother, The
Ancient Mariner, which sprang out of the sea, just facing it
and slightly to the left. Three faces of The Old Man Of The
Mountains were easily accessible. But the North face offered
to the tripper who ventured on to its unformed tracks a series
of almost insurmountable tricks, traps and obstacles that might
have been the mischievous result of some corbusian calcula-
tion, giving an ascent from that side all the certainty of a
throw of the modular dice.

Occasionally the Customs and Excise men came here for
a day's training and, all day long, in their bloodstained green
and white striped tracksuits they struggled to inculcate into
their apprentices the rudiments of creeping and crawling,
without which contraband smuggling would become a very
boring and tiresome adventure.

On that day, The Old Man Of The Mountains was deserted. Except for Clementine. Clinging closely to the rock,
making sure of every foothold in the granite features, she
slowly scaled the craggy face of the yetistone.

On previous days it had been child's play to reach the
summit from the Eastern, Western and Southern flanks. But

75

the smooth unflinching stone of the North offered not a single foothold, nothing immediately obvious on which the fingers could grip.

She found herself practically flat on her stomach against an almost vertical slope. Three yards above her, an overhanging projection would allow her to get a grip. That was where the real work would start—for the whole of the upper part of The Old Man Of The Mountains was overhanging. But before that she still had to surmount the three yards up to the ledge.

She hung out over space by the tips of her sandals, caught in a long cleft which ran diagonally across the slope. The earth that had settled in this narrow cleft was sufficient to enable small plants to grow there. The green line that this made was like the mossy slit of the roseless buttonhole of a commuting science master, or like a gigantic model of the parting in his vanishing hair.

Clementine took long, deep, slow breaths so that she could hoist herself up like a fly on a wall. Three yards. Only three more yards. Less than twice her own height.

Looked at closely, there were plenty of things to grab and get a hold on. The whole problem was to look closely enough to see them; but not to look so closely that it would be obvious that they were absolutely insufficient to prevent the climber from falling.

She put her hand on two of the mock projections and scrambled up.

Through the tight material of her pants the rock pressed, slashed and caressed her knees. Her feet rose a foot above the thin green belt.

She took another breath, looked round and started off again. Ten minutes later she was standing on the ledge, ready for the last lap. Her forehead was damp and her dishevelled hair was sticking to her temples. The smell of her own vegetable perspiration filled her nostrils.

Space was so limited here that she could hardly move.

Turning her head, she could see The Ancient Mariner with his collar of foam from an unusual angle. Already high in the sky, the sun brought clouds of dancing spangles round the knuckled reefs of the cliff.

The Old Man Of The Mountains, above her, ended against the sky, pointing into space like the spine of a three-quarters open book, slightly tilted and standing on end. An acute angle, shooting out into infinity, and that had to be followed.

Clementine flung back her head, looked up at the acute jutting angle which was the only course she could take, and purred with soft pleasure. The other angle, between her legs, was growing warm and moist.

II

On all fours the three little scoundrels galloped round the room where they were locked before they were given their three oak lock feed. They were beginning to get out of the habit of sleeping twenty-four hours a day and enjoyed giving their little backsides a bit of rest by using their knees for a change. Noel and Joel yelped. Alfa Romeo, more dignified, slowly circumnambulated round a little low coffee table.

Timortis watched them. He often joined in their games with them now that they were more like miniature human beings than larvae. Due to the climate and the care with which they were looked after, they were astonishingly advanced for their age. The first two had smooth pale blond hair. The third was as dark and curly as the day he was born, looking a year older than his brothers.

They had a natural gift for dribbling. The carpet was marked by a little damp stain every time they stopped, the stain being momentarily united to the mouth of its author by a long, frail, supple and shimmering thread.

Timortis paid special attention to Alfa Romeo. With his nose to the ground he was using up the remains of his energy by going round the table as fast as he could. His movement came to a halt and he sat down. But his eyes rose to the top of the table.

'Well, what's your opinion of that?' asked Timortis.

'Yuk!'...said Alfa Romeo.

He put his hand up to the table. Too far. Still in his sitting position, he got closer to it and, seizing the edge firmly and deliberately between his fingers, he stood up.

'You made it!' said Timortis. 'That's the way to get things done.'

'Oh! Yuk!' replied Alfa Romeo, letting go, falling down hard on his bottom and looking round in surprise.

'You see,' said Timortis, 'you shouldn't have let go. It's very simple when you know how. In seven years time you'll be in the choir, in twenty you'll have got your degree, and five years after that you'll be married.'

Alfa Romeo shook his head as if he didn't think so, and was back on his feet in no time at all.

'Well,' concluded Timortis. 'Well, we'll have to go and tell the bootmaker or the blacksmith. They bring kids up the hard way here, you know. And once a horse has been shod it doesn't feel it any more. That's the way your mother wants things to be.'

He left them alone. What a life! And no-one to psycho-analyse. The little maid was just as impossible as ever. No progress to report there.

'I suppose I'll be the one to have to take you down, sweeties,' he said. 'It's weeks since I've set foot in the village.'

Alfa Romeo had started going round the coffee table again, but standing up this time.

'Well, well!' observed Timortis. 'You certainly learn quickly. Maybe you'll beat my time-table. At any rate, you'll be somebody for me to talk to.'

Joel and Noel began to show some signs of agitation and Timortis looked at his watch.

'Yes, yes, yes,' he said, 'it's time. And it's even past your time. But don't be impatient—nobody's perfect.'

Joel started crying. Noel joined in. Their brother sat still and looked down his nose at them.

It was nearly half past three when Clementine got back. She found Timortis still sitting in the same place. He was perfectly calm and collected and did not even seem to hear the caterwauling crescendo coming from the terrible twins. Alfa Romeo, as calm and contented as Timortis himself, was sitting on his knees, deep in the fascinating game of pulling his russet beard.

'So here you are at last!' said Timortis.

The left leg of Clementine's pants had been completely ripped off. And she herself had a large cut bruise—red and purple—on her cheek.

'It looks as if you've been having a good time,' he said.

'Not bad,' she replied coldly. 'And how about you?'

Her flat tone contrasted visibly with the physical excitement with which every fibre of her body was still impregnated.

'What a din!' she remarked—equally objectively—a minute later.

'Well,' said Timortis, 'they're thirsty. They need you, you know, just as much as your old rocks do.'

'I couldn't come any quicker,' she said. 'I'll take the one who's been behaving himself best first.'

She took Alfa Romeo off the psychoanalyst's knees and sat down in the other armchair. Timortis discreetly turned his head away. It embarrassed him to see her giving them her breast because of the network of blue veins that crept across her transparent white skin. And besides, such things as giving children their feed seemed to him to be very far from the right use to which a breast should be put.

'You know he can walk . . .' went on the psychiatrist quietly.

She jumped and violently snatched the nipple from the baby's lips . . . The child looked up and waited in silence.

'He can . . . walk?'

She put him down on the floor.

'Walk then! . . .' she shouted.

Alfa Romeo grabbed at her torn trousers and hoisted himself up. She lifted him up again, slightly perturbed.

Joel and Noel, still screaming, came over on all fours.

'What about these two?' she asked.

'Not yet,' said the psychiatrist.

'Good,' she approved.

'You seem to be upset that he can walk?' hinted Timortis.
'Oh!' mumbled Clementine. 'They won't go far yet, the poor chicks.'

Alfa Romeo had finished. She grabbed Noel and Joel by their reins and caught them.

Timortis stood up.

'Then I presume that I may assume,' he queried, 'that you still love them?'

'They seem to be fine little fellows. Brave *and* tough,' replied Clementine. 'And besides, they need me. Are you going out?'

'I need a break,' observed Timortis.

'Call in at the blacksmith's,' said Clementine. 'See him about Alfa Romeo.'

'Why do you want them to be brought up like farm children?'

'Why not?' said Clementine drily. 'It's not hurting you, is it?'

'It is,' replied Timortis.

'Don't be such a snob!' said Clementine. 'I want my kids to be plain and simple.'

He left the room. Alfa Romeo watched him go and his expression was as morose as that of a sandstone saint after a particularly brutal bombing.

III

THE MAID appeared.

'You wanted me?' she said.

'Take the children. Change them and put them to bed,' said Clementine.

She looked her up and down and remarked 'You're looking bloody well.'

'Ah!' said the maid. 'D'you think so?'

'Are you still sleeping with Timortis?' asked Clementine.

'Yes,' said the maid.

'Tell me what he does to you.'

'Well,' said the maid, 'er, he covers me.'

'Doesn't he ask you any questions?'

'Does he!' said the maid. 'Does he! Before I've even had time to get in the mood, there he is asking me his questions.'

'Don't give him any answers,' said Clementine, 'and don't sleep with him any more.'

'Don't think I could do without it now,' said the girl.

'You disgust me. You'll be in a fine state if you find you're going to have a baby.'

'Hasn't happened so far.'

'But things like that do happen,' murmured Clementine with a shudder. 'Anyway, you'd be better off not sleeping with him. That kind of thing is absolutely revolting.'

'But I don't see anything revolting,' said the girl, 'because of the way we do it.'

'Get out,' said Clementine.

Whitarse picked up the three children and went out.

Clementine went back to her own room. She took off her

torn clothes, dabbed herself with eau-de-Cologne, washed the bruise and cut on her face and stretched out on her back on the floor to do her exercises.

When she had finished them she rose from the floor to her bed.

Next time she wouldn't be late for their feed. It doesn't hurt children to have to wait like that sometimes. All that babies want to do is eat when they're hungry. Nothing else matters to them at all.

Angel, sprawled out on his bed in an attitude of the most complete desolation, raised his eyes when he heard somebody knock three times on his door.

'Yes?' he said.

Timortis went in and made an obvious observation. 'Naturally you've still got nothing to do . . .'

'Still nothing, naturally,' replied Angel.

'How're things?' asked the psychiatrist.

'So-so. I've got some kind of a fever.'

'Let's have a look.'

He went over to him and felt his pulse.

'You're right,' he agreed.

Then he sat on the bed.

'Shift your feet.'

Angel moved over a little and Timortis, once he had sat down, began to pull his autumnal beard.

'What have you been doing lately?' he asked.

'You know perfectly well,' said Angel.

'Looked for a girl?'

'Found a girl.'

'And been to bed with her?'

'I can't . . .' said Angel. 'As soon as I get her between the sheets an attack comes on.'

'And Clementine's still not interested?' said Timortis.

'Not a chance,' said Angel. 'And all the others bring on this fever too.'

'You must have a guilty conscience,' remarked Timortis.

Angel smiled at the sarcasm.

'You didn't like it when I said that to you one day,' he remarked too.

'Well,' said Timortis, 'it's not a very nice thing to hear said about yourself . . . especially when you've got no conscience at all.'

Angel didn't answer. He looked extremely uncomfortable. He had unbuttoned his collar and was gulping in great draughts of the mild May air.

'I've just come from your wife,' said Timortis, trying to get him to stop thinking about himself. 'The kids are shooting up like the devil. Alfa Romeo can stand already.'

'Poor thing,' said Angel. 'He's too young . . . He'll grow bandy.'

'No, of course he won't,' said Timortis. 'If he can stand up, then it's because his legs are strong enough to hold him.'

'We should just let nature take its course . . .' murmured Angel.

'Your wife's sending me to fetch the blacksmith,' said Timortis. 'Don't you think she's bringing them up a bit too much the hard way?'

'I can't do anything about it,' said Angel. 'She did the suffering—not me. And that gives her the right.'

'I don't agree,' said Timortis. 'Why should something as useless as suffering give anybody at all any rights at all over anything at all?'

'Does she really treat them badly?' asked Angel, without pursuing that topic.

'No, of course not,' said Timortis. 'She's harder on herself. But that's no reason either. It all shows a lack of confidence and makes her jolly bad company.'

'I think she really loves them,' said Angel.

'Oh, she does . . .' replied Timortis.

Angel shut up. It was obvious that he wasn't well.

'You ought to find something to do,' said Timortis. 'Why don't you build yourself a boat?'

'I haven't got a boat . . .' replied Angel.

'I said "Build yourself a boat".'

'That's a good idea,' groaned the prostrate invalid.

Timortis said no more and stood up.

'Well, I'll go and fetch the blacksmith,' he said, 'since she insists.'

'Go tomorrow,' suggested Angel. 'Let the poor little thing have another day's freedom.'

Timortis shook his head.

'I don't know what to make of you,' he said. 'If you're against the idea, why don't you say so?'

'I'm in a very inferior position,' said Angel. 'Anyway, I think she's right. She's their mother, after all.'

Timortis shrugged his shoulders and went out. The wide tiled staircase rattled under his rapid footsteps. He crossed the hall and went into the garden. Spring sprinkled the earth with a million miracles of exploding colour, flickering pyrotechnically like sumptuous slashes in the billiard-tables of glittering green grass.

IV

THE NEXT day being a Wednesday, Timortis was careful to avoid going through the main street—and the square where the Old Folks Fair was held—as he went into the village. He took a side turning before reaching the crowded fork and followed a little path, full of nettles, benjamint and lousewort (called stinkroots by the local farmhands), which ran round the backs of the houses.

Cats were stretched out on the tops of walls or along window sills, lazily licking up the sun.

All was as quiet as the grave. Despite the permanent boredom that never stopped nagging at him, Timortis let himself relax and felt his empty cells, to use a tissue of truth, begin to function.

He knew that the scarlet stream ran brinkful past the houses on the right, and he knew that a little further on it turned sharply to the left. So he wasn't entirely surprised to see the narrow path do the same at exactly the same sharp angle and, at the same time, he felt himself logically obliged to assume that the whole group of farms lining the road all went back to an equal depth.

A few hundred yards ahead of him a group of people seemed to be involved in some complicated ceremony or operation. As he hurried towards the scene of action, a terrifying yell pierced his sensitive eardrums. A cry of surprised pain, it was wrenched into the air in such a way that it sounded very close to anger, although none of its passive undertones escaped Timortis's alarmed notice.

86

He hurried still faster, his pace and his pulse increasing with every step. The country people were crucifying a horse on a great rustic oak gate. Timortis went closer. Six men were holding the animal down on to the wooden framework. Two more men were busy nailing down its front left leg. The nail had already gone through the ankle. It was an enormous carpenter's nail with a great gleaming head. And a thread of dark glistening blood ran down the animal's smooth brown coat. Timortis needed no more explanation of the yelp of pain that had drawn him to the spot.

The country people went on with their work and took no more notice of Timortis than if he had been somewhere miles away, such as in The Hovering Islands. Only the horse stared at him with its great brown eyes streaming with tears, and bared its long teeth to give him a feeble fleeting apologetic smile.

'What on earth has it done?' asked the psychiatrist quietly.

'It's a stallion, and it fell into sin,' answered one of the five or six men who looked briskly round at him.

'That's nothing very serious,' said Timortis.

The man who had answered him spat on the ground and refused to answer any more. They were now nailing the stallion's right leg, and Timortis felt a shiver of pain shoot through each of his nerve-ends as he saw the tip of the nail go in and disappear, and then split the gleaming coat that was tarnished with anguish as it was rammed in with a heavy hammer. Just as before, the horse gave a short sharp horrible cry. Its shoulders broke under the abnormal tension that the executioners had put on them in their efforts to nail the limbs to the heavy gate. The animal's joints were all distorted and bent. Its hoofs made an acute angle between them to frame the expressive head. Flies, already thrilled by the sight and smell of the blood, were coming to paddle in the pools gathering round the vicious nails.

The men holding down the back half stepped back and then let go with the soles of their clogs against the bottom

87

rail of the gate. Not one detail of the operation skipped Timortis's frozen attention. He could feel a razor blade stuck inside his throat and only managed to swallow it with the greatest difficulty. The stallion's belly shuddered and its gargantuan pizzle seemed to shrivel, collapse and then press inside the skin to bury itself.

From the other side of the road there came a buzz of voices. Two men—one middle-aged and the other a youngster—that Timortis had not noticed coming, were now almost there. The eldest one had his hands in his pockets. He was big and hairy, his bare arms coming out of a tight woollen vest, and a red leather apron was flapping round his legs. The youngster, a pathetic weakly apprentice, was struggling along with a heavy iron cauldron filled with glowing coals, out of which was sticking the handle of a spiked hook that had been plunged in it to get red hot.

'The blacksmith's here . . .' somebody said.

'Really,' Timortis could not help himself saying under his breath, 'you're treating this poor animal far too severely.'

'It isn't an animal,' said one of the farmhands, 'it's a stallion.'

'But it's done nothing serious.'

'It was free,' said the man. 'All it had to do was stop itself falling into sin.'

'But that's what stallions are for,' said Timortis.

The apprentice put down the cauldron and revived the fire with a pair of bellows. His master dug amongst the coals for a few moments, twisting the spiked hook. Then, when he felt that it was ready, he grabbed it tightly, pulled it out and turned towards the stallion.

Timortis looked away and ran. His thumbs stuffed in his ears, his fists covering them, he ran madly and awkwardly with his elbows against his neck, shouting loudly to stop himself hearing the hopeless clamours of the horse. He stopped only when he had reached the little square which he knew was near the church. His hands dropped down, back to the

88

sides of his body. The scarlet stream, which he had just crossed on a light wooden bridge, ran smoothly, deeply, ripple-free and still. A little further on, Glory Hallelujah was swimming, struggling to get his breath, trying to drag on to his vessel a shred of pale flesh and bone that crumbled and disintegrated under his teeth.

V

CAUTIOUSLY, TIMORTIS looked round. Nobody had noticed his wild flight. The calm egg of the church was broken only by the blue stained-glass window, a hole through which it could be sucked out. A sound of singing came from inside. Timortis walked all the way round the church. Then, without hurrying, he went up the steps. And then he went inside.

Standing in front of the altar the priest was beating time. A choir of twenty or so children were singing a communion anthem. In order to hear its tricksy words better Timortis went closer to the altar.

> *Calvary was landscaped*
> *For the final test*
> *Happiness is shitshaped*
> *But Jesus is the best*
> *Folktales fill a figleaf*
> *Hair may fill a chest*
> *Grandad's filled with roastbeef*
> *But Jesus Christ is best.*
> *Lean Pisas*
> *May tease us*
> *With holy gravity*
> *Gold tweezers*
> *May squeeze us*
> *Dry of necessity*
> *Not Caesar's*
> *Fat fees as-*
> *Sure renderings so free*

As Jesus
Bucksheesus
Lapped Lord of Luxury . . .

By the time they had reached this last line the psychiatrist realised that the vicar must have written the hymn himself and gave up listening to the words as it would be easier to ask him for a copy of them later. The music had restored a little of the lost calm to his troubled spirit. Not wishing to disturb the vicar during his energetic rehearsal, he sat down quietly and waited. It was cool in the church. The voices of the children tarzanned their way through the frozen lacy music of the structural members. Letting his eyes wander here and there, Timortis noticed that the covered pulpit had been steadily set up in its right place again, and that two tremendous hinges at its base now allowed it to be knocked over without doing any damage to it. He realised that he hadn't been back in the place since the three imps were christened and thought that verily time passes—and, in verity, time passed, for twilight was already softening the hard edges of the blue squares of stained-glass and the voices of the children began to sound sweeter. Thus it is with music and darkness whose balmy association puts a soothing dressing on the salad of our souls.

He went out in peace and thought that he had better go and see the blacksmith if he wanted to get out of being beaten up by Clementine when he got back.

Evening was about to fall. Timortis set off for the village green, his nose following the smell of burning hoof and horn which was vaguely wafting from that direction. In order not to lose his way he closed his eyes and let his nostrils guide him to the dark shop where the apprentice was kindling the furnace of the forge by heavily pumping away at a pair of bellows. A horse was waiting at the door for its last shoe. It had just been clipped, all except the lower half of its four legs, and Timortis looked admiringly at its round rump, its

proud buttocks, its smooth and gently concave back, its powerful chest and its crewcut mane like a bristly briar hedge.

The blacksmith emerged from the black hole. Timortis was
sure that it was the same man that he had seen an hour earlier
coming along the path to torture the stallion.

'Good-morning,' said Timortis.

'Morning,' replied the smith, blackly.

At the end of a long pair of pincers in his right hand he
held a piece of red hot iron. From the end of his left arm
hung a heavy hammer.

'Lift up your leg,' he said to the horse.

It obeyed, and in a second it was shod. Vivid blue smoke
belched out from the carbonised hoof to fill the air. Timortis
coughed in the sudden obscurity. The horse put its foot back
on the ground to test the shoe.

'How's that feel?' asked the smith. 'Not too tight?'

The horse nodded to say *No*, nestled its head against the
blacksmith's shoulder, and he patted the end of its muzzle.
Then the animal went off at a jaunty trot. The floor was
sprinkled with heaps and mounds of hair, just like a barber's.

'Whoa there!' the smith's black voice called to his apprentice. 'Are you going to come and sweep this mess up? . . .'

'Yes, guv,' answered the pale voice of the apprentice.

The smith was about to go back inside, so Timortis put
his hand on his arm.

'Just a moment . . .'

'What?' said the smith.

'Could you come up to the house on the cliff? One of the
boys has started to walk.'

'Is it all that urgent?' asked the smith.

'Yes, I'm afraid it is,' said Timortis.

'Can't he come down here?'

'No.'

'Oh, all right. I'll be there. Just let me see what's in my
book,' said the smith.

He went back into his forge, knocking into the apprentice

92

who, armed with an old broom, was beginning to collect all the clipped horsehair into a disgusting looking pile. Timortis followed the smith as far as the threshold. It was extremely dark inside, but the blinding glare from the flaring orange furnace splattered flickering shadows over everything. Close to the source of light, Timortis could pick out the anvil and, on an iron work-bench at its side, the silhouette of something that looked vaguely human, attracting grey metallic reflections from the light coming in through the door.

But the smith had already turned round, having checked with his diary, and came back to Timortis. His brow blackened when he saw that he had been followed.

'Keep outside,' he said. 'This isn't a peep-show.'

'Sorry,' mumbled Timortis, more intrigued than ever.

'I'll be round tomorrow,' said the smith. 'In the morning, about ten. Get everything ready. My time is precious.'

'Of course,' said Timortis. 'And thanks.'

The man went back into his forge. The apprentice had finished collecting in his harvest of hair and had just set light to it. Timortis hurried away before the stench had the chance to make him faint.

On the way back he noticed a little tailor's and haberdasher's shop. Through the lighted window he could clearly see a little old lady just putting the finishing touches of broderie anglaise on to a green and white dress. Timortis stopped and thought for a moment, then went on his way again. Just before reaching home he remembered that Clementine had been wearing exactly the same dress a few days earlier. A green and white striped dress, with collar and cuffs of broderie anglaise. Yet none of Clementine's clothes came from the village. Or did they?

VI

TIMORTIS GOT up. The whole night's efforts to get the maid to talk had been fruitless. And, as always, they had ended up by copulating in that strange quadruped position—the only one she would accept. Timortis was bored with this exhausting and exhaustive mutism, and needed the perfume of the girl, gathered in the young undergrowth of the dewy jungle that he had been exploring between her thighs and that still lingered on his hands, to console him for having been unable to drag anything more out of her than hopelessly vague responses to his mercilessly precise questions. When she wasn't there he would lose his temper and would think of any stupid thing to argue with her about, but the next time she came back he would be put off by her natural inertia and silence that were too ingrained for him to be able to fight against them, too simple to be able to engender anything more violent in him than total discouragement. He sniffed at his palm, imagined himself stalking his prey, staking his claim, calming his stake . . . and such thoughts caused his weak flesh to be moved despite its willing spiritual lassitude.

Finishing freshening up, but carefully avoiding washing his hands, he thought he would go and have a word with Angel. He had to talk to somebody.

As Angel wasn't in his bedroom, a fact demonstrated beyond all possible doubt by the fact that replies were absent after a triple series of three successive knockings, he verified divers other rooms by the same method and concluded that the gentleman in question must have gone out.

94

Sounds of sawing came from the garden. So he went down there.

Turning off along a bushy path he furtively sniffed at his fingers. The smell was still there.

The chugging sound of the saw grew sharper. Then he saw Angel, outside the garage, in blue jeans and shirtsleeves, sawing through a heavy piece of wood supported across a pair of trestles.

Timortis went over to him. The rough end of the piece of wood, all split and broken, fell on to the earth with a dull thud. A heap of fresh resinous yellow sawdust had already piled up like an egg-timer between the trestles.

When Angel saw Timortis he stood up, put down his saw and held out his hand to the psychiatrist.

'You see,' he said, 'I'm taking your advice.'

'Is it going to be a boat?' asked Timortis.

'It is.'

'D'you know how to build a boat?'

'I'm not going to expect it to take me round the world,' said Angel. 'I'll be happy so long as it floats.'

'Make a raft then,' said Timortis. 'That's square. And far simpler.'

'Yes,' said Angel, 'but it wouldn't be as beautiful.'

'More like a water-colour,' said Timortis.

'Precisely.'

Angel put down his saw and picked up the piece of wood that he had just sawn in two.

'What's that for?' asked Timortis.

'I don't know yet,' said Angel. 'I'm just cutting off the rotten bits first. I must have good materials to work with.'

'But you're giving yourself twice as much labour ...'

'It doesn't matter. I've got nothing else to do.'

'Hm. Strange,' murmured the psychiatrist. 'Don't you think you could work unless you got all your materials straight beforehand?'

'I could—but I wouldn't like it much,'

95

'How long have you been like that?'

Angel looked at him with a suspicious flicker in the corner of his eye.

'Now look here, is this going to be an official interrogation?'

'Not at all! . . .' objected Timortis, passing his fingers under his nose once again, pretending to be breathing with only one nostril in order to clear it.

'Hankering after your old profession?'

'No, no, no,' said Timortis. 'But if I'm not going to be interested in other people, who *do* you want me to be interested in?'

'In yourself, of course,' said Angel.

'But you know perfectly that I'm nothing.'

'Why don't you ask yourself why? That would already be a start towards finding something to fill yourself up with.'

'Mere trifles,' said Timortis.

'And still nobody to psychoanalyse?'

'Nobody . . .'

'Why not try the animals? They're doing that now, I hear.'

'How do you know?' said Timortis.

'Oh, I must have read it somewhere.'

'Mustn't believe everything you read,' replied the psychiatrist in a superior tone.

The inside of his right thumb had really retained a most characteristic perfume.

'Try it, all the same,' said Angel.

'I'll tell you something . . .' began the psychiatrist—and then he stopped abruptly.

'Tell me what?'

'No,' said Timortis, trying to end that topic, 'I don't think I'll tell you after all. I'll find out for myself whether it's true or not.'

'Was it a supposition?'

'A hypothesis.'

'All right,' said Angel. 'After all, it's your business.'

He went back to the garage. The back of the car could be

96

seen through the open door and, leaning against the wall on the right, stacks of planks weighing against each other with a supple concave inflection.

'You're certainly not short of wood,' assessed Timortis.

'I think it's going to turn out to be a fairly large boat,' said Angel.

He went in and selected a plank. Timortis looked up at the sky. Not a single cloud.

'I'll leave you then,' he said. 'I'm going into the village.'

'Good luck!'

The saw started sighing again shortly after, and the sounds decreased accordingly as the distance between the garage and Timortis grew greater. By the time he had reached the garden gates he could not hear it any more. He set off along the powdery dust of the road. While he had been in the garden talking to Angel he had suddenly remembered the big black cat that was always perched on a wall at the far end of the village. One of the few creatures that might possibly approve of him and accept him.

That wall must have been one of the cat's favourite spots. He hurried along to make sure. At the same time he held his thumb close under his nose and breathed in deeply. The perfume materialised into living shapes. The robust curves of the maid's back with himself clinging to her rounded thighs which flexed and quivered as he battered and rammed into her. Imaginative images which made walking much easier.

VII

THE WIND was dragging straws across the road, straws that it had wrenched from the tops of the dunghills and siloes as it passed, from under the narrow cracks of farmyard gates, straws found flying outside barns from which they had been rejected, old backbreaking straws from haystacks that had been long forgotten in the sun. The wind had got up early that morning. It had crumpled the surface of the sea, skimming the icing off the spindrift, climbing the cliff-face, making all the strident briarbells ring like lost castrated cattle on misty moors. Then it swung round the house, hacking out whistles for itself at every slightest corner, raising here and there a light-hearted tile, rolling away the remains of last autumn's leaves from the gutters, their dull copper filigree having escaped the appeal to merge into the baser metal of compost. It dragged skeins and veils of grey powder across the highway, rasping over the bald cracked skin and thick dry crusts of antique parched puddles.

A whirlwind was forming on the outskirts of the village. Swishing twigs, wild oats, looping grass began to gyrate at the summit of a wobbling cone of purring aerial jelly. The pointed tip dodged here and there, like the doodling lead in a pencil tripping along and running over the curve of a vertical graph. At the top of the high grey wall was something soft, black and spongy. The summit zoomed towards it in an unpremeditated zigzag. It was the empty, weightless carcase of a black cat, a cat with no substance, impalpable and dry. The whirlwind whizzed at it, rolled it down into the road, dislocated its gaunt lank bankrupt envelope like a discarded sheet of newspaper blowing along a beach with great awkward seven-league strides, stretching taut sharp threads of sound between the tips of the high long grass—and the phantom of the cat left the ground in a caricature of a somersault and fell back on to it in an anamorphosis of its original shape. A fast leap with the wind whisked it flat against a hedge, then it was whirled up again like a boneless puppet for the next waltz. Then the cat took a sudden bound over the little hill where the road turned. It cut madly across fields; it ploughed through the green shoots of newborn ears of corn, electrifying itself on each of the needle spikes, sparking at every contact, flying from point to point like a drunken crow . . . and empty with the perfect emptiness of dried vegetation, like the last straws from ancient haystacks long forgotten in the sun.

VIII

TIMORTIS LEAPT on to the road, gulping the fresh air. He noticed a million new odours which set off a jumble of new memories inside him. For a week now he had been absorbing every fragment of the mental substance of the black cat. He went from surprise to surprise and found it extremely hard to learn how to manage in this complex and violently physical world. It was not true that he had also inherited from it an altogether new way of walking; his physical habits and his basic reflex movements had been too profoundly acquired, too thoroughly assimilated to be capable of much alteration through coming into contact with those of a black cat. Its feeble proportional intensity explained the small effect that it had. He laughed now at his attempts to convince and persuade himself that he felt the need to scratch his ear with his foot or sleep curled up in a ball with his knuckles under his chin. But he hung on to a series of desires, sensations and thoughts which he still found enormously attractive, even though he knew how shallow they were. Take catmint and catkins. His increased perception told him that clumps of them were to be found a few yards ahead. And yet he deliberately turned his back on them, taking another route into the village by following the path round the cliff. An idea had struck him, he had found it good, and he was letting it guide him.

He reached the edge of the escarpment and easily found a hardly discernible little path that had probably been made by tumbling rolling stones. Without a moment's hesitation he had taken it, and turning his back on space, used his hands to help him scramble down. He had a few moments of fright when stones broke loose and fell away under his feet but there was no doubt about it that his movements showed a supple sureness that he had never noticed before. Within a few moments he was at the bottom of the cliff. The low tide revealed a narrow ribbon of smooth pebbles below a frame of jagged rocks tapped with deep pools. Timortis, quickening his pace, hurried over to one of them. He crept up to the edge, selected a suitable spot and then squatted down with his sleeves rolled back. His cupped fingers skimmed the water.

Ten seconds passed. And then a little yellow fish showed its head behind a green reed. It could hardly be noticed against the vegetation at the bottom of the pool, but Timortis could see its graceful gills and his heart began to thump with a delicate delight.

With sudden sure aim his arm shot out. He grabbed the quivering animal and brought it to his nostrils. It smelt really good.

Licking his lips, he opened his mouth and snapped off the palpitating fish's head.

It was delicious. And the depths of the pool were full of them.

IX

ANGEL LAID the screwdriver and chisel on the bench and wiped his forehead with the back of his cuff. He had just completed the starboard. The bright copper nails made a pretty pattern like red sequins along the curves of the clear wood. His boat was taking shape. It rested on a cradle of oak pointing out towards the sea. Two oak rails led from it down the face of the cliff.

The three children were playing nearby with the heaps of sawdust and shavings which filled a corner of the workshop. Their development had been curiously rapid. All three of them could walk now in their little iron clogs. Only Alfa Romeo's feet still bled a little in the evenings, but Joel and Noel were tougher and their skin had soon hardened.

Angel was surprised. It was time for their feed and the maid hadn't come. But the children still had to be fed. Then he suddenly remembered that the maid had had to go out. He looked at his watch with a sigh. Actually Clementine was getting better at not forgetting to give them their feed and if he should ever complain to her about it, however slightly, she would always justify herself insolently with a kind of hateful hensureness. And Angel was usually embarrased to see the children watching them ironically and going over to take their mother's side.

As he looked at them he caught Alfa Romeo's seaching eye which worried him even more than the others. With a tinge of anger he told himself that they were only getting what they deserved. All that he himself asked for was to be allowed to make a fuss of them now and again, to pick them up on his knees and kiss them—but he found that he was never asked.

'They only like people who scold them,' he thought, rather spitefully.

All the same, he went over to them.

'Come and have something to eat, my lads,' he said.

Joel and Noel opened their mouths and groaned.

'Want Tina,' said Joel.

'Tina,' repeated Noel.

'Well, Clementine's not here,' said Angel. 'So come along with me and we'll try to find her.'

Taking dignified steps, Alfa Romeo walked on ahead. Angel held out his hands to the pair of twins. Without taking them they got to their feet in a cloud of sawdust and shavings and clumsily ran after their brother. Angel felt sticky and nervous. But all the same he went on following them from a distance because the hanging garden was full of snares and traps and, however irritated and annoyed he may have been, he would have hated anything to happen to them.

He reached the door of the house a second after them and caught up with them inside. Noel called out for his mother in a shrill voice and Joel imitated him.

'Shut up!' said Angel, with a certain forcefulness.

They stopped, astonished.

'Come into the kitchen,' went on Angel.

He was rather surprised to find nothing ready for them. She might have got their feed ready all the same. He sat them down awkwardly in front of bowls of bread and milk and went to the door while they noisily gobbled and slobbered. He narrowly missed bumping into Timortis.

'Haven't seen Clementine, have you?' he asked him.

With a feline gesture the psychiatrist put his hand over his ear.

'Prr ... er ...' he replied, without compromising himself.

'Give over your cats' tricks,' said Angel. 'You don't need them any more than I do. And tell me where my wife is.'

'I'm sorry,' said Timortis, 'but I went into the dining-room by mistake. You'll find her there.'

'And what's that supposed to mean?' groaned Angel.

He pushed Timortis aside and hurried out furiously. The psychiatrist crept after him. It was obvious that Angel wanted to translate his disgust at his own incompetence with the kids into anger, but Timortis was careful to avoid stressing this for him.

Angel prepared a cutting sentence. He rarely lost his temper, but when he did, it was always because of the children. He should have given more time to them. He was on edge. His heart was thudding away with suppressed fury. She didn't care about anybody.

He burst open the door—and stopped stock still. Clementine, with her pants down round her ankles, was stretched out on the dining table, moving breathlessly as if in a trance. Her hands were convulsively contracting and clutching at her sides. Her hips circled, her thighs rose and fell on the polished table top, fluttered as her legs opened still wider and an almost inaudible cry escaped from her lips. Angel stood there for a moment, stupefied, and then took a step backwards. His face turned slowly purple. He closed the door again and walked quickly out into the garden again. Timortis stopped on the steps when he saw him disappearing round the corner of one of the paths. He retraced his own steps and went back into the kitchen.

'I wonder . . .' he murmured to himself.

With less than half-a-dozen swift and accurate sweeps he cleared up the mess made by the three little buggers. Full now, they were happily burbling amongst themselves. He wiped their faces and pushed them outside.

'Run along and play with daddy . . .' he said.

'Want Tina . . .' said Noel.

'Tina . . .' said Joel.

Alfa Romeo said nothing, but trotted off towards the workshop followed by his brothers. Timortis frowned deeply for a te, hesitated for another of only fifty-nine seconds, and then went back into the dining-room. Flat on her stomach this time, Clementine was still deep in her obscene thrashing on the table-top. The psychiatrist took a whiff of the air in the room. Then he sadly withdrew and crept back upstairs to his own room. He stretched out on the bed, trying to purr, but without much success. He had to admit to himself that in spite of all his efforts he still could not do it very convincingly. In fact, had the black cat that he had psychoanalysed several weeks ago really known how to purr? And then he went back to thinking about a more interesting subject—Clementine. Perhaps he should have just touched her. He smelt his fingers. Something of the maid still lingered on them, but it was already a day old and was very faint now. It's true that he was comfortable on his bed, but the woman below must still be jigging away on the downstairs table. He sprang up on his bed, put his feet on the floor, went downstairs, and stopped outside the dining-room door. He put his ear against it. Not a sound now. He went in.

Clementine, still half-naked, was asleep. At least, she had stopped moving and was lying with her cheek against the table-top, her naked buttocks sticking up and being the first thing he saw. Timortis sensed something. He went nearer. She moved slightly when she heard him and turned over on to one shoulder. Timortis stopped and stood as still as a statue.

'Excuse me,' he said. 'I thought I heard you call.'

Her eyes were dark with worried bewilderment.

'What am I doing on this table?' she said.

'Er . . .' mumbled Timortis. 'I don't know. Perhaps you were feeling the heat . . .'

Then she realised that her clothes were down.

'I had a dream . . .' she began.

Then, like Angel a few moments earlier, she blushed to the very roots of her hair.

'Did I? . . .' she went on.

Then she sat up, making no attempt to cover her naked thighs.

'Oh, but you know the way I'm made,' she murmured.

Deflated, Timortis said not a word.

'I suppose I must have got worked up about something or other,' she said, beginning to put her clothes straight again.

'It looks like it . . .'

'Oh, well,' said Clementine, 'I just don't know. I was going to give the children their feed and then I . . . Well, here I am.'

She felt the top of her head.

'I seem to remember being turned over on this table . . . I've got a bump on my head.'

'Perhaps it was a succubus . . .' said Timortis.

She had hitched up her pants again and was smoothing her hair.

'Perhaps. Ah well! Things like this do happen,' she concluded. 'I thought I could manage to do without it. I'll go and get their feed ready.'

'They've had it,' said Timortis, factually.

The darkness came back into her face.

'Who gave it to them?'

'Your husband,' said Timortis. 'And I cleaned them up afterwards.'

'Did Angel come in here?'

'Yes,' said Timortis, flatly.

She pushed past him and her quick sharp steps led her into the garden. She was almost running by the time she had reached the turning in the path. Timortis went back upstairs, cogitating. Therefore he was. But only him.

X

ANGEL HAD picked up his chisel again and was busy on the other side of the boat. He was just putting in a screw when Clementine appeared, flushed through having rushed down after him. When the twins saw her they let out a joyful yelp and Alfa Romeo went up to her and took her hand. Angel looked up, took in the scene and situation, and bent over his work again.

'Who fed them?' she snapped.

'I did,' Angel replied drily.

She found something surprising in his tone.

'And what do you think gave you the right to do that?'

'That's enough of that,' said Angel, brutally.

'I'm asking you what gave you the right to feed these children. Didn't we agree that you were to have nothing to do with them?'

Before her mouth had time to close itself again, his full speed slaps landed on each side of it. She trembled with shock. Angel, as white as a sheet, was trembling with rage.

'I said that was enough!' he roared.

His rage seemed to subside and disappear as she put a shaking hand to her cheek.

'I'm sorry,' he said after a few moments, 'but sometimes you do go too far.'

The children began to shout and Alfa Romeo bent down to pick up a nail. Going up to Angel he drove it into his leg with every atom of his tiny force. Angel did not move. Clementine began to laugh—with a lightly hysterical laugh that was choked with tears.

'Stop it, stop it, stop it!' repeated Angel, tense and taut. She stopped.

'Actually,' he went on, 'I don't think I am sorry. I'm only sorry I didn't hit you harder.'

Clementine tossed her head and strode off. The three children followed her. Every few steps Alfa Romeo looked back and flung a black look at his father. Angel stood there, dreaming. On the screen of his dreams he projected the scene which had just taken place. Embarrassed, he changed it. Then he saw his wife again, stretched out on the dining-table, and the blushes soaked up to his forehead and down to the back of his neck. He knew then that he would never go back inside his house again. There was enough sawdust and shavings in the shed to sleep on comfortably—and the Spring nights were quite warm. He felt a slight irritation on his left leg. He bent down to pull out the sharp golden point of the nail. On his moss green lawn trousers there was a brownish stain, about the size of a drawing-pin. It was laughable. Poor little caterpillars.

XI

20 May

TIMORTIS DESERTED the house too after Angel had decided
to live in his workshop. He didn't feel in the least bit comfortable alone there with Clementine. She was far too motherly on
far too different a plane. Not that he could see any harm in it,
for he wasn't lying when he had insisted on his own emptiness
and in implying therefore that ethical values meant nothing to
him. But he found it physically embarrassing to be near her.

Stretched out in a distant corner of the garden where the
thamosucko potweed grew plentifully, imparting courage and
decision to its users, he thoughtlessly munched and tugged
at a few angular stalks. He was waiting there for Katey Whitarse who had promised to come and meet him and spend the
end of the long monotonous day with him. The thought of the
kind of relief she would bring forced him to check with his
hand the creases in his trousers. As usual, the day would
end with one of Psyche's hat tricks below the psychiatric
belt.

He could hear a crunch on the gravel and sat and waited.
Waddling clumsily on flat feet, trailing the cape of her thick
uniform behind her, the maid appeared and plumped down
beside him.

'Finished your work?' he asked.

'All finished,' she sighed. 'The kids are asleep.'

She had already started to unbutton her dress, but Timortis stopped her.

'Let's talk for a while first,' he suggested.

'That's not why I came,' she pointed out. 'I don't mind

109

doing our other exercises, but I don't care for your exercises in style.'

'There's one thing I must ask you,' he said.

She took off her clothes and stretched out on the grass. In this secluded corner of the garden they were in their own little Eden. Neither Angel nor Clementine would come down there and there wasn't the slightest risk of anyone surprising them. To teach her the value of patience, Timortis undressed himself too, but she was careful not to look at him. Naked, side by side on the grass, they were both slightly ridiculous. She turned round flat on her belly, and then rose on all fours.

'I'm waiting,' she said.

'Oh, bugger,' complained Timortis. 'Look here. In the first place, I'm fed up with this stupid position.'

'Why don't you get on with it?' she said.

'It's unputtupable with,' said Timortis.

He roughly pushed her and sent her off her balance. Before she had time to get up again he had nailed her down on her back and was on top of her. She fought back like a tiger.

'No, no, no,' she shrieked. 'Don't do it like that! Not like that! You maniac!'

Timortis held her down more tightly still.

'I'll let you go,' he said, 'if you'll tell me why you don't want me to do it in any other way.'

'I don't want to,' she grumbled.

He pressed down on her still tighter. He was ready to force his way into her whenever he wanted.

'If you don't tell me why, then I'm going to do it like this.'

Now she began to cry with anger.

'No . . . Go away . . .' she burbled. 'I don't want you to. You're too horrible. You're disgusting . . .'

'Oh, come on!' protested Timortis, 'you must be completely off your rural rocker!'

'I just don't want to talk!' she said.

'But you will!' snarled Timortis.

He bent down his head and grabbed the tip of one of her buxom breasts between his teeth.

'If you don't tell me why, I'll nibble your nipple right off,' he threatened, with his mouth full and with a certain amount of difficulty.

He felt like laughing—which had a certain effect on his potentialities. However he must have bitten her rather harder than he intended because she screamed and then melted into unceasing tears. He took pitiless advantage of this to force her.

'All right. I'll tell you why,' she wailed. 'But get off me this very moment.'

'Will you tell me everything?' said Timortis.

'I promise,' she said. 'Get off . . . Get . . . Oh! . . .'

Timortis loosened his grip on her and rolled back out of breath. She had been hard to hold down. As soon as she was free she sat up.

'Tell me then,' he said, 'otherwise I'll start all over again. Why do you have to do it like that? What's the point?'

'I've always done it that way,' she said.

'Since when?'

'From the very first time.'

'Who was that with?'

'My dad.'

'But why like that?'

'Because he didn't want to look at me. He didn't dare.'

'Was he ashamed?'

'We don't know what that means here,' she said, coldly.

She was holding her breasts in her hands, but kept her knees raised and apart. 'I suppose that's her idea of modesty,' thought Timortis.

'How old were you?'

'Twelve.'

'I can see why he didn't dare to look at you.'

'No, you can't see why,' she said. 'He didn't want to look at me because he said I was too ugly. And since it was my father who said it, then he must have been right. And now,

look, you've made me disobey my father and I'm a bad girl.'
'D'you like it?' asked Timortis.
'What?'
'The way you do it?'
'Shut up. That's not the kind of question you should ask a lady,' she said. 'D'you want to do it now or not?'
'Not always in the same way,' said Timortis. 'Men get tired of even the best things.'
'You men! You filthy, dirty pigs! You're all the same, all of you. Pigs! Pigs!' she said.
She got up and looked for her dress.
'What are you doing?' asked Timortis.
'Going back. I feel ashamed of myself.'
'It's not your fault,' remarked Timortis.
'It is,' she said. 'I shouldn't have—right from the start.'
'If you had told me a little more about things,' said Timortis, 'I could have tried to help you. But you're so uncommunicative.'
'The mistress told me right,' groaned the little nurse. 'I don't think I'd better see you any more.'
'Just too bad,' snapped the psychiatrist. 'I'll get over it.'
'And I won't tell you another thing. I'm not here just to satisfy your filthy habits.'
Timortis grinned and began to get dressed again too. He'd never seriously hoped to psychoanalyse this poor creature. He'd soon find somebody more worthwhile. He slipped on his shoes and stood up. She was still simpering.
'Flip off,' he said bluntly.
Sniffingly she obeyed. She must hate him. He smiled when he thought that, from this point of view at least, it had been a successful analysis. And then, leaping into the air with a light bound, he caught a late butterfly flitting past and happily swallowed it down.

XII

THERE WAS a small flat area of gravel paving in front of the steps leading up to the house where the children liked to play when they had finished their lunch while they waited for their nurse, who was waiting on the grown-ups, to put them to bed for their afternoon nap. They could easily be seen from the dining-room windows. As Timortis always sat facing this direction, this responsibility fell on to him. Sitting opposite him, Clementine was absent-mindedly amusing herself by picking up crumbs of bread and rolling them into little pellets —an unrewarding task if ever there was one (and there was). The only times they saw each other now were at meals. She seemed to want him to go on living in her house, but generally kept the conversation down to a very mundane level. And he did not dare to venture on to anything personal.

Katherine Whitarse, sullen, surly, scowling and dumb, brought in a dish which she put in front of Timortis. He took off the lid.

'Help yourself first, Clementine, please,' he said politely.

'No, no, no. It's for you,' she said. 'Just for you. A special delicatsy.'

One side of her mouth curled upwards in a lightly sarcastic smile. He looked at the dish more carefully.

'Why . . . It's catsmeat!' he yelled, full of joy.

'Exactly,' said Clementine.

'I wish it had been raw,' remarked Timortis, 'but it was a very kind thought, all the same . . . You're an angel, Clementine.'

'I'm very fond of you,' she said. 'But I couldn't have put up with watching you eat it raw.'

'Of course not,' said Timortis, helping himself to a long straggling slice. 'Talk to me about catsmeat! It's better than all the mice and birds in the world.'

'I'm delighted that you're so delighted,' she said.

'A bird,' observed Timortis, 'isn't bad, of course. But, oh, those horrible feathers! . . .'

'True,' said Clementine. 'But you have to take the rough with the smooth. And what about mice?'

'They're purely for fun,' said Timortis. 'There's hardly any food on them.'

'Well,' she said, 'at least we've extended the range of your tastes. Which was what I wanted. What are you working on at the moment?'

'I suppose,' said Timortis, 'that you're being so kind to me because you know that your little maid has given me the brush-off.'

'Maybe,' she said. 'And I must admit that the news didn't displease me. What have you found to replace her in the village? You seem to go there fairly frequently.'

'Oh!' said Timortis. 'There's not much there, you know. I see quite a lot of Glory Hallelujah.'

'I'm talking about women,' said Clementine.

'I never bother to look for them,' said Timortis. 'Did you know that cat had been doctored? I don't really believe it, but it does influence me a little, all the same.'

He was lying.

'Hm. I know you're on the prowl,' said Clementine.

Timortis looked at the three children outside who were going round and round behind each other until they drove themselves giddy.

'Let's change the subject,' he said.

'Have you been poking around in my frillies?' she suddenly asked.

Timortis was so astonished that he did not answer immediately.

'I beg your pardon?'

'You heard me!'

'No,' he replied, 'I haven't. What d'you take me for? What would I expect to find in your frillies? I've got all the clothes I need.'

'Oh . . . skip it!' she reassured him. 'Perhaps I've made a mistake. I just had the feeling that somebody fiddles around with everything now and again. No reason why it should be you, of course.'

He jerked his chin towards the maid who had her back turned towards them.

'Oh, no!' said Clementine. 'Surely not. Anyway, why should she want to keep quiet about it? It wouldn't matter to me. I never wear them. Or hardly ever.'

XIII

'THAT'S IT,' said Angel, standing up.

He'd just sawn halfway through the wedge which was holding the boat on its rails. It was complete. Thirty feet long, its clear wood curved up at the phront like a stubby phallic Pheonician phlick-kniphe, equipped with a single outrigging light spar beam which, so far, was attached to the body of the boat simply by supports of gleaming bronze. There was no bridge, but simply the hump of a low cabin somewhere near the back of the deeply curved deck. Timortis looked up and examined the bottom of the shell. Eleven pairs of double-jointed feet stuck out at equal distances all along its length.

'It should go like a bomb,' he remarked.

'Hope so,' said Angel.

'You've done jolly well,' went on Timortis, 'for an amateur.'

'I'm not an amateur,' replied Angel.

'Well then,' Timortis went on further, 'you've done jolly well for a professional.'

'I'm not a professional either,' said Angel.

'What are you then?' asked Timortis, beginning to grow irritated.

'Don't start asking your questions again. It's a deplorable habit you've got.'

Timortis could have lost his temper, of course, but that would not really have conformed with his temperament, so he restrained himself. He tried to find something suitable to say to a man on the point of going. Away for a long time. In a hopelessly unsound boat. And yet . . . And in spite of the eleven pairs of articulated ankles.

'Still on the same terms with your wife?'

'Uhuh,' said Angel. 'She's a . . .'

But he stopped himself.

'Oh, it doesn't matter. I've got nothing more to say about it. Women don't belong to the same world as men. But I shan't miss anything.'

'What about the children?'

'Luckily,' said Angel, 'I've hardly got to know them yet. So that won't hurt me.

'But they'll miss you,' insisted the psychiatrist.

'I know,' said Angel. 'But all of us miss something. So it might as well be something important.'

'Children who're brought up without a father . . .' started Timortis.

'Listen,' said Angel, 'there's no point in going over all that again. I'm off. I'm going. Got it? And that's that! "

'You'll get drowned,' said Timortis.

'It'll be just my luck not to.'

'Don't be so commonplace,' remarked Timortis scornfully.

'Voluptuously commonplace,' corrected Angel.

'What can I possibly say to you?'

'I can see your problem,' sympathised Angel, sarcastically. 'My turn to ask questions now. How are you getting on with your great ideas?'

'I'm getting absolutely nowhere at all,' said Timortis. 'So far I've had one mangy black cat and that's been my lot. I tried with a dog, but as it was straight after the cat it did nothing but keep starting up horrible fights, so I had to give it up. But it's a man I really want. Or a woman . . . A human being, at any rate.'

'Who are you off to see now?'

'I'm going to meet the blacksmith's maid. The tinker-woman's going to introduce me.'

'Oh, so you've been seeing the tinkerwoman then?'

'Oh, I don't know what she is. The dressmaker, then. It's all a bit funny. I think she makes your wife's dresses, doesn't she?'

'Never on your life,' said Angel. 'Clementine brought everything she's got here with her. You know she never goes to the village.'

'She's making a mistake,' said Timortis. 'It's full of interesting things.'

'Get along with you,' snorted Angel. 'They're all driving you out of your tiny mind.'

'It's true. But the place is still full of interest. In any case ... Um ... Oh well! ... But there's something very funny. The dressmaker's got copies of all your wife's clothes. Or all the ones I've seen her wearing here in the house.'

'Hmm?' said Angel, barely impressed.

He looked at his boat.

'I'll have to be going soon,' he said. 'Like to take a trip with me?'

'You're not going to go just like that, all the same? ...' said Timortis, knowing he was powerless to stop him.

'Yes I am. Not today, maybe, but this is the way I'll go.'

He went over to the block that he had half sawn through and raised his arm. With a carefully measured and calculated silent karate stroke he broke the piece of wood in two. There was a violent crack. The boat trembled and shivered. The thoroughly greased oak rails cut down through the hanging garden and boomeranged straight downwards through to the sea. The boat slipped along like an arrow and plunged out of sight into a cloak of smoky spray stinking of burning tallow.

'It must be there by now,' said Angel after twenty seconds. 'Come down with me and look. We'll see if it works.'

'You're crazy,' said Timortis. 'Launching something from this height.'

'It went marvellously,' said Angel ... 'The higher the risk, the finer the fall.'

They slithered down the escarpments of the slope, but not

as quickly as the boat. The weather was finer than ever and the cliff alive with the buzzing perfumes of the plants, and the chattering and twittering of the insects. Angel had put his arm affectionately round Timortis's shoulders. The psychiatrist felt himself falling. He liked Angel a lot and he was scared.

'You're going to be careful, aren't you?' he said.

'Naturally.'

'Have you got enough food?'

'I've got some water. And I've got my rod and some lines.'

'Is that all?'

'I'll be able to catch fish. I'll be tied to the apron-strings of the tide . . .'

'Aha! What a complex, what an oceanic complex you've got!' fulminated Timortis.

'Don't be so commonplace,' said Angel. 'I know your explanations about getting back to the womb. From tide to apron-strings. It all boils down to the same old thing. Get along with you and analyse your natives. This isn't a Maytree Ark that I've built here. I've had my bellyful of mothers.'

'Because the one you're thinking about is your wife,' said Timortis. 'But you must miss your own.'

'As a matter of fact, I don't. I never had a mother.'

They were looking out over space. Angel was the first to scramble on to a little ledge at the beginning of the way down. The boat could now be seen, far below their feet. Timortis saw that the rails ran almost horizontally into the water after their practically vertical plunge down. With the speed that it had been going, the craft should have been at least three hundred yards out at sea. He said so.

'There was a safety cable holding it back,' said Angel.

'Oh, good!' nodded Timortis, without understanding what he was talking about.

Underfoot the pebbly beach was overpopulated with crackling echoes. Angel, lithe and energetic, grabbed the end of a light springy rope. Slowly the boat drifted back to the shore.

'Jump on board,' said Angel.

Timortis obeyed. The boat began to wobble. Once on board it seemed larger. Angel sprang on too and disappeared inside the cabin.

'I'll unfurl the sails,' he said, 'and then we're off.'

'Not for good, hey?' protested Timortis.

Angel's head popped up.

'Don't worry,' he said, smiling. 'I'm not altogether ready yet. Not for another week. This is just a trial.'

XIV

TIMES SO many the road had taken Timortis into the village that it had become as flat and featureless for him as the corridor of a madhouse and as bald as a close-shaven beard. A plain and simple path, the shortest distance between two known points, as simple and straight as a line is a line is a line, without depth or breadth, simply does not exist. And shortened this road was by well-known feet, by steps already taken (by walking feet and walking steps—not three feet make one yard or metrical feet; not pairs of household steps). He had to set himself puzzles, entangle himself in symbolic logic, turn his simple ideas upside down, mix them all together in order to get to the end of the road not only without boredom but even at all. But he always managed to get to the end of it each time. He sang too.

> *Hear the cannon*
> *Hear the trains*
> *Light green candles*
> *In my brains*
> *Gangrene moulds*
> *The longest nose*
> *Choirboys hold*
> *The sprinkling hose*
> *See the salmon*
> *Snap the chains*
> *Of caravans*
> *On pearly plains*

Cankers rot
The four-walled room
Filled with froth
The foam of doom.

And all the songs everybody knew, had known, would ever know. Poor Timortis. How stupid he was. But it didn't matter. He couldn't see (or hear) himself. So he got to the village, since it's already been printed up there that he did. And the weighty cloak of the village fell about his shoulders and smothered him. Thus he arrived at the (as he thought) tinker-woman's door, although she was really the dressmaker (and deservedly so).

He went 'Knock! Knock' twice.

'Come in!'

Timortis went in. It was just as dark inside as it was in all the other houses of the village. Bits of brass gleamed darkly in the shadows. The floor of worn and tarnished red tiles was covered with little lengths of cotton, remnants of material and handfuls of hayseed for the deuced little red hens, beeseed for the honeygolden cocks, and seaseed for the queer little silver fish.

The old dressmaker was even older and was sewing a dress.

'Oho!' Timortis said to himself.

'Are you making that for Clementine?' he asked, in order to get to the bottom of the question and put his heart at ease. Hearts and bottoms are well-protected organs that are easy to look after—a little question now and again is all they need.

'No,' she said.

It was then that Timortis noticed the blacksmith.

'Oh, good morning,' he said, as if he were greeting an old friend.

The smith came out of his corner. He was always an impressive figure, but even more so in the black shadows, for the impression remained vague there and seemed all the more impressive because of it.

122

'What are you doing here?' he asked.

'I've come to see the lady.'

'You've got no business here,' judged the blacksmith.

'I wanted to find out what she was doing,' stated Timortis. 'These dresses are exactly the same as Clementine's, so naturally I'm intrigued.'

'You're going to a lot of trouble for nothing,' said the smith. 'There's no copyright on them. Anyone can make 'em if they like.'

'People don't usually copy dresses in such detail as that,' said Timortis sternly. 'I think it's indecent.'

'Don't use language like that,' snarled the smith.

His arms were tremendously thick. Timortis scratched his chin and looked up at the sagging ceiling decorated with dozens of dead flies on sticky spirals of dangling paper.

'So, to cut matters short,' he said, 'she's going to go on with it.'

'I order them,' said the blacksmith in a grim threatening voice. 'And I pay for them.'

'Oho,' said Timortis. 'For your lovely young wife, I presume.'

'Not got one.'

'Oh. Er, er . . .' began Timortis. 'But actually,' he said, changing his mind, 'I should like to know what models she copies them from.'

'She doesn't copy them,' said the smith. 'She sees them. And then she copies them from what she's seen.'

'Ha, ha!' said Timortis with grim emphasis. 'And now pull the other one.'

'I'm not pulling anybody's leg,' blathered the smith.

At that moment Timortis guessed—and verified—that the old, old dressmaker's eyes were really false eyes painted on her closed lids. The smith followed his eyes to see what he was looking at.

'They're painted on so that people don't notice anything

123

from the street,' he said. 'If you hadn't barged your way in here, you wouldn't have seen anything either.'

'But I knocked first,' said Timortis.

'You may have,' objected the smith, 'but if she can't see, then she didn't know it was you when she said "Come in".'

'But she did say "Come in" all the same.'

'Of course she did,' said the blacksmith, 'because she knows her manners, the silly old cow.'

The dressmaker had just started on a little bunch of pleats under the belt of the dress. It was a pretty but plain white crimplene dress that Clementine had been wearing the day before.

'But can she really work with her eyes closed?' persisted Timortis, trying to convince himself by being astonished and affirmative at the same time.

'You'd be wrong to say with her eyes closed,' blacked the smith. 'Your eyes aren't closed just because you put down your lids in front of them. They're still open underneath. If you roll a rock in front of an open door, then the door's not closed because of that. Nor's the window, because it's not your eyes you use when you want to see long distances and you don't understand anything at all.'

'Well!' said Timortis, gasping for breath. 'If you think all that nonsense is going to make it clearer for me, then you've got an uncommonly high opinion of yourself.'

'Nothing I've got is common,' said the smith, 'and I've certainly got nothing in common with you. Let this old trout get on with her work and leave us alone!'

'All right,' said Timortis. 'All right. All right, then . . . I'm off!'

'Good riddance,' said the smith, approving his action.

'Goodbye, Mr Timortis,' said the dressmaker.

She snapped the thread with her teeth, like a nun who had sent her scissors to be sharpened. Timortis, slightly vexed, went out like a gentleman. He fired one ultimate arrow.

'I'm off to poke your maid.'

'Fat lot of good that'll do you,' said the smith. 'I've poked her already and I don't recommend it. She don't wiggle her bum.'

'Then I'll wiggle mine for both of us,' Timortis reassured him. 'And I'll psychoanalyse her at the same time!'

He found himself proudly back in the street. Three pigs were going by, marking time and grunting. He kicked the third one violently up the arse. The pig considered this to be most unjustifiably vicious and Timortis took up his path again.

XV

THE BLACKSMITH'S maid, who was called Rosebag, slept with whoever happened to be the apprentice at the time, in the lean-to over the forge. The apprentices were always snuffing it, but the maid, hardened to the business, stayed put, especially since the smith himself had giving up infiltrating himself into her bed like an overflowing tributary. There was no need to worry about the apprentice. Permanently dead beat, there was never anything doing with him. All he did was sleep. Although at that very moment he wasn't sleeping. He was down in the forge, stoking up the furnace. Timortis saw him when he got there and went straight into the workshop that was filthy with soot in spite of Rosebug's cleaning up.

'Hello, young fellow,' said Timortis.

The apprentice murmured something like 'Morning' under the arm into which he had tucked his pale head, since it was the jovial custom of visitors to the forge to give him a clout round the ear as they went through. These apprentices were always striking while the iron was hot, so it was only justice that they too should be struck in return.

'Your guv'nor isn't here,' said Timortis, positively.

'Nope,' certified the young lad.

'I'm off then,' said Timortis.

He went out and turned left, ran all the way round the house, into the yard, up the wooden stairs at the side of the building, ending up in a dark gloomy corridor lined with rough wooden panelling.

On the right, under the lowest slope of the roof, was Nose-rag's room. Straight ahead there was a big wide door, behind which the guv'nor slept. The wall on the left screened an alcove in the guv'nor's bedroom which took up three-quarters of the floor space and was situated, being separated from it simply by the partition on the right, in close proximity to Nosebag's bedroom. It was a simple but practical piece of planning.

Timortis went in without knocking first. The girl was sitting on her bed reading a seven-year-old newspaper. News took a long time to reach the village.

'Ah,' said the psychiatrist, 'taking an interest in current affairs?'

He was trying to be friendly and managing it about as naturally as a pair of polyhydrae performing a solo on the parish shittapump.

'I've got the right to read,' said Rosenag aggressively.

'These bloody peasants are bloody hard to bloody well manipulate,' thought Timortis.

Nosebud's bedroom offered only lukewarm comfort. There was a scrubbed floor, the bare whitewashed walls and the roofbeams—themselves held together by ropes, rafters and purlins—under rows of tiny slates. The whole thing effectively and efficiently layered with thin dust. Furniture?

1 bed

1 table

1 bucket, all purposes, for the use of. And in a corner, a coffer for her (i.e. the girl's) things (of strictly limited number).

This monastical simplicity titillated the lubricious atheist lurking inside Timortis who doted on raw flesh and might so easily have dominated his outside when he came to think about it.

He went to sit by her side on the squeaky iron bed. There wasn't anywhere else.

'What have you been doing nice since I last saw you?' he asked.

'Well ... Oh, nothing,' she said.

She went on reading, finished the column and then folded up the paper and put it under her pillow.

'Take off your clothes and lie down on the bed,' said Timortis.

'Oh, sod,' said the girl. 'If the guv'nor comes back, I'll have to put them on again and get his grub ready for him.'

'Not at this time of day,' said Timortis. 'And, anyway, your guv'nor's not here. He's at the dressmaker's.'

'Then he's bound to come back afterwards,' she said.

Then, after thinking for a moment, she added, 'But he won't disturb us then.'

'Why not?' queried Timortis.

'It's always the same when he comes back from there,' said the girl. 'But why d'you want me to take my clothes off?'

'It's the indispensable basic beginning for a perfect psycho-analysis ...' said Timortis, pleonastically and pedantically.

She blushed. Her hand held her little pointed collar tight round her neck.

'Oh! ...' she said, lowering her eyes. 'Even the guv'nor's never dared do that to me.'

Timortis's frowning brow was covered in wrinkles. What had this one understood? But how could he ask her?

'Er ...' she murmured. 'I don't know whether I'm clean enough for that ... You won't like it ...'

Timortis began to see. It was a kind of village code.

'Psychoanalysis is ...' he began.

'Wait a moment ...' she muttered. 'Not for a minute ...'

The room was lit by a little window in the slope of the roof. She stood up and whisked an old curtain out of the chest, then draped it over the little rectangular pane of glass. A little daylight still squeezed through the dark blue material and made the sloping roof look like a cave.

'The bed's going to squeak,' said Timortis, deciding to

postpone his psychoanalysis until a little later. 'Perhaps it might be best to put your paillasse on the floor.'

'That's a good idea . . .' she said, beginning to grow more enthusiastic.

He felt the smell of her sweat filling the room. Her damp must have been very moist. So it wouldn't be all that unpleasant after all.

XVI

THE HEAVY tread on the wooden stairs wrenched them out
of their drowsy reverie. Timortis quickly pulled himself together and extricated himself from the sprawling girl who was
half on the paillasse and half on the floor.

'It's him . . .' he whispered.

'He won't come in here,' was all she could murmur. 'He
always goes straight into his own room.'

She started to wriggle herself against him.

'Stop it!' protested Timortis. 'I can't start again yet.'

She obeyed him.

'You'll come back and psy . . . thingummy me, won't you?'
she said in a husky voice. 'I liked that. It was good.'

'Yes, of course I will,' said Timortis who had no traces of
excitement left in him.

He'd need another ten minutes at least for the urge to come
back. Women have no delicacy.

The guv'nor's footsteps, very close now, shook the whole
corridor. The door of his room squeaked as it opened and
then slammed to. On his knees, Timortis listened carefully.
Still on all fours, he crept quietly to the wall. A little ray of
light shot through it and suddenly stabbed him in the eye. A
knot must have been missing from the wood in the partition.
Advancing towards the source of the ray of light which he
followed with his creeping fingers, he soon found the hole in
the plank and stuck his eye over it, not without a certain
small amount of hesitation, and sprang back again imme-

diately. He felt as if he could be seen as clearly as he could see himself. But, by using his powers of reasoning and wit, he reassured himself that this could not be so, and got back earnestly to his observation post.

The blacksmith's bed was immediately beneath the peephole. It was an unusually low bed and had no blankets. Just a mattress, with a tightly stretched sheet over it, was to be found between the four posts—and not even a sign of the regulation reskinkajurassic eiderup that was to be found down every street of the village.

Surveying the rest of the room he saw, first of all, the smith, from the back, and naked from the waist up. He appeared to be engaged on some very delicate task. His hands were invisible. Then they suddenly rose into view and sunk out of it again as they seemed to pat somebody with something. They went back to the centre of his own belt where the buckle sprang apart. His trousers fell, revealing his enormous legs, as sturdy as oaks, as hairy as palms. Underneath he had dirty interlock pants which also fell in their turn. Timortis heard a soft sound. But he could not watch and listen at the same time.

The smith kicked his bare feet free of his pants and trousers and, with wide open arms, turned round and went towards the bed. He sat down. Once again Timortis had moved backwards when he had seen him coming. But springing back again he immediately glued his eye to the hole once more. He even refused to move when he felt Noserug come over to him and he muttered to himself that he'd give her a belting kick in the cakehole if she tried to distract him from his pressing business. Then his muttering to himself ceased because his heart suddenly stopped. He could now see what the blacksmith's back had been hiding until then. In a white crimplene dress, it was an incredibly lifelike robot made of bronze and steel, carved into the shape and image of Clementine. With a strange dreamlike step it slowly walked towards the bed. Light coming from a lamp which Timortis could not see clothed its delicate features with rippling reflections and

131

the gleaming metal of the hands and fingers, polished to the softness of satin, scintillated and shone like precious jewels.

The automaton stopped. Timortis looked at the smith who was breathing heavily in his delicious impatience. With one simple movement the metallic hands rose to the collar of the dress and effortlessly ripped it off. The white material fell to the floor in shreds. Timortis, fascinated, took in every detail of the smooth skin of the breasts, the undulating thighs and the miraculous mechanical joints at the knees and shoulders. The robot smoothly stretched out on the bed. Timortis fell over on his back again. With the tips of his toes he brutally pushed over the maid who was trying to excite him again from her side. He scrambled around feverishly for his trousers. He'd left his wrist-watch in the pocket. He looked at it in the vague glow coming from the roof-light. A quarter to five.

Ever since the day when he had caught her on the dining-room table, Clementine had gone up to her room every day at half-past four to take, as she said, a short nap. At this very moment, while the steely thighs of the moving statue were plunging the smith into the depths of ecstasy, Clementine, up in the the house on the cliff, was crumpling the sheets with her bird-like fingers and gasping with satisfaction too.

Timortis grew more and more excited as he crept back to the partition. He had no inhibitions now about looking straight through the hole. At the same time his fingers groped for Rosedug's trembling body. She was delighted, although she had no real idea of what was going on. 'These country folk are more civilised than people think,' Timortis said to himself as he concentrated more firmly on watching the smith.

XVII

FEET IN the water, trousers rolled up, and shoes in his hand, Timortis stared stupidly at the boat. He was waiting for Angel —and the boat was waiting for him too. Angel came tumbling down the cliff again, his arms filled with blankets and his last jerrican of water on top of them. He was wearing mellow yellow translucent oilskins. He bounced and sprang across the pebbly creek until he reached Timortis. Whose heart would have broken if there had been room enough inside his tightening chest.

'Don't stand there like that with your shoes in your hand,' said Angel. 'You look like an old age pensioner on a Sunday outing.'

'I don't care what I look like,' replied the psychiatrist.

'And leave your beard alone!'

Timortis reached dry land again and put his shoes down on a large rock. When he raised his head he saw the bigdippering track made by the boat's rails disappearing high up over the rocky clifftop.

'It'll scare the living daylights out of me whenever I see that thing,' he said.

'Of course it won't,' said Angel. 'There's nothing to be scared of in that.'

He lightly sprang on to the supple gangplank leading on board. Timortis did not move.

'What are all the pots of flowers for?' he asked when Angel appeared again.

'Haven't I got the right to take flowers with me?' asked Angel, aggressively.

'Of course. Of course you have,' said Timortis. Then he added 'What will you water them with?'

'Water,' said Angel. 'It rains out at sea too, you know.'

'I suppose it must,' agreed Timortis, sounding as if he didn't really suppose so at all.

'Don't pull that face,' said Angel. 'You'll make me ill. Don't tell me you're losing a friend!'

'I think I must be,' said Timortis. 'I've grown to like you a lot.'

'So have I,' said Angel. 'But you can see I'm still going, all the same. One doesn't stay in a place because one likes certain people ... One goes because one can't stand certain others. Ugliness is the only thing that really makes us get anything done. We're all cowards.'

'I don't know if it's cowardice,' said Timortis, 'but it's bloody painful.'

'To stop it hurting you for too long,' said Angel, 'I've added a few slightly dangerous complimentary complications to my craft. I've got no provisions, there's a little hole in the bottom, and there's hardly any water. All right? Does that make up for it?'

'What a bloody bloody fool,' groaned Timortis agonisingly.

'It may,' went on Angel, 'still be a cowardly action from the moral standpoint, but from a physical angle, it's simply a rather tough undertaking.'

'It isn't being tough, it's just being stupid,' said Timortis. 'Don't get them confused. And then, how much cowardice is there standing on that moral point of yours? We aren't cowards because we don't love someone or because we stop loving them. That's just the way things are.'

'We're going to lose ourselves again,' said Angel. 'Every time we have a conversation together we get lost in the things we've done too much thinking about. That gives me another reason for leaving. It'll stop me giving you lousy ideas.'

'D'you think the others give me better ones?' mumbled Timortis.

'True. I'm sorry. I was forgetting your famous emptiness.'

Angel grinned and plunged back into the belly of the boat. He sprang back out again almost immediately as a soft sound, like a mixture of snoring and purring, began to be heard.

'Everything's working,' he said. 'There's nothing to keep me any more. I can go. Anyway, I prefer her to bring them up alone. I'd be bound not to agree with what she'd want to do, and I hate arguments.'

Timortis watched the clear water swelling over the pebbles and the seaweed. The beautiful still sea hardly moved, just disturbed by an occasional lapping like little damp lips opening and shutting. He lowered his head.

'Oh, damn! . . .' he said. 'Don't try to be funny.'

'I was never any good at telling jokes,' said Angel. 'But I'm forced to in this case. I can't go back now.'

He hurried down the gangplank and pulled a box of matches out of his pocket. He bent over, struck one, and set fire to the end of the launching pad.

'If I do this,' he said, 'you'll soon forget all about it.'

As they watched it a light blue flame shot into the air. It turned yellow, spread, raced along the track and the wood began to blacken as it crackled. Angel jumped on board again and flung the gangplank back on to the shore.

'Aren't you going to take that with you?' said Timortis, taking his eyes away from the flames.

'No need to,' said Angel. 'I'll tell you something. Children scare me to death. There you are! So long, old man.'

'So long . . . you soppy bastard,' said Timortis.

Angel smiled, but his eyes were gleaming in a strange and unusual way. Behind Timortis the fire was still huffing and puffing. Angel disappeared inside his cabin. An angry bubbling sound could be heard and the articulated feet began to churn up the water. He climbed out again and ran to the tiller. The boat was already gaining speed and the space between it and the shore rapidly increasing. The greater the acceleration, the greater the increase in distance. When it had reached its full speed it appeared, light and slender, to be walking on the calm water in the midst of a daydreaming wreath of foam. In the distance Angel raised a puppet's arm. Timortis waved back. It was six in the evening. The fire was sizzling and groaning and the psychiatrist had to move away from it, wiping his face and his eyes. A good excuse. A majestic spiral of thick black smoke, slashed with vivid orange, rose from the face of the cliff. In heavy volutes it went up and over the clifftop, and then rose almost straight up into the sky above.

Timortis shuddered. Then he realised that for the last few minutes he had been miaowing. With a miaow of regret, of regret mingled with pain, like the complaint of a cat that has just been doctored. He closed his mouth and stepped into his shoes again. He slowly went back towards the cliff. Before beginning to climb up it, he took one last look at the sea. The rays of the sun were still powerful enough to pick out a tiny object that was scintillating on the surface of the water like a legendary knockless monster. Or a water-scorpion. Or a water-spider.

Or like something which walked alone on the water, with Angel, all alone, on board.

XVIII

SITTING AT her window, she looked out at herself framed in space. In front of her the garden had piled itself up on the cliff end and was letting the long tongue of the sun lick across its curls in one last diagonally sweeping caress before the twilight. Clementine felt tired and thought inwardly about her home.

Lost deep inside herself, she gave a sudden jump when the distant steeple struck a quarter past six.

With a brisk step, she went out of the room. They weren't in the garden. She went downstairs, her suspicions roused, and went straight to the kitchen. When she opened the door the first thing she heard was the sound of Whitarse doing the washing in the wash-house.

The children had dragged a chair over to the sideboard. Noel was holding it firm with both hands. Standing on the chair, Alfa Romeo was handing down slices of bread to Joel, one after the other, from the bread basket. The pot of jam was still on the seat of the chair between Alfa Romeo's feet. The warpainted cheeks of the twins were sufficient evidence of the use to which the spoils of their raiding expedition had already been put.

When they heard their mother coming in, they looked round and Joel burst into tears followed closely by Noel. Only Alfa Romeo did not flinch or falter. He very deliberately took another slice of bread, bit squarely into it as he very care-. fully turned round and sat down beside the pot of jam. He chewed precisely, defiantly and unhurriedly.

137

Thinking that she had once more let the time for their feed go by, Clementine was filled with shame and remorse, even fiercer than the annoyance she felt when she happened to arrive home late. Even Alfa Romeo's defiantly provocative attitude completed the way his brothers had reacted. Standing up for himself and for what he was doing he had the feeling, as they did, of having brought off something forbidden. He obviously imagined that his mother was deliberately punishing all three of them, that she didn't want them to have their feed. And this reflection hurt Clementine so much that she almost burst into tears herself. However, in order to stop the kitchen turning into a vale of tears or a wailing wall, she managed to stem the flow of her mercilessly titillated lachrymal glands.

She went over to them and picked up Alfa Romeo in her arms. Stubbornly, he went stiff. She kissed him, very softly and very gently, on his jammy cheek.

'My poor darling,' she said with great tenderness. 'His horrid wicked mummie forgets her baby's feed. Come along now and we'll make up for it with a gorgeous big chocolate milk shake.'

She put him down on the floor again. The twins' tears had suddenly stopped flowing and they scrambled over each other with joy as they rushed over to where she was. They rubbed their grubby tear-stained faces against her black-sheathed legs while she went over to the fitment to take down the beakers which she filled with milk. Alfa Romeo stared hard at her, fascinated, but still clutched his crust of bread defiantly in his hand. Slowly his wrinkled brow began to relax. His eyes shone with tears, but he still refused to give in. She gave him a big wheedling smile. He smiled back, with a timid little smile like a rare smoky-grey squirrel.

'You'll see how much you'll love me now,' she murmured, almost to herself. 'You'll never have anything to reproach me with again . . .'

But with bitterness she went on, completely to herself, saying that so this was the situation, they could feed themselves, they don't need me any more. Perhaps they even know how to turn the taps on already.

Don't worry. It's not too late. Things could easily change back. She'd give them so much, so much love. She was going to give them so much wonderful love that their whole lives, interwoven with her good deeds and her loving care, would lose all their meaning if she were not always by their side.

As her eyes glanced out of the window at just that moment she saw some thick black smoke rising up from below, from somewhere near the workshop. It was the burning launching path that had been used for the boat.

She went out to see better. The three little boys were jabbering behind her. But she had no real need to check up. She knew within herself what the meaning of the fire was. The last obstacle had been removed from her path.

The timber of the shed crackled and roared. Pieces of blackened wood flew up and bounced down on the roof. Timortis stood still at the door, contemplating the blaze. Clementine put her hand on his shoulder. He jumped, startled, but said nothing.

'So Angel's gone?' asked Clementine.

He nodded his head.

'When all that rubbish has burnt itself out,' said Clementine, 'you'll get the maid to help you clear it up. The space will make a marvellous playground for the children. We'll make a covered porch. Then they'll be able to play there like little princes.'

He was astonished by her boldness and audacity, but saw when he looked at her that there was no point in arguing.

'Of course you can do it,' she assured him. 'My husband could have done it perfectly well. He was handy. I hope the children will take after him.'

THIRD PART

I

'I'VE ALREADY been here four years and x days,' Timortis said to himself.

His beard had grown much longer.

II

A THIN, snivelling, drivelling, driving, persistent, pernicious rain was falling and everybody had a cough. The garden was waterlogged and swampy. The sea could hardly be distinguished from the equally grey sky. The wind across the bay chopped the air diagonally, sweeping the willowy rain according to its wispy windy will.

What can you do when it rains? Nothing. Except stay in your room and play. Joel, Noel and Alfa Romeo were staying playing in their room. They were playing at dribbling. Alfa Romeo, on all fours, was making his way round the border of the carpet and stopping when he came to the red spots in the pattern. Then he bent down his head and let a gob of dribble drool out. Noel and Joel were following in his trail behind him and trying to dribble in the same places. A very tricky operation.

The rain still went on falling. Clementine, in the kitchen, was making all sorts of gorgeous things for them with sugar and milk and spice. She had grown fatter. And she had given up using make-up. She was far too busy looking after and working for her children to bother with things like that. When she had finished she went up to relieve the guard. As she opened the door Whitarse was scolding them.

'You little horrors. You're foul and filthy.'

'But it's raining outside,' stated Alfa Romeo, who had just created a smashing trickly dollop of spit.

'It's raining outside,' repeated Joel.

'Raining,' said Noel, more concisely.

It's true that it was pelting down at that moment.

'And who's going to clear up all this mess that you've been making?'

'You are,' said Alfa Romeo.

Clementine went in. She had overheard these last few words.

'Of course you're going to clear it up,' she said. 'That's what you're paid for. Haven't the poor little darlings got the right to enjoy themselves? Do you like this kind of weather?'

'Bloody nonsense,' said Whitarse.

'Be quiet!' said Clementine. 'And get back to your ironing. I'll take over up here.'

The maid went out.

'Dribble away to your heart's content, my pets,' said Clementine. 'If you find that it's fun to dribble, then dribble . . . dribble . . . dribble . . .'

'Don't want to dribble any more,' said Alfa Romeo.

He stood up.

'Come on,' he said to his brothers. 'We're going to play trains.'

'Come and give me a big sloppy kiss,' said Clementine.

'No,' said Alfa Romeo.

'No,' said Joel.

Noel said nothing. It was the only possible remaining abbreviated course that he could take.

'Don't we love our poor old mummie any more?' asked Clementine, down on her knees.

'Of course we do,' said Alfa Romeo. 'But we're playing trains. You'd better get on if you don't want to be run over.'

'Wait a second then! I'm climbing in now!' said Clementine. 'In we get. Mind the doors!'

'You shout,' said Alfa Romeo. 'You can be the guard with the whistle. I'm the driver.'

'So am I,' said Joel, starting going choo choo choo.

'So . . .' began Noel.

But he went no further.

'Oh, my darling little darlings!' said Clementine.
She started to kiss them.
'Don't do that. Whistle!' said Alfa Romeo. 'We're there!'
. . . .
Joel slowed down.
'Well!' said Clementine, her voice hoarse with having done
so much shouting, 'what a speed your train goes at! Come
and have your pudding now.'
'No.' said Alfa Romeo.
'No,' said Joel.
'Just for my sake,' said Clementine.
'No,' said Alfa Romeo.
'No,' said Joel.
'Then you'll make me cry,' said Clementine.
'You wouldn't know how to,' sneered Noel, wrenched out of
his normal laconicism by the outstandingly presumptuous
remark made by his mother.
'Oh, so I wouldn't know how to cry, eh?' said Clementine.
And she burst into tears.
But Alfa Romeo stopped her straight away.
'No,' he said. 'That's not how to do it. You just don't know.
You go woow woow woow. But we go eugh eugh eugh.'
'All right then . . . Eugh eugh eueueugh!' said Clementine.
'That's still not right,' said Joel. 'Listen.'
Gripped by the situation, Noel managed a big salty tear.
Not wishing to be left out, Joel produced one too. But Alfa
Romeo never cried. Even though he was very sad. Perhaps he
was even in despair.
Clementine began to get worried.
'But these are real tears! Alfa Romeo! Noel! Joel! Stop
this horrible game, my poor pets! My dear, dear darlings!
My baby babies! Look, look, look! Stop crying like that!
What's the matter?'
'It's because you're wicked!' bellowed Joel, lamentably.
'Horrid!' snapped Alfa Romeo, furious.
'Yep!' yelled Noel, louder than the other two put together.

146

'No, no, my darlings! I was only pretending. Look, it was only a joke! Stop, stop, stop. Otherwise you'll drive me mad!'

'I don't want any pudding,' said Alfa Romeo, starting to bawl once again.

'Don't want pudding!' said Joel.

'Don't want!' cried Noel.

When they reached such an emotional pitch, Joel and Noel always relapsed into baby language.

Clementine cuddled them and kissed them, completely knocked off her balance and lost as to what to do next.

'My little darlings,' she said. 'All right, then, We'll eat it later. Not now.'

Everything stopped as if by magic.

'Come and play at boats,' said Alfa Romeo to Joel.

'Oh, yes! Boats!' said Joel.

'Boats!' concluded Noel.

They all scampered away from Clementine.

'Leave us alone,' said Alfa Romeo. 'We're busy playing.'

'I am leaving you alone,' said Clementine. 'Shall I sit here and knit?'

'Go out of the room,' said Alfa Romeo.

'Go in the room next door,' said Joel. 'Come on, boat!'

Clementine sighed and sadly left them to play alone. She'd have liked them to be tiny again and all sweet and cuddly. Like they were the first day when she'd given them her breast to feed at. She put down her head and remembered.

III

Melancholy Timor Mortis
To the village went again—
Life, once long, now growing short is;
King Remorse begins to reign.
As vacant as a holiday
In one fixed spot he seemed to stay . . .
The sea was black, the sky was grey,
Like slimy eggs the muddy clay
Soiled boots once polished far away . . .

A bird shrieked.—'Damn you! Damn!' said Timortis. 'You frightened the life out of me. Yet everything started off all right. From now on I shan't talk about myself except in the third person. That'll be an inspiration.'—He was walking, he was always walking. In the winter the hedges that were like wet socks on either side of the road were decorated with down from the eider ducks and drakes (being their winter off-spring, just as gentlemen's gentlemen are always the gentlemen in question's offspring) and all these little ducklings, down under the hawthorn bushes, made beautiful artificial snow by scratching their tummies with great swirling swoops of their immature beaks. The remaining lower parts of the hedgerow were still fresh and green, foaming with thistledown frogs, holy toads and effervescent water, taking its good time without hurrying for the droughts of Julember.

'I've been taken in,' continued Timortis. 'I've been had by this jinxeyed village. When I got here I was a young psychiatrist full of vim and vigour, full of hope and expectation. And now I'm a young psychiatrist with no verve, no knack and no go-ahead at all. And no ambition certainly makes a big difference. And I owe it all to this rotten dump. This disgusting bloody village. The first Old Folks Fair I'd ever seen. Now the Old Folks Fair means nothing—certainly nothing shocking—to me; I bash the apprentices with the rest; and I've already treated Glory Hallelujah as badly as the others because if I didn't I'd be doing harm to myself. Well, it's time to put an end to all that. All that's over. I'm going to put my shoulder to the wheel and my nose to the grindstone and put my back into some real hard work!' That was the kind of thing that Timortis was saying to himself as he went on his way. The things that a man's brain can calculate for a man to do without are absolutely incredible. It certainly makes you think.

The road moaned, groaned, squeaked and wailed under Timortis's plodding feet. Splattered. Squelched. Mashed. Belched. Splashed. Highly picturesque rooks and ravens croaked and cawed in the sky above, but they did it silently because the wind carried their sounds in the opposite direction.

'Why,' thought Timortis, suddenly, 'aren't there any fishermen here? The sea is right on the doorstep, full of seaspiders, scabs, crabs, scallawags and shellable edibles. So why not? Why not? . Why not? . . Why not? . . . Why not? . . . .'

'Well . . . it must be because there's no port!' He was so delighted with the reasoned answer that he had come up with that he smiled at himself with supersmugness.

The head of a fat brown cow peered at him over the top of a hedge. He went over to say *Good Morning* to it. He called out to it as it was looking the other way. When he got right up close he saw that it was only a severed head stuck on a pointed stake. Obviously a cow that had been punished. A piece of writing had been nailed to the stake too, but it had fallen into the ditch. Timortis picked it up and read a mixture of mud and message. 'Next . . . Smudge . . . time . . . Smudge

you will . . . Smudge . . . give . . . Smudge . . . more milk.
Smudge. Smudge. Smudge.'

He shook his head in angry annoyance. He simply couldn't
get used to it. He had just about learnt to put up with the
treatment of the apprentices . . . Oh, but not the animals. He
let the piece of writing flutter away. Winged insects had de-
voured the eyes and nibbled away the nose of the cow and it
looked like an old woman who was finding it a great joke to
be eaten away by cancer.

'Something else for Glory Hallelujah,' he said. 'It's bound
to fall on his shoulders again. And he'll get some more gold
for it. Useless gold, since he won't be able to buy anything
with it. So it's the only thing with any value. In fact, it's
priceless!'

> *Thus Timortis on his way*
> *Conturbating as of old*
> *Found profound new things to say—*
> *Arguments in praise of gold.*

'Well, well, well,' Timortis said to himself. 'I'm getting back
some of my old form. Although, of course, the object of this
evidence has no importance, since it is through the design
based on it that Glory Hallelujah is placed in a situation where
his accumulated gold has neither rhyme (*sic*) nor reason (*sic*).'

'After all, I couldn't care less about gold—but at least it's
got me another hundred yards along this road.'

The village came into sight. Glory Hallelujah's barge was
floating aimlessly (apparently) amongst the rubbish on the
surface of the scarlet stream. When the boat came up level
with him, Timortis thumbed a lift and sprang on board.

'Hallo,' he said, jovially. 'What's the latest?'

'I've got no news,' answered Glory Hallelujah.

Timortis felt something that had been in the back of his
mind all morning suddenly spring into shape.

'Here,' he said, 'how about asking me back to your place?
I've got a few questions I'd like to ask you.'

150

'All right,' said Glory Hallelujah. 'Why not? Let's do that. Just excuse me for a moment.'

Then, as if he had been projected downwards by an atomic catapult, he shot into the river. Even though he was shivering. He propelled himself towards some particular piece of debris that was floating on the top and picked it up expertly between his teeth. It was a tiny hand. Covered with inkstains. He climbed back on board again.

'Tut, tut,' he said when he looked at it. 'Old Charlie's boy's been refusing to do his homework again.'

IV

'REALLY, THIS village horrifies me more and more,' Timortis said to himself as he looked at himself in the glass.

He had just trimmed his beard.

V

CLEMENTINE FELT hungry. She no longer ate anything herself at lunchtimes as she was so busy fussing around and feeding her three growing boys. She went to see if her bedroom door was closed and turned the key in the lock. All quiet. Nobody likely to come in. She went back to the middle of the room and lightly loosened the belt of her cotton dress. She looked at herself modestly in the wardrobe mirror. Then she went over to the window and closed that too. Then over to the cupboard. She took her time, savouring each minute as it passed. She took the cupboard key which was hanging from her belt on a light leather plait. She looked at it and slipped it in the lock. It smelt musty inside the cupboard. To be more—and even perfectly—precise, it smelt of dead meat. The smell came from a cardboard boot box. Clementine picked it up and greedily sniffed at it. In the box, on a saucer, the remains of a piece of steak were reaching the summit of putrifaction. A clean and pure kind of rottenness, without flies, without maggots and without worms. It was growing delicately green, and, quite simply, it stank. Horribly. She put her finger on the meat and felt its condition. It readily crumbled. She smelt her finger. Just rotten enough. She carefully took the steak between her thumb and index finger and elegantly bit into it, taking care to bite off a neat sharp mouthful. It was easy to do because it was so tender. She chewed slowly, giving as much attention to the slightly soapy consistency of the pheasanty high flesh, which gave her an acid sensation behind her cheek, as to the powerful perfume exhaling from the cardboard box. She ate half of it and then put it back in the box that she pushed into its secret and primitive hiding place. By the side of it there was a wedge of cheese in approximately the same condition, sticking to its abandoned plate. She prodded it with her finger, licked it, and repeated the process several times over. Sadly she closed the cupboard door again and went to the bathroom to wash her hands. Then she stretched out on her bed. This time she was determined not to bring it up. She knew she wouldn't. This time she would manage to keep it down. You simply had to be hungry enough. She'd be careful to watch that in the future. At any rate, the principle of her theory should succeed. All the best pieces for the children. She smiled when she thought of how she had started. She'd been happy then to eat the remnants and finish off the fat that they'd left on the edges of their plates. Or swallow the crusts from their slices of bread and milk that they always left lingering round the edges of their breakfast bowls. But anybody could do that. Every mother. It's only normal. Peach skins had been slightly harder. Because of the horrible feel of velvet on her tongue. Yet that was still only small fry—and, anyway, lots of people eat the skins with the fruit. But she had been unique in letting the peelings go bad first. Her children fully deserved every bit of this sacrifice. And the more horrible it was, the more foul the smell, the greater was the impression she had of consolidating and confirming her love for them, as if the torture that she was inflicting upon herself through what she was doing could give rise to something purer, truer. And all those moments of the past, every minute that she had ever spent thinking about something other than her children, would have to be atoned for and made up for.

But she was still vaguely unsatisfied and not completely happy, because so far she had been unable to force herself to swallow down maggots. And she knew she was cheating by stopping the flies from getting at the odds and ends that she selected from the larder throw-outs. And possibly, in the end, her maternal sins would be visited upon her children . . .

She would try again tomorrow.

VI

'I'M WORRIED out of my life,' Clementine said to herself, leaning her elbows on the window sill.

The garden was growing golden in the sunshine.

'I don't know where Noel and Joel—or Alfa Romeo—can be. At this very moment they might be falling into the well, or eating poisoned fruit, or getting arrows in their eyes if some village child is playing with a cross-bow on the road, or catching tuberculosis if one of Koch's bacilli should come this way, or going into a trance through breathing some over-scented flowers, or getting themselves stung by a scorpion brought back by one of the village children's grandfathers—a famous explorer recently returned from the land where scorpions grow—or falling from a treetop, running too fast and breaking a leg, playing with the water and drowning, coming down the cliff-face and tripping and breaking their necks, skinning themselves alive on a piece of old barbed wire, contracting tetanus . . . Or they're going down to the bottom of the garden and turning over a stone. Under the stone they'll find a little yellow cocoon just about to hatch itself out as they watch. It will fly into the village, slip into the shed where a mad, wild bull is locked, and sting it on the tenderest part of its nose. The bull rushes out of the shed, demolishing and destroying everything in its path. It's charging along the road, heading for the house, it's raging mad with fury, tearing up everything that it comes across and leaving tufts of black hair on everything it brushes against. On all the hedges of prickly vine. Just before it reaches the house it charges head first into a heavy cart drawn by an old half-blind horse. With a single blow the cart is smashed into smithereens and a splinter of metal whirls up into the air to a prodigious height. Perhaps it's a screw, a putlog, a wingnut, a hobnail, a spokeshaft, a horseshoe, a spinnaker, a crochet-hook, a sprogget, a hub-spoke, a countersunk rivet that's been cartwritten, then broken after being repaired by hand-forged butt-straps, bonds and wedges . . . And the needle of iron shrieks and whistles as it whizzes through the clear blue sky. It's gone over the garden gates. My God, it's coming down. It's coming down, lower and lower. As it hurtles down it breaks off the wing of a flying ant. With one wing wrenched off the ant loses its balance and all sense of direction and stability. Smashed and broken it wobbles in the air up above the trees. Suddenly it pounces down to the lawn. My God! Noel, Joel and Alfa Romeo are there! The ant falls, lands on Alfa Romeo's cheek, finds a spot or two of jam still sticking there and . . . and stings him! '

'Alfa, Alfa Romeo! Where are you?'

Clementine had rushed out of the bedroom, quite beside herself, and was shouting all the way down the stairs. She rushed down them as fast as she could. In the lobby she crashed into the maid.

'Where are they? What have you done with my children?'

'They're asleep,' replied the astonished maid. 'It's time for their afternoon nap.'

Oh well! It hadn't happened this time. But it might easily have. She went back up into her room. Her heart was still beating like a hollow sonic boom. It's definitely too dangerous to let them out in the garden by themselves. In any case, they must be stopped from looking to see what's underneath stones, whatever happens. You never know what might come out from under a stone. Venomous woodbugs, poisonous spiders, stinging cockroaches which can pass on colonial diseases against which there are no known remedies, needles with spells put on them by some sadistic white witch-doctor on his flight from the village after the murder there of eleven people he had been treating and whom he had forced to change their wills in his favour—an infamous fraud discovered by a young medical student, a strange young man with a bushy red beard . . .

'What has Timortis been up to lately?' she thought to herself when she got to this point (or vice-versa). 'I hardly ever see him at all nowadays. Just as well, maybe. Using the fact that he's both a psychiatrist and a psychoanalyst as an excuse, he'd want to start meddling with the education of Noel, Joel and Alfa Romeo. And what would give him that right? We may well ask. Children belong to their mothers. Since they've gone through all the suffering of having them, then they must belong to their mothers. And not to their fathers. And their mothers love them. And so they have to do what their mothers want them to. Their mothers know better than they do what they need, what's good for them, what will make them stay children for as long as possible. Chinese feet. The Chinese squeeze their children's feet into special shoes. Or bind them up. In little vices. Or toe-screws. Or steel moulds. Whatever it is that they do, it's all worked out so that their feet will stay tiny. And they should do the same with the whole child. Stop them growing up. They're so much nicer, so much better, when they're younger. They don't worry about anything. They don't need anything. They don't want to do anything naughty. Later, they're going to grow. They'll want to extend their domain. They're going to want to see what's beyond the horizon. With all the new risks that that will entail. If they go out of the garden there will be at least a thousand supplementary risks and dangers. Did I say at least a thousand? I meant at least ten thousand. And that's no exaggeration. Everything must be done to stop them going outside the garden. Even there they already run an incalculable number of risks every time they venture into it. There could be a sudden gust of wind to break off a branch and kill them. Or if it should rain again, while they're all warm and sticky after playing horses or trains or cops and robbers or whatever game they're most fond of at the moment, then the sudden shower could force them to catch pulmonary emphysema, or pleurisy, or a cold and a chill, or an attack of rheumatism, or polio, or typhoid, or scarlet fever, or chicken pox, or measles, or that new disease they haven't even given a name to yet. And if a storm should brew up . . . There'd be thunder. And lightning. There might even be—who knows?—some kind of atomic fallout. Ionisation phenomena. Its name's horrible enough for it to be something really terrible. Sounds like inanition. And so many other things could happen. And if they went outside the garden things would obviously be much worse. But don't let's think about that now. There's quite enough to be getting on with trying to exhaust all the things that might happen *inside* the garden. And when they're bigger . . . Oh, dear! Oh, dear! Oh, dear! Yes, they're obviously the two most terrifying things. That they'll grow up—and that they'll go outside the garden . . . So many dangers to be prevented. It's perfectly true that a mother must be able to see everything that might happen. But let's leave that for a moment. I'll think about all that a little later on. I certainly won't forget it. They'll grow up—and they'll go out. But I want to concentrate on the garden for the moment. Even in the garden alone, the number of accidents that could take place is enormous. Simply enormous! There's the gravel on the paths. How many times have I said how ridiculous it was to let the children play with it. Suppose they should put some in their mouths and swallow it? Nothing would happen straight away. Everything would go on as usual for a time. And then, three days later, they'd get appendicitis. Immediate emergency operation necessary. Who would do it? Timortis? He's no doctor! The village quack? There's only a vet there! So they'd die . . . just like that! After going through the most horrible agony and suffering. Fever. The sound of their screams. No, not their screams . . . They'd only be able to groan, and it would all be even more horrible. And there'd be no ice. Impossible to find any ice anywhere

158

to put on their burning stomachs. Their temperatures are going up and up and up. The mercury's gone over the top. The thermometer bursts. And a sliver of glass goes straight into Joel's eye as he watches over the sufferings of Alfa Romeo. It's bleeding. He'll have to lose his eye. And there's nobody to look after him. Everyone's busy with Alfa Romeo whose groans fade more and more into a grim silence. Making the most of the disorder and fuss, Noel slips into the kitchen. A bowl of water is boiling on top of the stove. He's hungry. Naturally nobody's had time to give him his feed with his brothers so ill. They've all forgotten. He climbs on a chair in front of the stove. To reach the pot of jam. But the maid has put it a bit further away than usual on the shelf because she'd got a speck of flying dust in her eye. Things like that would never happen if she swept up a bit more carefully. He leans forward. He slips. He falls into the bowl of boiling water. There's just time for him to let out one piercing shriek—just one—and then he's dead. But his little arms and legs still go on struggling, like crabs that are flung live into boiling water. He goes red like the crabs. But he's dead. Noel!'

Clementine rushed to the door and called the maid.

'Yes, ma'am.'

'Don't you dare give us crab for lunch.'

'I wasn't going to. There aren't any. We've got roast beef and croquette potatoes.'

'Don't you dare, all the same.'

'Very well, ma'am.'

'And don't ever dare do crab again. Or lobster. Or shrimps. Or scampi.'

'Very well, ma'am.'

She went back into her room. Wouldn't it be better to cook everything while they were asleep and then let them eat it cold. In that way there'd never be any fires alight when they were up and about. And keep the matches strictly under lock and key too, of course. But we do that already. And the boiled water we use for them to drink—we'll boil it in the evenings after they're in bed. It's a good job I thought of the boiled water. Microbes lose all their malignancy once they've been boiled and boiled and boiled. Yes, but what about all the things they shove into their mouths when they're in the garden? That garden! We almost ought to stop them going into the garden. It's no more healthy out there than being in a nice clean room. A beautifully, scrupulously clean room that's scrubbed out every day—of course that must be better than any garden. Although they could catch cold from the tiles on the floor. But they could do that in the garden too. There are just as many draughts out there. And there's the damp grass. A spotlessly clean room. But it's true that there's still the risk from the tiles. Or they could cut themselves on them. The arteries of their wrists. And as they've done something stupid, they're scared to tell anybody. And so the blood pours out. Gushes out. And Alfa Romeo grows paler and paler. Joel and Noel cry and Alfa Romeo's lifeblood trickles away. The door is locked because we've all gone out shopping. The sight of the blood frightens Noel and he tries to get out of the window to call for help. Look at him climbing on Joel's shoulders. He can't get his balance. He wobbles, falls and is injured, wounded too. It's his neck. The carotid artery. Within a few minutes he's dead. His face dead white. It's impossible. No. . . It couldn't happen in a locked room . . .

She tore out of her room and, like a lunatic, rushed into the room where the three little boys were soundly sleeping. Through the slits in the shutters the sun was making a rosy glow on the pink walls. All that could be heard was the light scuffling sound of their regular breathing. Noel moved slightly and made a funny little noise. Alfa Romeo and Joel were smiling in their sleep, lying flat out, relaxed and inoffensive, their little fists unclutched and open. Clementine's heart was beating too quickly. She left them alone and went back to her own room. But this time she left all the doors open.

'I'm a good mother. I think of everything that might possibly happen to them. Every accident that they might run into is thought of in advance. But I'm not talking about the dangers they'll have to risk when they're bigger. Or when they go outside the garden. No ... That kind can wait until a little later. I'll give plenty of thought to them then. Full consideration. But I've got plenty of time. Plenty of time. There are so many catastrophes to imagine already, the way things are. So many catastrophes. So many. I love them because I think of all the most terrible, the worst possible things that might happen to them. So that I'll be prepared. And ready to prevent. I don't spare myself anything when I imagine these dreadful things. They're forced on to me. I'm responsible for them. They depend on me. They're my children. I've got to do everything in my power to help them escape from the innumerable calamities that lie in ambush for them along every path they might take. The angels. How should they know how to look after themselves, or know what's good for them? I love them. And it's only for their good that I think of all these things. It's not as if I do it for my own pleasure. It makes me shudder to think that they might eat poison ivy or laurels. Or sit on the damp grass. Or have a branch fall on their heads. Or slip into the well. Or roll over the top of the cliff. Or swallow pebbles and stones. Or get stung by ants. Or by beetles. Or get thorns in their fingers. Or scratched by thistles. Or pecked by birds. They might smell the flowers. So strongly that a petal will go up their nostrils. They'll get a blocked nostril. It'll go up into their brains. They're dying. They're so small. They tumble into the well. They're drowning. The branch crashes down on to their heads. The tile breaks. There's blood everywhere. Blood. Blood . . .'

She could take no more. Silently she got up and tiptoed back into the children's room. Then she sat quietly on a chair. From there she could see them all. All three of them. They were sleeping. A deep dreamless sleep. Little by little she too began to relax and give in. All anxiety and worry began to fade and disappear. Now and again she started in her sleep, like an old sheepdog dreaming of its flock.

VII

'HRUMPH!' SAID Timortis to himself as he reached the village, 'this must be the thousandth time that I've been to this satanical outback and this wretched road hasn't got a thing left up its sleeve to show me. Although it's true that it doesn't stop me from trying to find out something else for myself, all the same. Anyway, for once there's something new to break the monotony.'

Every wall had a poster stuck on it. White posters with mauve printing. Done, no doubt, with the help of some kind of duplicator.

GALA PERFORMANCE
THIS AFTERNOON
etc., etc., etc.

The show would take place in the garage behind the vicarage. It appeared to have been organised by the vicar.

No sign of Glory Hallelujah on the scarlet stream. He must be out of sight, round the bend. People were emerging from the houses in their Sunday best—that is to say they were dressed as if they were going to a funeral. The apprentices were kept at home. So that they shouldn't feel sorry for themselves they gave them extra kicks on show-days and holidays so that they'd be happy that they'd been left alone for the rest of the afternoon.

Timortis now knew every corner, every long cut and every short cut. He crossed the village green where the Old Folks Fair was always held and went past the school. A few minutes later he went all the way round the church to get a ticket from the box-office that was being run by one of the vicar's special hand-picked choir-boys. He bought an expensive ticket so that he could get a good ring-side view of what was going on. And then he went straight into the garage. Other people were bustling in in front of him, and others were pushing along behind. At the garage door another choir-boy tore half of his ticket or, more precisely, tore the whole of his ticket. When it was in two halves he gave him one of them back again. A third choir-boy was showing every branch of a very large family to their seats. Timortis waited for him to come back and show him to his seat—which did not take very long. The three choir-boys were wearing their poshest gala outfits which consisted of long red skirts, hairy little skull-caps and shreds and fragments of ragged lace at the edges of everything. The third boy snatched Timortis's half-ticket and led the psychiatrist to the centre of the centre stalls. The vicar had loaded into the garage everything that his church contained in the way of chairs. There were so many chairs gathered together and stuffed in there that in certain places there was nothing but chairs. Chairs on top of chairs. Chairs sitting on other chairs so that there was no room for people to sit on them. But in this way they could sell a great many more tickets.

Timortis sat down in his seat, reluctantly boxing the ears of the choir-boy who seemed to be expecting a tip—and who scarpered off without waiting for anything more. If there had been anything more it would, no doubt, have consisted of a set of several matching thumps. It was only natural that Timortis should not show himself publicly to be in opposition to the curious village customs, however much such carryings-on may still have disgusted him. Feeling embarrassed and awkward, he looked elsewhere and began to examine the stage that had been set for the show.

In the middle of the shed, framed on all four sides by the church chairs, a perfectly geometrical ring was standing. It

163

had been set up in the centre of four carved posts that were held up by strong metallic wires, and between which purple velvet ropes were stretched. Two of the poles showed nothing more than overfamiliar scenes from A Child's Life of Jesus. There was Jesus picking his toes at the side of the road; Jesus gulping down a pint of cider; Jesus going fishing; etc. In short it was a miniature collection of belligereligious imagery. In contrast the two other poles were conceived on a much more original plane of relief. The one on the left, closest to Timortis, looked more like a big fat trident, standing with its prongs in the air and covered all over with infernal bas-reliefs, certain of which were fit (or, more fittingly, unfit) to make a friar flush, a brother blush, a priest empucify or a canon collapse. Or a Jesuit colonel explode. The last post, in the form of a cross, bore—in a more everyday fashion—the effigy of the vicar, naked, but seen from the back. He was deeply engaged in searching for his collar-stud under the bed.

There seemed to be no end to the crowds of people coming in and the noise of the moving chairs, the oaths and curses of the people who couldn't find anywhere to sit down because they'd tried to be too economical by buying the cheapest seats, the piercing cries of the choirboys, the powerful heady perfume rising from the feet of almost every member of the audience, and the whines and groans of a handful of Old Folks recently purchased from the Fair and who had been brought there specially to be pinched and punched during the intervals, made a generous contribution to the spiritual feeling and general atmosphere of a Sunday Benefit Gala ... Suddenly there was the noise of a tremendous scratching and scraping, like a worn record revving up, and a thunderous voice burst out from a loud-speaker that Timortis, as he raised his eyes, noticed looped over a beam just above the ring. After a few seconds he recognised the vicar's voice and, in spite of the bad quality of the masonic reproduction, the gist and thread of his discourse could easily be followed.

'This simply won't do!' he yelled as an exordial exhortation.

'Ah! Aha! Ahah!' went the crowd, delighted by such a delightfully diverting declamatory debut.

'Certain amongst you gathered here today, inspired by a sordid, avaricious and malicious mentality, have attempted to scorn and scoff at the teachings of the Wise Books. These wretches have dared to buy cheap, and therefore bad, seats. But they shall not be seated! This afternoon's Gala Performance is a Luxury Show provided by the auspicious patronage of God, that creature of luxury. Whomsoever in these circumstances refuses to act luxuriously shall receive the punishment of the wicked and roast externally in hell on crackling log fires, on poor peat flames, on scumsparks, if not just on smouldering dry straw.'

'Give us our money back! Give us our money back!' cried the ones who hadn't been able to find anywhere to sit down.

'You'll get nothing back. Sit down as best you can. Or don't sit down at all. God couldn't care less. We've put other chairs on your chairs, with their feet in the air, to drive it into you that they're hardly worth being sat on, even by other chairs, at the measly price you've paid for them. Shout, protest as much as you like. God is luxury. God is beauty. All you had to do was buy more expensive seats. Those who wish to can pay a supplement. But they won't get any better seats for it! Making amends does not imply automatic absolution.'

They were beginning to find that the vicar was becoming a trifle abusive. Hearing a loud noise of breaking wood behind him, Timortis looked round. He saw the blacksmith standing up in the centre of the cheap seats. He had a chair in each hand and was smashing them against each other. The second time he did it, the chairs split into matchwood. With all his strength he threw the pieces into the wings. The fragments hurtled through the taut curtain. That was the signal. Everybody with rotten tickets grabbed the chairs that were in their way and started to smash them up. Those who weren't strong enough passed them along to the smith.

The bits and pieces flew into the midst of the uproar and slashed out a violent path for themselves through the space between the two halves of the curtain. A luckier aim than the others shook the curtain-rod that was holding it up. The vociferating vicar could still be heard over the loud-speaker.

'You have no right to do this! The God of luxury despises you and your miserable morals, your stinking socks, your piss-stained breeks, your grubby black collars and your yellow tartared teeth. God preserves no Paradise for watered gravy, no Paradise for tough old parboiled chickens, no Paradise for long, lank, bony, jady crocks. God is a great silver swan. God is the sapphire eye in the centre of a shimmering, twinkling delta. God is the diamond eye eternally winking at the bottom of a golden chamber pot. God is the voluptuousness of twenty-four carats, the great platinum mysteries, the hundred thousand rings of the courtesans of Malamponia. God is an ever-lasting green candle carried by a bishop of velvet. God lives in precious metals, in liquid pearls, in boiling mercury, in ethereal crystals. God is looking down at you, turdy filthy brutes that you are, and is ashamed of you . . .'

Immediately he pronounced the forbidden word, the crowd, including even those who were sitting comfortably, began to mutter amongst themselves.

'That's enough, vicar! Get on with the show!'

Chairs started flying through the air again, wilder than ever this time.

'He is ashamed of you! You are drab, dull, dirty, disgusting! You are the dishrags of the world, potato peel in the soups of heaven, unloved nettles in God's garden. You are . . . Ouch! Oh, ououuochouchouch!'

One chair, that had been aimed more accurately than the others, had managed to completely unhook the curtain and the vicar could be seen behind it, jumping about and dancing

166

in his underpants in front of the microphone while rubbing the crest of his cranium.

'Get on with the show, you vile old vicar!' cried the furious crowd with a single voice.

'All right! All right! Ouch!' said the vicar. 'Here it comes then. We're going to start!'

The tumult immediately subsided. The chairs were almost all occupied now and the choir-boys rushed to close in round the vicar. One of them held out a roundish brown object in front of him. He plunged his hand into it. Another choirboy did the same thing with his other hand. The vicar slipped on a splendid blinding yellow dressing-gown and sprung limping out into the ring. He had brought his microphone with him which he hooked up over his head on a specially provided wire.

'Today,' he announced without any further preamble, 'In ten rounds of three minutes each I shall fight the devil before your very eyes!'

There was a murmur of incredulity in the crowd.

'Do not mock!' shouted the priest. 'Those who don't believe me have only to keep their eyes open to be convinced.'

He made a signal, and the curate flashed out of the wings. A pungent smell of sulphur filled the air.

'Exactly one week ago,' announced the vicar, 'I discovered the startling fact that my curate was the devil.'

The curate casually spat out a lazily vivid but beautifully sharp and polished sword of flame. Although he wore a long Kathakali dressing-gown, the thick bushy hair on his legs and his forked boots could be clearly seen.

'Give him a round of applause!' proposed the priest.

There was a soft crackle of unenthusiastic clapping. The curate looked disappointed and upset.

'What could delight God more,' roared the priest, 'than such a sumptuous combat. This is the kind of thing that the Roman emperors, supreme lovers of luxury, excelled at organising.'

167

'Shut up!' yelled a member of the audience. 'We want to see some action!'

'Good,' said the vicar. 'Good. Very well then. I've only one more thing to say. And that is that you're a lousy load of miserable morons.'

He opened his dressing-gown and let it fall to his feet. He had two choir-boys to serve him as seconds; the curate had nobody on his side. The choirboys set out the bucket, the stool and the towel, and the vicar slipped in his gumshield. The curate simply said a single cabbalistic syllable and his jet-black dressing-gown went up in flames round his shoulders and disappeared in a cloud of crimson smoke. He chuckled satanically and began to limber up with a little shadow-boxing. The vicar looked pale and scribbled a quick but accurate sign of the cross in the air.

The curate objected. 'Hey, vicar, no hitting below the belt *before* we start!'

The third choir-boy whacked a heavy hammer on the side of a copper cauldron. The curate, who had been waiting in his corner under the totemised trident, came out into the centre of the ring. The audience had given out a great satisfied 'Ah!' of relief at the sound of the witch's gong.

The devil took up the attack from the very first in short right hooks. With every third blow he broke through the vicar's defences. But the vicar showed that he had a very pretty way with his legs. More precisely, with both his legs. They were chubby and fat and extremely agile, in spite of their inequality. The vicar countered with direct jabbing punches from the right, trying to keep his adversary at a distance. Taking with both hands the opportunity offered when the devil put down his guard to better butcher the vicar with a bilateral assault from the flank, the vicar doubled in with a left to the heart that caused the curate to swear diabolically. The crowd roared its applause. The vicar acknowledged this by strutting and swaggering and got an unexpected uppercut bang in the mandibles which he took right on the jaw. Then with a rapid sequence of lefts the devil blacked his right eye for him, putting it through every shade of grey until he reached the climax. He seemed as if he wanted to display his entire repertoire of fancy punches. Red marks began to appear on the bodies of both men and the vicar was beginning to grow breathless.

As the curate closed in with a left hook, he said to him 'Get thee behind me! ...'

This made the curate laugh so much that he had to hold his sides and the vicar took his chance and landed a couple of corkers straight on his conk. The blood shot straight out like a Florentine fountain of a pretty pissing cherub. Almost immediately, the sound of the gong rang out and each of the two adversaries went back to his separate corner. The vicar was immediately surrounded by his three choir-boys. The crowd applauded wildly because there had already been gallons of blood. The devil snatched up a jerrican of petrol, took a great swig from it, and a fantastic salvo of filigree flame forked out from his lips to gently grill the microphone wires. The crowd applauded even louder. Timortis thought that the vicar had been putting up a good fight, both as a defender of the faith in his title, and as organiser of the show. The idea of raising the devil and bringing him into play seemed an excellent one to him.

The little choir-boys were carefully patching up the vicar. But he didn't seem to be terribly fit and well and big bruises were becoming visible over various parts of his anatomy.

'Round Two!' announced the boy with the clanging gong as it boomed out.

This time the devil seemed to have made up his mind to finish it all off before the end of the round. He attacked like a madman without allowing the vicar a single second to get his breath. A hailstorm of blows rained down (if it is not against the rules to say that hail may rain). The vicar snapped out without a break and even got in one or two himself to the great displeasure of the bloodthirsty mob. And then, making the utmost of a tiny pause, he brought both fists down in a single punch on top of the curate's head while at the same time kneeing him viciously up the bracket. Every bone in the devil's body snapped in turn, each accompanied by an appropriately anatomical yelp of pain or anguish.

And with a single voice all the over-excited and exquisitely happy children exclaimed 'Foul! Foul! Come on vicar!'

'Disgraceful!' confirmed the devil as he rubbed the end of his broken nose while displaying all the signs of acutest agony and suffering.

The vicar, delighted, wriggled with pleasure. But the devil was only making a feint of throwing a faint and brusquely flung himself on to the vicar and dealt him two terrible hooks to the liver followed by an uppercut to the jaw which was involuntarily blocked by the vicar with the help of his left eye. Which promptly closed.

Luckily for the vicar, the gong rang out again. He rinsed out his mouth several times and had a big raw juicy steak applied to his eye. It had a little cut in its middle so that he could look through it and see if his eye was capable of carrying on the battle. Meanwhile the devil was showing off by doing a few simple tricks to keep the crowd amused. One trick in particular was a great success. This was when he suddenly let down his shorts and showed the old tinkerwoman his bare behind.

In the middle of the third round, which began even more painfully for him, the vicar, while protecting himself with one hand, treacherously pulled the microphone wire which he had rigged up over his head. Immediately the loudspeaker came unhooked and fell on the curate's head. It knocked him out flat. The vicar proudly paraded round the ring with his fists clenched over his head.

'I have won by a technical knock-out,' he proclaimed. 'Through me, God has won another victory. This great God of luxury and riches! God is the winner! In three rounds!'

'Boo! Boo! Boo!' yelled various voices in the audience.

Most of the village people remained dumb for a moment because it had all happened so quickly. And then they too began to protest because they had got so little value for each minute at the price they had paid for their expensive seats. Timortis began to grow worried, feeling that everything was about to be spoilt.

'Give us our money back, vicar!' cried the crowd.

'Never!' he answered.

'Money back, vicar!'

One chair flew, closely followed by a second. The vicar sprang out of the ring. A storm of chairs landed on his back.

Timortis was slipping along towards the exit when something hit him behind the ear. Instinctively he turned round to hit back. After smashing in his opponent's teeth with his fist, he recognised who it was. It was the carpenter. After spitting out the whole contents of his mouth he collapsed. Timortis looked down at his fingers. His knuckles were broken in two places. He licked them . . . Then a great feeling of embarrassment came over him. He shrugged it off by raising and lowering his shoulders in reasonably quick succession.

'What does it matter? . . .' he thought. 'Glory Hallelujah's there to take it. Anyway, I already owe him a visit for clouting the choir-boy.'

He still felt like hitting somebody. So he knocked into everything and everybody that he came across. He bashed and bullied and felt greatly relieved and gratified to have been able to let fly into grown-up people for a change.

VIII

WHEN TIMORTIS pushed open Glory Hallelujah's door the old man was beginning to put his clothes on again. He had just had a bath in his massive golden tub and, having put away his old working clothes, was slipping into a sumptuous gold brocade smoking jacket. There was gold everywhere. The whole of the inside of the old house seemed to have been carved out of a single piece of the precious metal. Gold not only overflowed from all the coffers, but also covered the cutlery, the crockery, the chairs, the tables, everything. Everything was shining, everything was yellow. All this had struck Timortis the first time, but now he looked at it with the same indifference that he brought to everything that had no direct connection with his personal mania. Which is the same as saying that he no longer even noticed it.

Glory Hallelujah greeted him. He was astonished to see him in such a state.

'I've been in a fight,' said Timortis. 'It was after the vicar's gala. Everyone was fighting. He was fighting too, but he cheated. That's why everybody began to join in.'

'Delighted to find an excuse,' said Glory Hallelujah.

He shrugged his shoulders and raised his eyebrows in slow but resigned parallel motion.

'I . . . ' said Timortis. 'Er . . . I'm a little ashamed . . . Because I've been fighting too. So, as I was coming to see you anyway, I've brought a few spondulicks . . . '

A pile of golden coins trickled between his long, elegant fingers.

'Naturally,' murmured Glory Hallelujah, bitterly. 'It hasn't taken you long to get the hang of things. But put your clothes straight. Don't worry. I'll take your shame off you.'

'Thanks,' said Timortis. 'And now, shall we carry on with our interview?'

Glory Hallelujah swept the heap of golden coins into a gilt-bronze salad-bowl and, without a word, stretched out on the couch at the back of the room. Timortis went and sat by his side.

'Talk to me,' he said. 'Just let yourself go. Relax and let the words come out. We'd got up to where you were telling me about your schooldays, when you stole a balloon.'

Glory Hallelujah put his hand over his eyes and slowly began to speak. But Timortis did not begin listening straight away. Something else intrigued him. Just at the moment that the old man's hand rested on his forehead, he had thought that he had been able to see, although perhaps it had been no more than an illusion, the feverishly fugitive eyes of the old man flickering through the flesh of his palm.

IX

ON THE days when Timortis felt like being an intellectual, he would go into Angel's library and read. There was only one book there, but it was amply sufficient as it was an excellent encyclopaedic dictionary in which Timortis redis-covered, in alphabetical—if hardly logical—order and classifi-cation, the basic facts and ingredients of all those things which go to make up normal libraries, concentrated into one volume. It was a pity that it was so large, clumsy, awkward to handle and heavy.

He stopped, as he always did, at the double-page spread showing the flags. This was full of gay colour, and the words, noticeably less dense than elsewhere in the tome, relaxed the soul and soothed the spirit. The eleventh flag, counting from the left, showed a bleeding tooth on a black background and brought to his bruised mind on this baleful day a blissful vision of little wild hyacinths hiding in the woods.

X

THE THREE children were playing in the garden in a spot where they could not be seen too clearly from the house. They had chosen the spot themselves for a special reason. Pebbles, earth, grass and sand could be found there in equal and plentiful supply. There was also light and dark, dry and damp, hard and soft, mineral and vegetable, the quick animal and the dead insect.

They were not saying very much. Equipped with little iron spades, each was digging a trench for himself. Every now and again their spades would strike against something interesting which its excavating possessor would immediately scoop out and take along to put on the pile of previous discoveries.

After a hundred shovelfuls, Alfa Romeo stopped.

'Stop the dig!' he ordered.

Joel and Noel obeyed him.

'I've found a green one,' said Alfa Romeo.

He showed them a little sparkling object with an emerald glitter.

'And I've got the black,' said Joel.

'And me the gold,' said Noel.

They put the three objects down in a triangle. Very gingerly, Alfa Romeo linked them with thin dry twigs. And then they sat down, each one at an apex of the triangle, and waited.

In the centre of the three objects the earth suddenly caved in. A minute white hand appeared, quickly followed by another. The pale hands gripped the edges of the opening

175

and a shining form, four inches high, stood in the middle of the triangle. It was a little girl with long fair hair. She blew kisses to each of the boys and then began to dance. She danced for three or four minutes inside the triangle, never going beyond the limit of the twigs. And then suddenly she stopped, looked up at the sky, and sank back into the earth as swiftly as she had grown out of it. Where the coloured stones had been there were now only three very ordinary worn pebbles.

Alfa Romeo stood up and threw away the twigs.

'I've had enough of that,' he said. 'Let's play another game.'

Noel and Joel had already started digging again.

'We're sure to find something else,' said Noel.

At that moment his spade struck something hard.

'Here's an enormous stone,' he said.

'Let's see!' said Alfa Romeo.

It was a lovely yellow stone with gleaming streaks. He licked them to see if they were as good as they looked. Almost. The earth crumbled as it was bitten into. And in a hollow recess in the stone a tiny slug, yellow, too, was clinging.

'That one's no good,' said Alfa Romeo. 'You can still eat it, but it's not a good one. It's only the blue ones that make you fly.'

'*Are* there blue ones?' asked Noel.

'Of course,' said Alfa Romeo.

Noel tried the yellow one. Jolly good. Much nicer than plain earth, at any rate. Soft. And gooey. In short, it was smashing.

Now Joel, in turn, had just put the blade of his spade under a heavy stone. What a weight! And *two* black slugs.

He held one out to Alfa Romeo who showed a certain amount of interest in inspecting it, but passed it over to Noel. Joel ate the one he had left.

'Not really very marvellous,' he said. 'Tastes like tapioca.'

'They do,' said Alfa Romeo. 'But the blue ones are really good. They're like pineapple.'

'Are they really?' asked Joel.

'And afterwards—you fly!' said Noel.

'You don't fly straight away,' said Alfa Romeo. 'You have to do a lot of work first.'

'Perhaps we could do the lot of work first now,' said Noel. 'Then afterwards, if we find some blue ones, we'll be able to fly straight away.'

'Oh look!' said Joel, who had been busily digging away all the time. 'I've got a lovely brand new seed.'

'Show us,' said Alfa Romeo.

It was almost as big as a nut.

'You have to spit on it five times,' said Alfa Romeo, 'and then it will grow.'

'Are you sure?' asked Joel.

'Sure,' said Alfa Romeo. 'But you must stand it on a fresh leaf first. Go and find one, Joel.'

Out of the seed there came a miniature tree with pink leaves. Between its branches of filigree silver flew slender singing humming birds. The largest one was just as big as Joel's little fingernail.

XI

'ALREADY SIX years, three months, five days, two hours and seven minutes that I've been burying myself alive in this bloody backwater,' said Timortis to himself as he scrutinised his reflection in the mirror.

He was managing to maintain his beard at a steady medium length . . .

XII

TIMORTIS WAS just going out when he bumped into Clementine in the corridor. He never saw her now. Hadn't done so for months. The days flowed by so continuously and so furtively that he had lost all count of them. She pulled him back.

'Where are you off to in such a hurry?'

'Same place as usual,' replied Timortis. 'I'm off to see my old friend Glory Hallelujah.'

'Are you still psychoanalysing him?' asked Clementine.

'Er . . . yes,' said Timortis.

'It seems to be taking you a long time.

'Well, I want it to be complete, total and exhaustive.'

'You're getting a swollen head,' observed Clementine.

He took a step back because she was speaking straight at him and an undeniable whiff of musty carrion was wafting across on her breath.

'Possibly,' said Timortis. 'Anyway, he's beginning to become extremely transparent and I'm starting to get worried.'

'It certainly doesn't seem to be making you very happy,' said Clementine. 'You searched long enough before you got a client.'

'All my hopes stole away one after the other,' said Timortis. 'I had to fall back on Glory Hallelujah because he was the only one left. But I must confess that the contents of his cranium aren't particularly the right kind of thing to make the person he unloads them on to overflow with joy.'

'How far have you got?' asked Clementine.

'How do you mean?'

179

'Well, is the psychoanalysis very advanced?'

'Thank goodness it isn't going too badly,' said Timortis. 'But I can see that I'm nearly at the point where I'll have to start probing the most infamous details, and the fact is that I'm a bit scared of that. But all this isn't very interesting for you to talk about. What have you been doing lately? We don't ever see you at meal-times any more. Neither at lunch nor supper.'

'I like to eat in my own room,' said Clementine with a certain smug superiority in her tone.

'Oh, I see,' said Timortis.

He looked down—all the way down—at the young woman's figure.

'It doesn't seem to be doing you any harm,' he said simply.

'I only eat what I have to,' said Clementine.

Timortis desperately tried to find some other topic to keep the conversation going.

'Your spirits are as high as ever?' he asked flatly.

'I wouldn't know . . . Yes and no.'

'What's wrong then?'

'To tell the truth,' she explained, 'I'm afraid.'

'What of?'

'Not *of* anything. I'm just afraid *for* my children. The whole time. Anything—absolutely anything at all—might happen to them. And I keep picturing it. Oh, it could be the simplest possible thing in the world. I don't go racking my brains for things that could never happen. Or for all these crazy ideas that other people think of. No. Even confining the list strictly to only those things that *could* or *might* take place is enough to drive me round the bend. And I just can't stop myself thinking about it. I haven't even started thinking about what might happen to them if they went outside the garden—but luckily they don't even know that it has an outside yet. Anyway I'm putting off thinking about that for a moment, otherwise I'll go completely dotty.'

'But your children run no risks at all,' said Timortis.

'Children know more or less subconsciously what's good for them and they don't often get into serious trouble.'

'Don't you think so?'

'I'm sure they don't,' said Timortis. 'If they did, then neither you nor I would be here now, would we?'

'I suppose it's true to a certain extent,' said Clementine, 'but my children aren't like other people's.'

'Of course not,' said Timortis.

'And I love them so very, very much. I love them so much that I think I've thought of everything that could possibly happen to them in this house and in this garden. And I keep thinking about it all so much that I can't sleep any more. You can't imagine the number of accidents I've listed. Just try to imagine what a trial it is to be a mother when that mother loves her children as I love mine. But there are so many things to be done in the house that I can't be on top of them watching over them every single minute . . .'

'What about the maid?'

'Oh, she's just stupid,' said Clementine. 'They're in even more danger when she's with them than when they're on their own. She's got no sense or feeling and the further away from them that she is, the happier I am. And she's incapable of using the least little bit of initiative. Suppose that one day they should dig a little too deeply in the garden with their spades and come across an oil well there. The petrol would start gushing out and drown them all and she wouldn't have the least idea what to do. Can't you see how terrified I am? And it's all because I love them so much!'

'Indeed,' said Timortis. 'It strikes me that you've neglected nothing in your foresight.'

'There's one other thing that torments me,' said Clementine. 'And that's their education. The idea of sending them to school in the village fills me with terror. Of course, it's out of the question to think about sending them there alone. But I can't let them be taken in by *that* girl. An accident would be bound to happen to them on the very first day. I'll have to go myself. And if there are times when I can't go, then you'll have to replace me—if you'll promise me to be extra specially careful. Oh, but no, I don't think I can even risk that. I'll have to go myself. But we don't want to worry too much about their education for the moment. After all, they're still very young. Just the idea of seeing them walk out of the garden drives me so far out of my mind that I haven't yet been able to consider all the risks that would be involved with it.'

'Why not get them a tutor who could come home?' said Timortis.

'I've thought about that too,' replied Clementine, 'but I'll have to admit that I'd be jealous. It's stupid, I know, but it's also terribly clear and simple. I just couldn't bear to see them growing attached to somebody else rather than me. Now, if we had a good tutor here with them, they'd be bound to grow attached to him. And if he was a bad one—well, I just wouldn't want my children to have anything to do with him. It's not as if I had much faith in the school anyway, but at least they've got some teachers there, while the problem of a tutor seems practically insoluble to me.'

'The vicar would make a fairly conventional kind of traditional tutor,' said Timortis.

'I'm not very religious and I don't see why my children should be.'

'I don't think they'd run much risk of that with the vicar,' said Timortis. 'He's got some pretty healthy notions about religion and can only encourage the absolute minimum of followers.'

'He wouldn't put himself out to come here anyway,' cut in Clementine, and the solution of the problem came no nearer. 'They'll just have to go into the village.'

'But when you come to think of it,' said Timortis, 'there's never any traffic on that road. Or hardly ever.'

'Exactly,' said Clementine. 'There's so little traffic that nobody bothers any more. Then when something happens to come along it's a thousand times more dangerous. It makes me tremble even to think about it.'

'You sound like the Holy Lady of Lewisham,' said Timortis.

'Stop laughing at me,' said Clementine. 'No, seriously, I can't see any other answer except for me to take them there and back every time myself. But what else can you expect? When one loves one's children there are sacrifices that one is willing to make.'

'They didn't kiss you so much when you left them without their feed to go clambering over the rocks,' observed Timortis.

'I don't remember ever having done that,' said Clementine. 'And if I did, then it must have been while I was ill. At any rate, it's not your place to remind me of it. You know perfectly well that it was during the time that Angel was here. And when even his very presence was enough to make me want to run away from everything, including myself. But things have changed now, and the entire responsibility for their education falls on my shoulders.'

'Don't you think you might make them too dependent on you?' observed the psychiatrist, a trifle shamefully.

'Oh, but what could be more natural? These children mean everything to me. They are my only reason for living. So it's only just that they should always turn to me when they need anything.'

'Even so, and in spite of everything,' said Timortis, 'I still think you're exaggerating with all your worries . . . because you can't see anything else at the moment. Look, let's take an example . . . I'm surprised that you still let them use paper. In the first place they could scratch themselves with it. And then suppose the woman who had done up the roll had just poisoned her entire family with arsenic and had put the fatal dose down on the first sheet . . . That sheet would still be dangerously contaminated . . . Just by coming into contact with it one of your kids could drop dead . . . I think that you ought to lick their little bottoms for them . . .'

She gave it a moment's thought.

'Well,' she said, 'you know animals do it for *their* young . . .
So perhaps a good mother should too . . .'

Timortis looked at her.

'I think you really *do* love them,' he said, very gravely.
'And, when you come down to it and give it a bit of thought,
there's nothing so incredible or impossible about my story of
the old woman and the ars(sorry!)enic after all.'

'It's all enough to drive anyone mad with worry," said
Clementine, crushed.

She burst into tears.

'I just don't know what to do . . . I don't know what to do
for the best . . .'

'Take it easy,' said Timortis. 'I'll see what I can do to help
you. I've only just realised what a complicated problem it is.
But I'm sure we'll be able to sort it all out. Go upstairs and
have a lie down.'

She took his advice.

'This is what I call a genuine passion,' Timortis said to
himself as he went on his interrupted way.

He would have liked to experience something similar. But
as he didn't, he would have to do without it. But he could
always observe it from the outside.

He was teased and tormented by a vague thought that
refused to take shape. A thought so vague. So elusive. At any
rate it would be interesting to get the children's point of view.

But there was no hurry.

XIII

THEY WERE playing on the lawn in front of their mother's window. Less and less could she put up with them being out of her sight. For the time being she was happy watching them, following every detail of all their little movements and trying to guess what they would do next. Joel seemed less energetic than usual and lingered behind the others, copying everything they did lethargically. Slowly he stood up, felt his little trousers and looked round at his brothers. They began to dance round and round him as if he had just said something very funny to them. Joel pressed his fists into his eyes and it could be seen that he was crying.

Clementine hurried out of her room, down the stairs, and was on the lawn with them in a few seconds.

'What's the matter, darling?'

'Tummy ache!' sobbed Joel.

'Have you eaten something nasty? Has that silly idiot gone and given you something bad to eat again, my poor cherub?'

Joel was standing with his legs apart. He pulled in his tummy and stuck out his bottom.

'I've done it in my pants!' he whimpered, crushed and crimson.

Alfa Romeo and Noel's expressions were mockingly superior.

'He's a big baby!' said Alfa Romeo. 'He still does it in his pants!'

'What a baby!' said Noel.

'Come along with me, then,' said Clementine. 'And I want

you two to be nice to him. It isn't his fault. Come on, darling, come on. I'll put you on a nice clean pair and I'll give you a nice big spoonful of camphorated chlorodyne.'

Alfa Romeo and Noel turned green with envy and astonishment.

Joel trotted along behind Clementine, completely consoled.

'It isn't fair and it's just plain disgusting,' said Alfa Romeo. 'He does it in his pants and all she does is give him complicated colic-beans.'

'Yes,' said Noel, 'it's not fair. I want some too.'

'I'm going to try to do some in mine,' said Alfa Romeo.

'So am I,' said Noel.

They made the most tremendous effort that they were capable of. Their cheeks went from puce to purple, but still nothing came.

'I can't do a thing,' said Alfa Romeo. 'I've just managed a tiny weeny weewee.'

'Just too bad,' said Noel. 'We'll have to do without the colly-beans. But let's hide Joel's teddy.'

'What?' said Alfa Romeo, unable to believe that Noel had said so many words at once.

He thought about his proposal.

'That's a good idea,' he added, 'but we'll have to do it so that he won't be able to find it again.'

Noel's forehead crinkled laboriously. He was trying to think of a suitable hiding place. He turned his head to the right and to the left, seeking inspiration. Neither was Alfa Romeo doing nothing. Febrifaciently he was nudging his neurons.

'Look!' he said. 'Over there!'

By *over there* he meant the clearing where the maid hung out her washing on lines high up in the air. At the foot of one of the white posts between which the lines were stretched they could see the shape of her little step-ladder.

'We'll hide it in a tree,' said Alfa Romeo. 'We can use Tarse's ladder. Hurry up before he comes back.'

They ran as fast as their four legs would carry them.

186

'But . . .' puffed Noel, as he ran, '. . . he'll still be able to get it back . . .'

'No he won't,' said Alfa Romeo. 'See, we can move the ladder together. But he won't be able to do it by himself.'

'Don't you think so?' asked Noel.

'You'll see,' said Alfa Romeo.

They got to the ladder. Much bigger than it had looked from over there.

'We'll have to be careful not to tip it over,' said Alfa Romeo. 'If we do, we'll never get it the right way up again.'

Struggling along like a pair of old drunks they dragged the step-ladder away.

'Phew, it's heavy!' said Noel after ten yards.

'Hurry up!' said Alfa Romeo. 'She's coming back.'

XIV

'THERE!' SAID Clementine. 'Now you're nice and clean again.'

She threw the piece of cotton-wool into the pot. Joel was standing in front of her with his back to her. She had just cleaned him up and was still kneeling. She couldn't quite make up her mind about the next part of the operation.

'Bend over, darling,' she said to him.

Joel bent over, his elbows sticking out at each side. Delicately she pressed open his little buttocks—just a little—and began to lick. Gently and carefully. Scrupulously and conscientiously.

'Mummy, what are you doing?' asked Joel in surprise.

'Just making sure you're really clean, my darling,' said Clementine, stopping her work for a second. 'I want you to be just as clean as a baby puppy or a baby kitten.'

It wasn't even humiliating. And, when you got down to it, extremely natural. What a moron that Timortis is! Incapable of even understanding that. A thing like this is no trouble at all. And like this, at least she'd be sure that they'd never get anything else again. And since she loved them, nothing that she did for them could possibly harm them. Nothing! When you got down to it, she should even have cleaned them all over like that . . .

She got up and pulled up pensive Joel's pants. New horizons spread themselves out before her.

'Go back and play with your brothers, darling,' she said.

Joel scampered off. When he got to the bottom of the staircase he slipped a finger in his trousers because his little bum was still slightly damp. He shrugged his shoulders.

Clementine slowly went back to her room. It really hadn't tasted very nice when you thought about it. Perhaps a bit of beef would do her good.

Wash them all over like that. Yes, a good idea.

It's extremely dangerous, as she had often told herself, to put them in the bath. You've only got to look away for a second. Just turn your head, say, or bend down to pick up the soap that has slipped out of reach under the basin. And then, at that very moment, there's a terrible blockage in the pipes because a flaming meteorite has suddenly shot into the middle of the reservoir and—without exploding—managed to worm its way into the main conduit because of its crazy supernatural speed. And once it's stuck there, the water in all the channels begins to turn to steam and a shockwave (charming expression, *shockwave*) whizzes through. And, of course, a thousand times more water than before gushes through the pipes so that, in less than the time it takes to bend down and pick up the piece of soap—and, anyway, it ought to be a crime to sell soap in shapes like that, all oval and slippery, that can slip, slither and slide away without the slightest provocation, and fly anywhere, even splash into the water and send a microbe straight up a child's nose—anyway, in less than the time it takes to pick it up again, here comes the deluge, the sea-level rises, the child goes mad, swallows it all, chokes—and might even drown and die—his poor face bright purple—asphyxiated . . .

She wiped her perspiring forehead and closed the cupboard door again without taking anything. Her bed. Her kingdom for her bed. She'd have to lie down. Straight away.

XV

Still a little resentful, vexed and perplexed, Joel went back to find his brothers. With their spades in their hands they were deep in their digging and didn't even look up as he came along.

'D'you think we'll ever find another blue one?' Noel said to Alfa Romeo.

Joel, intrigued, lifted his nose in their direction.

'No,' said Alfa Romeo. 'I've told you they're the rarest of them all. You only find one in every hundred thousand billion.'

'They're just playing a trick on me,' decided Joel, getting back to his work with a rage.

'It's a pity it ate it,' said Alfa Romeo. 'If it hadn't done that, *we* might have been flying now instead.'

'I'm glad it was his,' said Noel. 'I'd be very sad if mine had gone.'

Very flamboyantly he put his arm round his soft golden teddy.

'Dear old Hunnimuzz!' he said with dramatic tenderness.

Joel, his eye obstinately stuck to the ground, attacked a small stretch of gravel with vigour.

The allusion to the bear made his heart miss a beat. Where was his one? He didn't want to look up, although he could feel a smarting sensation beginning to tingle behind his eyelids.

'He doesn't look very happy,' jeered Noel.

'Weren't the caulibeans very nice,' asked Alfa Romeo with profound sarcasm.

Joel refused to answer or look up.

'He still smells pongy,' said Noel. 'Doesn't surprise me that Phrognollipaws should fly away like that.'

Joel knew that if he spoke his voice would tremble, and he didn't want to give himself away. He could hardly see what he was doing. More and more tears were welling up to dim his eyes, but he concentrated on his pebbles. And suddenly he forgot his teddy bear, his tormenting brothers and all the things that surrounded him.

A beautifully seductive slug of the purest and loveliest lapis lazuli blue was slowly creeping over one of the pebbles that mapped out the depths of his territory as if it were marking out a boundary in liquid mother-of-pearl. His breathing stopped short as he stared and stared at it. With trembling fingers he tenderly picked it up and quickly slipped it into his mouth. His brothers' jeers only reached him now through a haze of joy.

He swallowed down the blue slug and stood up.

'I know perfectly well that it was you two who hid it,' he said with a tone of extreme confidence.

'Never on your life,' said Alfa Romeo. 'He went up there because he didn't want to stay with such a pongy poppa.'

'I couldn't care less,' said Joel. 'I'm going to fetch him back.

He had soon found the step ladder a few yards away from the tree, and then the tree itself where Phrognollipaws was nestling comfortably between two branches eight feet seven inches above the ground and carrying on an earnestly important conversation with a woodpecker.

Now he would have to fly. He spread out his arms, concentrated hard, and moved the tips of his fingers. That's how Alfa Romeo had said that you did it.

When his kicking heels flew past Noels' nose, Noel grabbed Alfa Romeo's arm.

'He's found one . . .' he whispered.

'So he has,' said Alfa Romeo. 'That proves I was right, see!'

The woodpecker didn't fly away when it saw Joel come along and sit down and make himself comfortable by the side of his bear and call down to his brothers.

'Aren't you coming up too?' he called, mockingly.

'No, we're not,' said Alfa Romeo. 'That's not funny.'

'Oh, yes it is,' said Joel. 'Isn't it?' he said to the woodpecker.

'It's great fun,' confirmed the woodpecker. 'But, you know, blue slugs aren't all that rare. The bed of irisis is full of them.'

'Oh, you needn't bother to tell me,' said Alfa Romeo. 'I'd have found them anyway. And, besides, they can always be turned blue with a lick of paint . . .'

But he set off for the iris bed all the same, followed by Noel. Joel overtook them on the way. He had left Phrognolli-paws up on his forked branch.

'We'll eat lots and lots and lots,' he said, 'and then we'll be able to fly ever so high.'

'One's enough,' snapped Alfa Romeo.

When Clementine came out, she saw the ladder on the lawn. She ran to look closer. Then she saw the tree. And, in the tree, Phrognollipaws, cosily perched on high.

Putting her hand to her heart she rushed across the garden, screaming and yelling for her children.

XVI

'I DON'T LIKE to have to tell you that you're wrong,' said Timortis. 'But don't let's rush things.'

'It's the only possible solution,' said Clementine. 'Look at it from whatever angle you like—this would never have happened if that tree hadn't been there.'

'Why not put the blame on the step-ladder?' suggested Timortis.

'Of course she should never have left the ladder standing there. But that's another story. She'll get her punishment— and I'll make sure it fits her crime. But surely you can understand that if that tree hadn't been there, then Alfa Romeo and Noel would never have thought of putting the bear up there where Joel couldn't reach it. That tree was the cause of everything. Anyway, just suppose he had tried to *climb* up it to get his teddy back, the poor sweetheart . . .'

'And yet some people,' said Timortis, 'think it's a good thing to let their children climb trees.'

'It wouldn't be a good thing for *my* children!' said Clementine. 'Just think of all the things that can happen with trees. You never know. Insects can gnaw away their roots and make the trees suddenly tumble over on top of the children. Or a dead branch could break, snap off and come down and crush them. Or it could get struck by lightning, go up in flames, follow the wind and cause a forest fire . . . Then the sparks would be carried into the children's bedroom and they'd be burned alive! . . . No, we'd be running far too many risks if we let the trees stay in the garden. So I implore you to take it on yourself to go into the village and to beg the men to come up here and chop them all down. They can take away half of them for themselves, and the other half can be used to keep us warm in the winter.'

'What men?' asked Timortis.

'Oh, I don't know . . . The interloppers, the pruning-men, the woodchoppers, or whatever they're called. Please, please get them to send me as many woodchoppers as they can spare. Is it very much to ask?'

'No . . . I suppose not . . .' said Timortis. 'I'll be off then. We mustn't leave any stone unturned, if you'll pardon the expression . . .'

And he got up. And went.

XVII

THE MEN came in the afternoon. They brought many iron and steel instruments with them, spikes, needles, hooks and crooks, and bright little braziers. Timortis saw them arrive. He was just coming back from a walk, and he stopped and stood back to let them go past him. There were five of them. And they had brought two apprentices with them. One was about twelve years old, pale, puny and pusillanimous. The other was a little older and had a black patch over his left eye and his right leg comically crippled.

One of the men touched his cap as he passed Timortis. It was the one he had agreed the price of the job with. In the end they had said they would accept the compromise proposed by Clementine—half of the trees for the woodchoppers themselves, and the other half to be left there for use in the house. She would have to pay extra if she wanted them to chop up the logs and bring them indoors.

The cockles of Timortis's heart closed their shells tightly and shrivelled up inside. Although they had no sentimental value for him—how could they for an individual born at an adult age and without any memories?—he was attached to the trees because of their anarchistic uniformity and their functional beauty. He felt that he was on intimate enough terms with them not to have to bother to talk to them, nor to write odes to them. But he loved the flickering reflections of the sun on their lacquered leaves, the jigsaws of shadow cut between them by its rays, and the leaves, the leaves, the leaves themselves. He loved the light living, bustling rustling sound in the branches and the smell of their evaporating sap in the warm evenings after the long days. He loved the forked tongues of the dragon-tree, the jaunty trunks of the great dumpy palms, the smooth cleancut limbs of the eucalyptus trees like tall, gawky, awkward schoolgirls who've grown up too quickly and overload their necks with cheap green copper bells and jewellery at weekends after emptying their mothers' scent-bottle down their necks. He admired the pines, so austere in appearance, yet always ready to discharge a few drops of odoriferous resin at the slightest flattering tickle. And he loved too the quenching shade of the canine quercetum of great tousled twisted oaks with their ouliporiferous silhouettes like wise shaggy dogs. The barktrees, the gingkos, the shaddocks . . . all the trees. They all had their own personalities, their habits, their desires—but all of them were friendly and lovable. And yet Clementine's astonishing maternal love completely justified their sacrifice.

The men stopped in the middle of the lawn and put down their tools. Then two of them picked up their picks and began to dig while the pair of apprentices, seizing spades several sizes larger than themselves, cleared away the earth that they had flung out. The trench quickly grew. Timortis had retraced his steps and was circumspectly considering all the activity. The apprentices were piling up the earth round the edges of the trench and trampling on it with all their strength to harden it into a broad low rampart.

When the workmen felt that the ditch was deep enough, they stopped their digging and climbed out. Their movements were slow, and their dull brown clothes made them look like prehistoric ladybirds burying their ancient forefathers. The apprentices, however, still went on clearing away the earth. And frantically, sweatingly, piling it up and ramming it down. As an encouragement, they each received a periodic belting. While they were doing this, three of the workmen who had gone back to the gates, came back dragging a wheelbarrow loaded with round logs about a yard long, like sleepers. They stopped their clumsy vehicle at the edge of the trench. Then they began to put the logs across it on the sole-plates of beaten earth prepared by the apprentices. They placed them carefully side by side, firmly fixing each one in position with a heavy hammer blow to make sure the whole construction was rigid. When the shelter was finished, they took their turn with the spades and began to cover the logs with earth. Timortis beckoned to one of the apprentices who went over to him.

'What are they doing?' he asked, giving him a tough yet timid kick in the tibias, both in spite of and because of his repugnance.

'It's the shelter,' said the apprentice, hiding his head in his arms and running off to join his companions. Who would let him have it too.

The sun was not shining that day, and the leaden sky gave off an unpleasantly livid glow. Timortis felt a shiver run up his back, but he wanted to see what was going to happen.

The shelter appeared to be finished. One after the other, the five men climbed down the gentle ramp that had been built at one end of the trench. They all insisted on trying it out. The apprentices didn't even attempt to follow them, knowing beforehand what would happen to them if they did.

The men came out again. They took their hooks, probes and spikes from their pile of tools. The two apprentices were busy with the braziers, blowing into the embers with all the strength of their weak lungs. At a word of command from their leader they rushed to pick up the hot and heavy iron stoves and followed the men to the first tree. Timortis felt more and more anxious and worried. It reminded him of that terrible day when they had crucified the profligate pony to a gatepost.

They put the first brazier down under a high date-palm and each man plunged one of his tools into it. In a similar way the second brazier was taken to the foot of the neighbouring eucalyptus. The apprentices began to blow into the flames again, but this time with the help of great leather bellows which they jumped on with their feet together. While they were doing this, the team leader was carefully sounding the trunk of the date-palm with his ear. He went all round it until he found the right spot. Then he stopped suddenly, stood up and made a red cross on the bark. The toughest of his four men pulled his crocket out of the red hot coals. It was more like an arrowhead than a hook, a sharp point with pale red barbs smoking in the heavy air. Taking careful, firm aim, he stood back, made doubly sure, and harpooned the trunk in the centre of the red cross. The apprentices had already run off with the brazier, and already one of his workmates was harpooning the eucalyptus tree in the same way. Then both men, as fast as their legs could carry them, rushed back to the shelter and disappeared inside it. The apprentices crouched down at the entrance, near the braziers.

The cluster of leaves at the top of the palm-tree began to tremble. Imperceptibly at first, then more and more quickly. As the quaking increased, Timortis clenched his teeth. A shriek went up, so anguished and intense, that all ears had to be stuffed. The trunk of the date-palm was shaking. And, every time it shook, the rhythm of the siren-like wailing grew faster. The earth at the foot of the date-palm began to crack and then split wide open. The unattainable, impossible note shattered the air, tore eardrums open, and in splitting echoes raced round the whole garden, seeming to reverberate against the low ceiling of the clouds. With one final tremendous effort, the stump was wrenched out of the earth and the long curved shaft crashed back towards the shelter. Now it jumped and danced over the earth, getting closer and closer to the trench, still letting out its insupportable, unbearable cry of pain. A few moments later, Timortis felt the earth tremble for a second time. It was the eucalyptus's turn to tumble. It did not cry out, but breathed thunderously in and out like a gigantic pair of lunatic bellows in a demonaic forge. Its silvered branches twisted round itself, or dug deeply into the soil as it struggled to reach the trench. At that moment the date-palm had reached the end of the ceiling of sleepers and began to hammer and thump on them with great powerful trembling contractions. But its power was already waning and the rhythm slowing down. The eucalyptus, more fragile, had already stopped. Only its leaves, like the blades of little daggers, were still occasionally twitching. The men peeped out of the trench. The date-palm made one last leap. But the man that it had seen and aimed for jumped smartly aside and gave it a Lizzie Borden of a whack with his axe. Then everything went quiet. Only long silent shudders still shivered through the length of the grey column. But even before it was all over the wood-choppers were making tracks towards the next grove.

Timortis, his feet riveted—if not rooted—to the earth, his head ringing and reeling, could not take his eyes away from them. When he saw the harpoon penetrate through tender bark for the third time, he could stand it no longer. He turned round and ran for the cliff. He ran and ran and ran. The air all round him was trembling, trembling with roars of anger and anguish at the piercing pain of the monstrous massacre.

XVIII

Now THERE was nothing left but silence. The trees were all lying on the earth with their roots reaching upwards, and enormous holes riddled the garden which looked like the heart of a bombed city. Great sad, dry, empty abcesses. The five workmen had gone back to the village and the two apprentices were left behind to saw up and stack the corpses into logs.

Timortis surveyed the disaster. Only a few clumpy bushes and low shrubs remained. There was nothing now between his eyes and the sky, which appeared to be suddenly strangely nude without its trellis of shadows. On the right of the house the clacking sound of a billhook could still be heard. The youngest of the two apprentices went by, swinging a long supple two-handed saw behind him.

Timortis took a deep breath, sighed, and went back into the house. He climbed the stairs. On the first floor he turned towards the children's room. Clementine was sitting there, knitting and keeping them company. At the other end of the room, Noel, Joel and Alfa Romeo were turning over the pages of picture books and sucking sweets. The bag of sweets was in the middle of them.

Timortis went in.

'It's all over,' he said. 'They're all dead.'

'Thank goodness!' said Clementine. 'I'll feel so much happier now. I'll have some peace of mind.'

'Is this all you've been doing?' said Timortis. 'Even while all that noise was going on?'

'I didn't pay any attention to it. I suppose it's only normal that timber should make a bit of noise when it falls.'

'Yes ... Oh, yes ...' said Timortis.

He looked at the children.

'Are they being kept in? They haven't been out for three days now. There's no danger for them out there now, you know!'

'Have the men finished all their work?' asked Clementine.

'There's only the sawing up to be done,' said Timortis. 'But if you're still scared, then I'll look after them. I think they could do with a breath of fresh air.'

'Oh yes!' said Alfa Romeo. 'Please let's go for a walk with you!'

'Please let's go!' said Noel.

'Well, be very careful then!' commanded Clementine. 'And don't let them out of your sight for a single second. I'd die of worry if I thought they weren't being looked after properly.'

Timortis went out of the room. The kids frolicked in front of him. All four tumbled down the stairs together.

'Mind they don't fall into the holes!' Clementine was still shouting after them ... 'And don't let them touch the tools.'

'Yes, yes, yes,' said Timortis, mezzavoce at mezzanine level —if there had been one.

As soon as they were outside, Noel and Joel galloped to the spot where the sounds of the billhook were coming from. Timortis slowly followed them with the dignified Alfa Romeo.

The youngest apprentice, the one who was about ten years old, was lopping the branches off a pine tree, As his blade rose and fell, fine whittlings and chips sprang out and the resin perfumed the air with its rasping odour. Joel selected a suitable observation post and stood there and watched, fascinated. Noel stood by his side, just a little behind, and looked over his shoulder.

'What's your name?' asked Noel, after a moment.

The apprentice's sad, miserable little face looked up.

'Dunno,' he said. 'Think it's Johnny.'

'Johnny!' repeated Noel.

'My name's Joel,' said Joel. 'And my brother's name is Noel.'

Johnny didn't answer. The billhook went up and down with a wretched regularity.

'Johnny, what are you doing?' said Alfa Romeo as he reached them.

'This,' said Johnny.

Noel picked up one of the chips to smell it.

'It must be fun . . .' he said. 'Do you always do this?'

'No,' said Johnny.

'Look at me,' said Alfa Romeo. 'Can you spit as far as that?'

Johnny looked at him dispassionately. A yard and a half. He tried—and managed more than twice the distance.

'Oh!' said Noel.

Alfa Romeo's admiration was sincere.

'You *can* spit a jolly long way,' he said, overwhelmed with respect.

'My brother can spit four times as far as that,' said Johnny, who wasn't used to being appreciated at home, and who was trying to pass on this embarrassing praise to somebody more worthy of it.

'Well then,' said Alfa Romeo, 'he must be able to spit a jolly long way too!'

The branch was only hanging on by a thread of fibre. It broke off at the next stroke, and the elasticity in the twigs made it bounce up again and fall to the side. Johnny pushed it away with his hand.

'Look out!' said Johnny.

'Aren't you strong!' said Noel.

'That's nothing,' said Johnny. 'My brother's much stronger than me.'

All the same, he tackled the next branch boldly and bravely, making some very big sparks fly as he lopped and chopped away.

'Take a look at that,' said Alfa Romeo to Joel.

'He'll be almost through it with a single blow,' said Noel.

'Yerrup,' said Alfa Romeo.

'But it's only *almost*,' said Noel, precisely. 'He hasn't quite managed it in one blow, all the same.'

'I could do it in one if I wanted to,' said Johnny.

'I dare say you could,' said Alfa Romeo. 'Have you ever cut straight through a tree in one stroke before?'

'My brother has,' said Johnny. 'A real live tree.'

The excitement of life could be seen flowing back into him.

'D'you live in the village?' asked Alfa Romeo.

'Yes,' said Johnny.

'We've got a garden,' said Alfa Romeo. 'And it's smashing fun there. Are there other boys as big as you in the village?'

Johnny pondered over this question for a moment, but was swept forward by honesty.

'Yes,' he said. 'Hundreds!'

'You must be at least . . .' said Noel, '. . . nine.'

'I'm ten,' corrected Johnny.

'D'you think I'll be able to chop down trees when I'm ten?' asked Alfa Romeo.

'Dunno,' said Johnny. 'It's not so easy if you don't know how.'

'Will you lend that to me?' said Alfa Romeo.

'What?' said Johnny. 'D'you mean my billhook?'

'Yes, that's right,' said Alfa Romeo, licking his lips round the word, 'your billhook.'

'Have a go, if you like,' said Johnny generously. 'But it's very heavy, so be careful.'

Alfa Romeo picked it up gingerly and lovingly. Johnny took the opportunity to spit copiously on his hands. Which, when Alfa Romeo saw it, made him give back the billhook with a certain amount of embarrassment.

'Why d'you spit on your hands?' asked Noel.

'That's what *men* do,' said Johnny. 'It makes your hands tough.'

'D'you think my hands will get tough too?' asked Alfa Romeo. 'Perhaps they'll get as hard as hardwood!...'

'I wouldn't know,' said Johnny.

Then he got back to his work.

'Have you tried digging in your garden to see if there are any slugs there?' asked Alfa Romeo.

Johnny sniffed as he studied the question, then spat out a splendid green gob. It went a stupifyingly surprising distance.

'Wow!' said Noel. 'Did you see *that*?'

'Yessirrup!' said Alfa Romeo.

Completely committed, rapt in fascination and interested excitement, they sat down to watch.

'My brother once found a dead man's bone,' said Johnny, 'while he was digging!'

They listened to him, but this time they weren't impressed. Timortis, standing above them, watched the curious quartet. He felt rather puzzled.

XIX

27 Octoptember

HE WOKE up with a start. Somebody was knocking at his door. Before he could answer, Clementine came in.

'Good morning,' she said, although the words obviously had no meaning for her.

She seemed to be completely out of her mind.

'Whatever's the matter?' asked Timortis, extremely intrigued by this interruption.

'Oh, nothing . . .' said Clementine. 'It's so stupid . . . I had a nightmare.'

'About another accident?'

'No . . . They just went out of the garden. And it won't stop haunting me.'

'Go back to sleep,' said Timortis, sitting up in bed. 'Don't worry. I'll take care of it.'

'Of what?'

'Now, don't worry.'

She seemed a little calmer.

'D'you mean to say that you can do something about their safety?'

'Yes,' said Timortis.

Always that same idea that refused to take shape. But this time she had given him something more precise to work on.

'Go back to bed,' he repeated. 'I'll get dressed. And then I'll come and see you as soon as I've arranged everything. Are they up yet?'

'They're in the garden,' said Clementine.

She went out and closed the door.

XX

'NOT LIKE that,' said Alfa Romeo. 'Like *this*! '

He was flat on his tummy in the grass and, by making the minutest movement with the ends of his fingers and the tips of his toes, he rose a foot above the earth. Then suddenly he shot forward three or four inches and looped a splendid loop in the air.

'Not too high,' warned Noel. 'Don't go over the rockery. They'll see us there.'

It was Joel's turn next, but he stopped when he got to the top of his loop and came back backwards.

'Someone's coming,' he whispered quietly when he was on his feet again.

'Who is it?' asked Alfa Romeo.

'Uncle Tim.'

'Play at pebbles,' commanded Joel.

All three of them sat down, holding their spades in their hands. Timortis appeared a few moments later, as had been predicted.

'Morning, Uncle Tim,' said Alfa Romeo.

'Morning, uncle,' said Joel.

'Morning,' said Noel. 'Come and sit down with us.'

'I've come to have a chat with you,' said Timortis, sitting in the place they had made for him.

'What would you like us to tell you?' said Alfa Romeo.

'Well now,' said Timortis. 'This and that. First of all . . . what were you doing just now?'

'Looking for pebbles,' said Alfa Romeo.

'That's fun, isn't it?' said Timortis.

'It's great fun,' said Noel. 'We play at it every day.'

'I saw some lovely ones yesterday on the road as I was going into the village,' said Timortis, 'but, of course, I couldn't bring them back for you.'

'Oh, it doesn't matter,' said Joel. 'There's loads here.'

'True,' mumbled Timortis, looking round him.

There was a pause.

'But there are plenty of other interesting things to see on the road,' remarked Timortis, tamely.

'Yes,' said Alfa Romeo. 'There are plenty of interesting things everywhere. We can see them through the gates. We can see all the road as far as the bend.'

'So you can,' said Timortis. 'But what about *beyond* the bend?'

'Well,' said Alfa Romeo, 'after the bend ... it must go on just the same.'

'A little further on ... there's the village,' said Timortis.

'With boys like Johnny?' said Alfa Romeo.

'Yes.'

Alfa Romeo turned up his nose.

'Ugh, he spits on his hands,' he sneered.

'That's because he works,' said Timortis.

'Does everybody who works spit on his hands?'

'Of course,' answered Timortis. 'They do it to stop the hair growing there.'

'And do they have fun?' asked Joel. 'Do all the boys in the village have fun?'

'They play together when it's playtime. But most of all they work. If they didn't, they'd be beaten.'

'We play together,' said Alfa Romeo, '*all* the time.'

'And then there's the service,' said Timortis.

'The service?' said Noel.

'Well, that means heaps of people in a great big room. Then a gentleman called the vicar comes and talks to them, dressed in lovely fancy embroidered clothes. And then all the people chuck stones at the old geyser.'

'You do use rude words,' observed Joel.

'Is that all they do?' asked Alfa Romeo.

'It all depends,' said Timortis. 'Yesterday afternoon the vicar had organised a lovely gala performance. He had a fight with his curate on a stage. They had boxing gloves on, and they punched and punched each other. At the end of it, everybody in the room had joined in the punch-up.'

'You too?'

'Bet your life!'

'What's a stage?' queried Joel.

'It's a kind of platform up in the air so that everyone can see. People sit all round it on chairs.'

Alfa Romeo went deep into thought.

'Do they do anything else besides fight each other in the village?' he asked, his interest becoming slightly aroused.

Timortis seemed uncertain about how to answer.

'Well, no . . . On the whole they don't do much else.'

'Well then,' said Alfa Romeo, 'in my opinion we're far better off by staying in the garden.'

Timortis hesitated no longer.

'Then I suppose that means,' he said, 'that you don't want to go outside any more.'

'Right,' said Alfa Romeo, 'not in the least. In the first place, we're already outside the house. And then we don't fight each other. We've got better things to do.'

'Such as? . . .' asked Timortis.

'Er . . . well . . .'

Alfa Romeo looked at his brothers.

'Looking for pebbles,' he concluded.

They went back to their digging, making it perfectly clear to Timortis that his presence was no longer required by them. He stood up.

'Doesn't it upset you that there aren't any trees left?' he asked before he left them.

'They were pretty,' said Alfa Romeo. 'But they'll grow again.'

'But how about climbing?'

Alfa Romeo said nothing. Noel answered for him.

'We've grown out of climbing trees,' he said.

Timortis, completely muddled and confused, went away without looking back. If he had, he would have seen three tiny silhouettes zoom up into the sky in a single jet and hide behind a cloud to release their suppressed laughter. Grown-ups' questions really are ridiculous.

XXI

ON HIS way back Timortis was taking long strides. His back was bent over, the hairs of his beard were hanging long and separate and straight, and his eyes were staring at the road. He was now extraordinarily opaque and reciprocally felt himself growing extremely materialistic. The multiplication of his interviews had shown a great advance. And probably no more would be needed. Timortis wondered. He was still worried. How was it all going to end? Whatever he did and said, however much he might drag out of old Glory Hallelujah, he would gain nothing more from it mentally. As a living person he had nothing more than his own experiences and memories, his own exploits, adventures and opinions. He couldn't manage to assimilate Glory Hallelujah's. Not all of them.

'Nonsense, nonsense!' he said to himself. 'Nature is fine and fresh, cool and beautiful, even though it is coming on for the end of the year. I love the Octoptember season with its seabathed climate. Octoptember, all ripeness and perfume. The hard black leaves and the prickly thistles of rusty barbed-wire; all the clouds moving in layers across the bottom of the sky; thatched cottages made of old honey. All these things. It's all so very pretty, with the earth soft and brown and warm. So what's the sense in worrying? Pure madness... Since everything will sort itself out in no time. But how long, how long this road is!'

A flight of sphinxwings overhead, setting off for the South no doubt, made him raise his eyes—although they had reached him first through his ears. Curious, their habit of singing together in single, thumping, fluttering and seemingly electronic chords. The leaders of the valentinian flight formation took the base on tympani and drums, those at the sides and in the middle were on cellos and violas, and the following chorus came in equally with the woodwind and brass—any harpsicorkscrewing stragglers chancing a few subtle, if diminished, harmonic embroideries and embellishments with arpeggios and clavicocktails of castanets. They all started and stopped together at the same moment, although the intervals between the chords were strangely irregular.

'Customs and habits of the sphinxwing,' thought Timortis. 'Who is going to make a study of them? Who *could* describe them? It would need a tremendous tome, printed on art paper, illustrated with colour plates due to a fertile mere-sinning walrus brush dipped in the nation's skeeter pot. Sphinxwings, sphinxwings, who will teach you to behave like human beings? Alas, will anyone ever be able to trap one of you? Sootwinged sphinxwings. Redbreasted sphinxwings. Hummingcanned sphinxwings. Mooneyed sphinxwings, piping and pattering like baby mice. Sphinxwings that fade and die as soon as the lightest of fingertips caresses your intangible feathers. Who die for the slightest cause. Even when you are looked at for a second too long. Listened to for a second too long. Or when people smile at you. Or turn their backs on you. When people take off their hats to you. When night does not come. When evening falls too soon. Subtle, tender sphinxwings, whose hearts swell inside you, fill you until they are all beat, beat, beat . . . in those places where other birds and animals have ordinary organs.'

'Perhaps other people don't see the sphinxwings as I see them,' said Timortis to himself. 'And perhaps I don't see them either. Or not altogether in the way I say I do. But, at any rate, one thing is sure. And that is that even if one doesn't see the sphinxwings, one has to pretend to see them. Anyway, they are so clear and obvious that it would be ridiculous to miss them.'

'I can see the road less and less clearly—that's one thing that's certain. I know it too well. And yet they say—though not me, I think—that the things we know best we find beautiful above all others. Or perhaps my overfamiliarity with it leaves me free to appreciate other things in place of it. Like the sphinxwings. Therefore perhaps the statement can be rectified. We find that things that don't interest us very much are beautiful above all others because they allow us to see what we want to see in place of them. Perhaps I shouldn't put it in the first person plural. So let's get back to the singular. I find . . . (*see above*).'

'Oho!' Timortis said to himself. 'I'm being very wise and profound suddenly. Whoever would have thought it, eh, whoever would have thought it? Anyway, this final definition shows my abnormal common sense. And there's nothing more poetic than common sense.'

The sphinxwings passed swiftly backwards and forwards overhead, swerving at the most unexpected moments, tracing graceful figures in the sky, amongst which a persistent prolongation of the retinal images would have permitted the spectator to pick out shapes such as cartesian four-leaved clovers for St Patrick, and many other little curvilinear diversions, including the lovers' cardioid cardiograph—a graph in the shape of a heart.

Timortis went on looking at them. They flew higher and higher, rising in ever-widening spirals, until they no longer had any distinct outline. They were now nothing but black specks, capriciously sprinkled on to the clouds where they moved with collective animation. When they flew in front of the dazzling sun, Timortis was forced to blink his eyes.

Then, far out over the sea, he suddenly noticed three slightly larger birds who were flying so quickly that it was impossible for him to tell which species they belonged to. Shielding his eyes with his hand, he tried to see them more clearly. But they had already gone out of sight. They reappeared behind a distant jutting rock, describing a relentless curve, delving ever upwards, one behind the other, and always with the same terrifyingly supersonic speed. Their wings must have been beating so fast that they could not be seen. They were simply three streamlined silhouettes, almost identical.

The three birds swooped towards the formation of sphinx-wings. Timortis stopped walking to watch more carefully. His heart beat rather rapidly—with an emotional shock that he found hard to explain to himself. Perhaps it was the ease and grace of the flight of the new arrivals. Or perhaps the fear of seeing them attack the sphinxwings. Or perhaps that impression of careful rehearsal and premeditation given by their perfectly synchronised movements.

They zoomed up sharply, up the length of an imaginary slope in space, and their speed through the air took away your breath. Timortis thought that not even swallows could have followed them. And they must have been fairly large birds too. Not being sure how far away they were when he had first seen them, it was hard for him even to make a rough guesstimate of their size. But they had stood out against the sky infinitely more sharply than the sphinxwings which had now grown almost invisible, like the heads of tiny silver pins on the grey velvet of the sky.

XXII

28 Octoptember

'The days are growing shorter,' Clementine was telling herself. 'And the nights are getting longer. Which means that winter and spring are on their way. These are the cruellest seasons, breeding an infinity of dangers. An infinity of dangers, half-foreseen in the summer, but which do not spring into such vivid detail until these very moments when the days dwindle down, when autumn leaves begin to fall, when the earth begins to smell of warm, damp dog. Novembruary, the cold, spitgrey, drizzleridden, fogeared month. Novembruary rain can cause all sorts of damage in all sorts of places. It can furrow through the fields, flaunch the furrows into ravines, and carry off the enraptured ravens. Or it can suddenly freeze. And then Alfa Romeo catches double bronchial pneumonia. Here he is coughing and coughing. Spitting blood. And his worried mother, sitting by the side of his bed, puts her hand on his poor, slender, sunken face. It breaks her heart to see him like that. But she must stay with him. But she can't look after the others at the same time. So out they go without their wellingtons. And catch colds too. Each of them catches a different kind of disease. It's impossible for her to look after all three of them at the same time. She'd wear her feet off running from one room to the other, in and out of all those doors. But she'd do it, she'd do it, even on bleeding stumps, leaving trails of bubbling scarlet and crimson on the cold tiles. She rushes from one bed to another with the tray and the thermometer and the pills and the bottles of medicine. And then suddenly the microbes from each of the three separate

rooms float up in the air, join together in some dark triple combination, and result in a filthy cross-breed hybrid, a monstrous crobe, so hideous that it is visible even to the naked eye. And it has the unique and unusual property of provoking the growth of terrible soft tumours, great ghastly ganglions. In soft, melting, laocoon-like rosaries round the childrens' limbs as they lie in bed. Then the swollen ganglions burst, the microbes come streaming out of the sores—all, all because of the rain, the greydull Octoptember rain. And the Novembruary winds that come with it. But there are no branches left for the wind to fling down on the heads of the innocent. No weighty branches to be wrenched from no trees. But suppose the wind should seek revenge, smack its brutal breath on to the surface of the sea, send showers of spray shooting over the soaking cliff. On one of the drops of spray is a tiny insect, a minute shell. Joel was watching the waves. Oh! (it was nothing, a speck of dust brushing by!) the shell has landed in his eye. In and out in a flash. He rubs his eye with his cuff. It's gone. Nothing left but an imperceptible scratch. But from day to day the scratch lengthens into an immense split. And Joel's eye—for God's sake!—Joel's eye looks like the eyes of old people that have turned into coagulated whites of eggs through staring at the fire for too long. And his other eye slyly surrenders to the sleeky evil and looks darkly up to the sky. For God's sake!—Joel has gone blind!... And the spray rises higher and higher over the cliff. Rises higher and higher over the whole of the earth. As white as sugar. And the earth, like sugar, softens under this spread of foam. Like sugar it melts. It melts, caves in, crumbles, runs, oozes. Like a cold lava. And Alfa Romeo and Noel—for God's sake!—are dragged down with the melting earth. Their weightless childrens' bodies float for one tiny instant on the collapsing crest of the blackish wave and then sink. And the earth, the earth clogs their mouths. Shout! Scream! Cry! Make people hear! Make people come! ...'

The whole house shook as Clementine howled and

screamed. But there were no echoes as she ran down the steps and into the garden, calling, sobbing, yelling for her lost children . . . All that she found was the palegrey weather and the distant sound of the waves. Then she thought that perhaps they were asleep. She rushed back in to the house, but half-way there she found a different idea taking hold of her. She darted over to the well and checked its heavy oak cover. Lurching, reeling, staggering, out of breath, she went back home. She went up the steps and searched all over the house, from the cellar to the loft, and then went outside again. All the time she went on calling for them, in a voice grown husky with emotion. Then, with a final stroke of intuition, she ran to the gates. They were open. She flung herself out into the road. Fifty yards outside the garden she met Timortis coming back from the village. He was walking slowly, his nose held high, lost in contemplation of the birds' flight.

She grabbed his collar.

'Where are they? Where are they?'

Timortis jumped. She was the last thing he had expected.

'What?' he said, trying to bring himself down to earth again and focus on what Clementine was saying.

His eyes, broiled by the lightness of the air, danced in front of him.

'My children! They've gone! The gates are open! Who opened them? My children have gone!'

'Of course they haven't gone,' said Timortis. 'I suppose I must have opened the gates when I went out. And if they'd have gone out too, then I'd have seen them."

'It was you!' yelled Clementine. 'You wretch! It was all your fault! So it's thanks to you that my children are lost!'

'But they're not in the least bit interested in going out,' said Timortis. 'You've only got to ask them for yourself. They don't want to go outside the garden at all. Not in the least.'

'That's what they may have told you! But if you don't think my children are clever enough to fool you! . . . Come on! Hurry! Run! . . .'

'Where have you looked?' asked Timortis, grabbing her by the sleeve.

Her words were beginning to make some impression on him at last.

'Everywhere!' said Clementine, sobbing. 'Even down the well!'

'This is a nuisance,' said Timortis.

His eyes automatically rose to the sky for a last time. The three black birds had stopped playing with the sphinxwings and were swooping down and diving back to the earth. In a sudden flash the truth dawned on him. And he immediately rejected it the following second. Pure fantasy! What a stupid idea! All the same, where could they be? And his eyes still followed the downward flight. They disappeared behind a curve in the cliff.

'Come back home,' he said. 'I'm sure they haven't gone outside the house.'

He was the first to run in. Clementine was sobbing behind him, out of breath. Yet she still found time to close the gates behind her once she was back inside them. As they got indoors, Alfa Romeo was coming down the stairs. Clementine flung herself on him like a wild animal. Timortis, feeling suddenly and strangely moved, did not look at her too closely. Clementine covered her child with kisses, asked him a million questions, babbled non sequiturs.

'I was up in the attic with Noel and Joel,' the boy explained as she listened carefully. 'We were looking at all the old books up there.'

Then Noel and Joel came down the stairs too. Their faces were bright and flushed, as if whipped blood were running through their veins. A kind of odour of liberty surrounded them. And when Noel hastily stuffed back into his pocket the silver lining of a cloud that was peeping out, Joel smiled at his brother's carelessness.

She did not leave them until late in the evening, spoiling them more than ever, showering them with tears and covering them with kisses, as if they had just escaped from some man-eating monster. She tucked them up in their little blue beds and did not move away until they were deep in sleep.

Then, and only then, did she go up to the next floor and knock on Timortis's door. She spoke for a quarter of an hour. He gave in, understanding completely. Then she went back to her own room and he wound his alarm-clock for the morning. The next day he would go early into the village to fetch the workmen.

XXIII

67 Novembruary

'COME AND see what they're doing,' Alfa Romeo said to Joel. He was the first to notice the new noise coming from the gates.

'I don't like to,' said Joel. 'Mummy will be upset if we do, and she'll start crying again.'

Alfa Romeo tried to make him change his mind.

'She won't find out,' he said.

'She might,' said Joel. 'And when she cries she kisses you while her face is all wet. It's horrible. And it's all warm.'

'I don't mind it,' said Noel.

'Anyway, she can't stop you looking,' said Alfa Romeo.

'Well, I don't want to upset her,' said Joel.

'It won't upset her,' said Alfa Romeo. 'She likes crying. And then she's got an excuse to pick us up and kiss us.'

Noel and Alfa Romeo went off together, with their arms round each other's necks. Joel watched them go. Clementine had told them not to go anywhere near the men while they were working. Naturally.

But at that time of day she's always busy in the kitchen and the noise of the frying and the banging of the saucepans stops her hearing anything that's going on outside. And when you get down to brass tacks it's not terribly naughty to go and watch the workmen so long as you don't talk to them, after all. What are Noel and Alfa Romeo up to now?

To make a change from flying, Joel began to run to catch up with the other two. He ran so quickly that he skidded on the gravel and almost fell at the turn in the path. He steadied

219

himself and set off again. He smiled to himself. He'd forgotten how to walk!

Alfa Romeo and Noel, their arms outspread, were standing side by side. And there, where the garden wall and the great golden gates should have risen up, Alfa Romeo and Noel found themselves, with some astonishment, face to face with nothing.

'Where's it gone?' said Noel. 'Where's the wall?'

'I don't know . . .' mumbled Alfa Romeo.

Nothing. Just clear, empty space. A total absence of every-thing—as sharp and sudden as a razor slash—rose up before them. Far above it was the sky. Joel was intrigued and went over to Noel.

'What's happened?' he asked. 'Did the workmen take the old wall away?'

'They must have done,' said Noel.

'There's nothing left,' said Joel.

'I don't know what it can be,' said Alfa Romeo. 'What have they done? It hasn't got any colour. It isn't even white. And it certainly isn't black. What *is* it made of?'

They went nearer.

'Don't touch it,' said Noel. 'Don't touch it, Alfa Romeo.'

Alfa Romeo hesitated for a while, then put out his hand. But he stopped before his fingertips quite touched the vacant space.

'I daren't,' he said.

'You can't see anything more where the gates used to be,' said Joel. 'Before you used to be able to see the road and the corner of the fields . . . Remember? Now it's all empty.'

'It's like when you've got your eyes shut,' said Alfa Romeo . . . 'yet we've got our eyes open. And we can't see anything more than the garden.'

'It's as if the garden was our eyes,' said Noel, 'and as if that—as if *that* was our eyelids. It's not black, and it's not white, and there's no colours . . . just nothing. It's a wall of nothing.'

'Yes,' said Alfa Romeo, 'that's what it is. She's had a wall built out of nothing so that we won't want to go out of the garden. This way, everything that isn't the garden is nothing —and we can't go there.'

'But isn't there anything else left?' said Noel. 'Is there only the sky now?'

'But that's enough for us!' said Alfa Romeo.

'I didn't think they'd have finished so soon,' said Joel. 'We could hear them hammering and talking. I thought we were going to look at them working. This is boring. I'm going in to see Mummy.'

'They might not have finished all the wall . . .' said Noel.

'Let's go and see,' said Alfa Romeo.

So Noel and Alfa Romeo, leaving their brother standing there, went off along the path which went round the inside of the wall, right from where it started, and which now formed the border round their new and unexpanding universe. They flew very swiftly, just above the earth, gliding under the low branches of the shrubs.

When they got near to the side of the cliff, Alfa Romeo pulled up sharply. In front of them was a long stretch of old rugged wall, with all its stones and the climbing plants which clung to the coping and hung over it like a bristling green crown buzzing with insects.

'It's the wall!' said Alfa Romeo.

'Oh!' said Noel, stopping too. 'But look! You can't see the top of it any more.'

It was slowly disappearing as if it were being conjured away by magic.

'They must be taking it down from the other side,' said Alfa Romeo. 'They're taking down the end of it now. We'll never see any more of it again.

'We can go on the other side,' said Noel, 'if we want to.'

'Oh!' said Alfa Romeo, 'we don't need to see it. Anyway, we have much more fun with the birds now.'

Noel said no more. He agreed. Therefore no further commentary was needed. Gradually the bottom of the wall surrendered to invisibility. They could hear the orders given by the team's foreman, the blows of the hammer and pick, and the subsequent cottonwool of silence.

Hurried steps rang out behind them. Alfa Romeo looked round. Clementine was coming along, followed by Joel.

'Come along, Alfa Romeo! Come along, Noel! Mummy's just made a lovely cream cake for your tea. Come along, come along! The first one to kiss Mummy will have the biggest slice of cake.'

Alfa Romeo stood still on the path. Noel winked at him and rushed into Clementine's arms, pretending to be frightened. She held him to her tightly.

'What's the matter, baby mine? Is he all sad? What's worrying you so much?'

'I'm scared,' whimpered Noel. 'There's no more wall.'

Alfa Romeo wanted to laugh. What an actor his brother was!

Joel, with a sweet in his mouth, tried to comfort Noel.

'It's nothing to be scared about,' he said. 'Look, I'm not frightened. I think it's prettier than the old wall, and we'll be much safer in the garden now.'

'My darling!' said Clementine, kissing Noel passionately. 'You wouldn't believe that your mummy would do anything to frighten you, would you? Come along now! Be good boys and come indoors for a nice piece of cake.'

She smiled at Alfa Romeo. He saw that her lower lip was trembling and he shook his head meaning No. When she began to cry, he looked at her strangely. And, then shrugging his shoulders, he finally went over to her. She caressed him convulsively.

'You beastly little devil!' said Joel. 'You've made Mummy cry again.'

He gave him a hard dig with his elbow.

'Oh no! Don't do that,' said Clementine.

Her voice was damp with tears.

'He's not a beastly wicked devil. You're all lovely and kind and nice and you're all three of you my little chicks. Come on, come on, come and see my lovely creamy cake. Come along!'

Joel began to run, and Noel ran after him. Clementine took Alfa Romeo's hand and dragged him with her. He joined in with them, but his eyes were the colour of mild steel. He didn't like her hand grabbing his wrist so tightly. It made him feel caught and uncomfortable. He didn't like her tears either. Something akin to pity forced him to stay by her side, although he felt ashamed of it. What he was doing embarrassed him . . . Like the day when, going straight into the maid's room without knocking, he'd found her standing naked in front of a bowl of water with all hair on her tummy and a red towel in her hand.

XXIV

'GOODBYE TO the trees,' thought Clementine. 'Goodbye to the trees and an expensive set of gates and railings. Two insignificant things, I know, but both of them rich in potentiality. And from now on quite a number of accidents of every shape and size are going to find themselves relegated to the domain of eventual death. They're lovely children; they're growing up; they're brimming with health. That's because I boil every drop of water they drink and take a million precautions over everything. As if they could ever be ill when I keep all the bad and evil things for myself. But I mustn't start taking things easily. My watch must be as strict as ever. Just as strict. There are still so many dangerous things left! Even if height and space are suppressed, there still remains the earth. The earth . . . Every kind of rottenness, grime and dirt and microbe all come out of the earth. I must cut off the earth too. Stretch a watertight raft—smothering every risk beneath it—from one wall to the other, from side to side. These walls, these marvellous walls, these walls of absence. They can't be walked through, they can't be banged into, and yet they make an ideal frontier. The purest kind of limitation. Why not a similar kind of earth? An earth annihilating the earth beneath. There'll still be the sky for them to look at . . . and, after all, the sky isn't very important. Oh, I suppose it's true that plenty of bad luck—or worse—could still fall on top of them from up there. But, although I don't on any account want to minimise the immense amount of risks hidden behind the sky, it must still be admitted—and I don't think I'm being a bad mother by overlooking, entirely theoretically, mind you!, this one aspect of the case—it must still be admitted that, as far as immediate dangers are concerned, the sky is the last thing to worry about. But the earth is another matter.'

'Perhaps I could tile over the garden! With quarry tiles. Or white glazed tiles, maybe. But just think of the reflection from the sun into their poor eyes! And suddenly the sun becomes white-hot as a semi-transparent cloud passes in front of it. By a bad stroke of luck the cloud happens to be exactly the same shape as a lens and acts as a kind of magnifying glass. The bunched-up sheaf of rays is all concentrated on the garden. The whiteness of the tiles reflects back the light with an unimagined strength and power. It springs up at the children and fences them inside a cage of rays. Their poor little fists go up to protect their eyes. But they are already trembling, groping, blinded by this furious energy. They fall. They can't see any more . . . For God's sake! Make it rain, make it rain! . . . I'll put down matt black tiles, Lord, matt black tiles. And yet all tiles are hard. So hard. Suppose they should slip . . . Slip after the rain. Or if they should trip over something. Then down they go . . . Noel's flat on his back. There was nobody to see him fall—and now there's an invisible fracture hidden under his fine golden hair. His brothers aren't treating him any more carefully than usual . . . And then suddenly, one morning, we find him going raving mad! We try to see what it is. Everybody's forgotten about his fall. The old sawbones can't make it out . . . And then, suddenly, his skull splits wide open, the fracture has gone all the way round, and off comes the top of his head like a lid. And a horrible hairy monster comes creeping out, trephinating its way through his brainbox. No! No! No! It mustn't be true! It can't be true! Noel, don't fall! You mustn't fall over! Be careful . . . Be careful! Where is he? . . . They're all asleep . . . there, beside me . . . All asleep. I can hear them breathing in their sleep. In their little beds . . . I must be careful not to wake them up. Be careful . . . Not a sound! But none of this would ever happen if the earth were soft and tender and springy—like a carpet made of rubber. Obviously that's the answer! That's what's needed! Rubber! That's it! A carpet of rubber stretching from wall to wall of the garden. And yet rubber burns . . . It could so easily catch fire. It melts and their feet are caught in the stickiness. The smoke chokes them! . . . Stop it! Stop it! Stop it! I don't mean it. I'm telling lies. There's no truth in all this. I don't want any of it to happen. It mustn't be true. It mustn't be possible. It was wrong to try to find something better than the wall. The wall. Of nothing. Nothingness. Obliterate, anul, remove the earth like the wall! They'll have to be got back. The men will have to come back. They must come back. And spread a carpet of invisibility, of utter absence, from wall to wall. They'll stay indoors while it's laid and put down, and then—when it's all finished—all dangers will have disappeared. Apart from the sky, of course. I've given that a great deal of thought—but for the time being I've decided that the most important thing to attend to is the earth. And make sure that there's no more possibility of any harm coming from it . . .'

She stood up. Timortis wouldn't object to getting the men to see about the earth. It was stupid not to have had it all done at once. But you can't be expected to think of everything. Not all at the same time. You've always got to be on the lookout. Always on the watch. And punish yourself for not having taken everything into account. Persevere. Improve upon improvement. A new world must be built for them—fit for them to live in without danger. A clean and pleasant and perfect world—as harmless and as inoffensive as the inside of a white egg floating on a cushion of feathers.

XXV

80 Marchember

ON HIS way back from placing the contract, Timortis went past the church. As the early hour left him plenty of free time, he thought he would go in and have a little chat with the vicar, whose ideas he always found pleasantly stimulating and amusing. He went into the oval of chiaroscuro, deeply inhaled the tasteful religious bouquet like a lecherous old rakehell, and went over to the half-open vestry door which he pushed to ninety degrees. Three little taps preceded this gesture and announced his arrival.

'Come along in,' said the vicar.

He was in his shorts and skipping with a rope in the middle of the cluttered little room. In his armchair the curate was enjoying a glass of lickliquor, very little of which was left. The vicar's limp ruined the elegance of his skipping, but nevertheless, he managed to get over it (and over the rope) very well.

'Goodmorning,' said the curate.

'All hail, Mr Vicar,' said Timortis. 'I thought I'd take the opportunity to call in on you and pay my respects as I was going past your front door.'

'Now that you've done that,' remarked the curate, 'how about a nip of parson's perdition?'

'Don't talk like that,' said the vicar reprimandingly. 'Only the language of luxury becomes the house of the Lord.'

'But we're only in the vestry, vicar of vicars,' observed the curate. 'Which is—as you might say—only God's bog, the Lord's loo, Jesus's john, Christ's can . . . There's a chance to relax out here.'

'Diabolical creature,' said the vicar, damning him with a look. 'I don't know why I still keep you here with me.'

'Oh, but it makes jolly good propaganda for you, vicar,' said the curate. 'And I come in handy for your gala performances, don't I?'

'By the way,' said Timortis, 'what are you thinking of giving us for the next one?'

The vicar stopped jumping up and down, carefully wound up his rope and then let it tumble, jumbled, into a drawer. He stuffed it in tight and pushed back the drawer. As he spoke, he wiped the perspiration from his podgy bolstered thorax with a pale greyish bath-towel.

'It'll be the greatest ever,' he said.

He scratched himself under the arm, then immediately switched to the depths of his navel. Then he shook his head.

'It'll be a show,' he went on, 'whose luxury and splendour will make secular spectacles—where the exhibition of creatures divested of all vestments, denuded of all raiment, serves as a pretext for setting off majestically elaborate scenery—pale in comparison. But more than that, the principal attraction will consist of an ingenious new method of approaching the Lord and getting closer to him. This is what I intend to do. A choir composed of Mary's little lambs, dressed in an unimaginable display of costumes, accessories and ornaments, will tow a golden balloon out as far as Jonah's field, each of them holding one of its thousand silver wires. To the dewy carousel of the cornelian keys of a steam organ, I shall take my place in the basket. Then, as soon as I've reached a suitable height, I shall tip out this curse of a curate, chuck overboard this bad egg, defenestrate this scoundrel of a sexton . . . And God will smile as he watches the unforgettable splendour of this fete and the triumph of his Word of luxury.'

'Hey!' said the curate, 'you might have told me before, vicar. I'll break my neck if you do that!'

'Diabolical creature!' growled the vicar. 'And what about your bat's wings?'

228

'I haven't flown on them for months,' said the curate. 'And every time I try, the carpenter sprinkles the contents of a whole salt-cellar over my bum and treats me like a bird.'

'Well then, it'll be just too bad for you,' said the vicar, 'and you'll get your neck broken.'

'Even so, you'll still be the one must put out,' mumbled the curate.

'Because I'll have lost you? It would be deliverance at last.'

'Ahem,' interrupted Timortis. 'I wonder if I may make a remark. It seems to me that together you make up both sides of an equilibrium. Each of you increases the value of the other. Without a devil, your religion would lose most of its reason for existing.'

'Precisely,' said the curate. 'I'm delighted to hear you say that. Come on, vicar, confess that I am your justification.'

'Clear off, chatting Satan,' yelled the priest. 'You're filthy. You're dirty. You're vermin. And you stink!'

The curate had heard all this—and much worse—before.

'And the rotten thing about you,' he added, 'is that it's always me who gets the rotten parts to play. I don't ever complain, but you still go on shouting and grumbling at me . . . If only somebody would intervene now and again.'

'And what about when I get the stones flung in my face?' said the vicar. 'It couldn't be you—could it?—who whispers in their ears, telling them to throw them at me?'

'If I had any say in it, you'd get more of them more often,' grunted the curate.

'Oh, get away with you. I'm not angry!' concluded the vicar. 'But don't start forgetting your duties again. God needs flower power. God needs Japanese incense. He must have sumptuous homage. Be given sumptuous presents. Gold, myrrh and miraculous visions. And beautiful adolescents like centaurs, with badges of sparkling diamonds. Suns. Dawns. And there you sit, ugly and lousy, like a mangy donkey farting in Our Lady's chamber . . . Let's change the subject. You make me lose my temper. I'm going to push you out of the basket

and that's all there is to it. There's no point in discussing it
further. I'm not putting up with any more.'

'Very well then,' said the curate. 'I just won't fall out.'

He spat out a tongue of flame which toasted the hairs on the
vicar's legs. And he swore, blasphemously.

'Gentlemen,' said Timortis, 'please!'

'Well now,' went on the vicar, coming down to earth again,
'to what do we owe the pleasure of your visit?'

'I was just going by,' explained Timortis, 'and I thought
I'd take the opportunity of coming in to see you.'

The curate stood up.

'I'll go then, Vic,' he said. 'I'll leave you to have a talk
with Mr Whateverisnamis. So long.'

'Goodbye,' said Timortis.

The vicar was sandpapering his legs to get rid of the toasted
hairs.

'What have you been up to lately?' he said.

'Getting along fine,' said Timortis. 'I've just been into the
village to fetch the workmen. There's still plenty for them to
do up at the house.'

'And still for the same reason?' asked the vicar.

'Still the same,' said Timortis. 'The idea that something
could happen to them drives her mad.'

'But if she thought that nothing might happen to them she'd
be just as mad,' stated the vicar.

'Very true,' said Timortis. 'That's why I thought at the
beginning that she was exaggerating the danger. But I must
admit that now this frenzy to protect them from everything
makes me feel a certain respect for her.'

'What splendid love!' said the vicar. 'This admirable luxury
of precaution! I hope that at least they've got some idea of all
the things she's doing for them?'

Timortis didn't answer straight away. He had never considered the question from this point of view and he hesitated for
a few seconds.

'That I wouldn't know . . .'

'That woman is a saint,' said the vicar. 'And yet she never comes to church. Can you explain that to me?'

'Nobody could,' said Timortis. 'But the fact is that there's no connection. You must see that. And that's the real explanation.'

'I suppose so,' said the vicar. 'I suppose so.'

After this they remained silent for a long time.

'Well then,' said Timortis, 'I'll be off.'

'Yes,' said the vicar. 'You'll be off.'

'I'll go then,' said Timortis.

And after saying goodbye to the vicar he went away.

XXVI

THE SKY was dogtoothed with dull yellow threatening clouds. It was cold. In the distance the sea was beginning to sing in a very unpleasant key. The garden crouched under the resonant metallic light that heralds a storm. No earth was left after the last transformation. All that stood out from the space and emptiness were sparse and far-spaced flower beds, and those small shrubs and bushes that had escaped when the trees were massacred. And the gravel paths remained intact, dividing the invisibility of the earth into two.

Furtively the clouds closed in on each other. As they met a dull, humming, buzzing sound could be heard at the same time as a ruddy glow sprang up between them. The whole of the sky seemed to be hanging concentrated above the cliff. When it had become nothing but a huge heavy dusty carpet, a great silence fell. And behind this silence, the wind could be heard coming, softly at first, then leaping lightly over the agile rooftops and swift chimneys, but soon growing harder, sturdier, wrenching a sharp, anguished, skirmishing zoom from every cornerstone it passed, bending and banging the weary heads of the flowers, chasing the first blade-edges of water before it as it went. Then the sky cracked with one wild blow, like a piece of dead china, and the hail began. Bitter stones exploding as they battered on the slates of the roof, sending up a spray of hard crystal gunpowder. Little by little the house disappeared in the deep, dark vapour. The hailstones struck still more savagely on the paths and sparks shot off and dropped back dead at each point of impact. The continuous jolts and shocks made the sea begin to rise and bubble like boiling black milk.

Once the first horrified shock was over, Clementine went to look for her children. Fortunately they were in their room. Quickly she gathered them all together round her in the big living room on the ground floor. It was completely dark outside and the sombre fog in which the windows were swimming grew alternately opaque and translucently phosphorescent in the lamplight.

'And all it would have needed would have been for them to have been outside,' she thought, 'for me to find them hashed into mincemeat by the hail, crushed under these eggs of black diamond, stifled by this dessicated dust which it is impossible to breathe but which insidiously fills up their little lungs. What kind of protection would do the trick? A roof? A roof built right over the garden? It would hardly be worth it. The house is just as good—even better; certainly tougher and stronger—than any superimposed roof. But wouldn't the house itself cave in if this hail went on for hours? For days and weeks? Shouldn't all the dead dirt and dust accumulated on the roof be enough to cave in the roof-trusses? What would be really needed is a room built of steel, a perfectly invulnerable room, a complete shelter. And they'd have to be kept in a powerful strongbox, a kind of safe of the type that highly priced jewels are always kept in. Caskets of unlimited strength, as indestructible and hard as the bones of time, are what they need. That's what must be put up here for them tomorrow. Tomorrow.'

She looked at the three children. Heedless of the storm, they were playing together, peaceful and relaxed.

'Where's Timortis? I must discuss the best possible answer to all this with him.'

She called the maid.

'Where's Timortis?'

'In his room, I think,' said Whitarse.

'Would you mind fetching him?'

233

The high-pitched sound of the frothing sea numbed the ear. There were no signs of the hail decreasing or breaking up.

A few minutes after the maid had gone out, Timortis appeared.

'I think I've got it,' said Clementine. 'I think I've found the final solution.'

She laid before him the results of her reflections.

'. . . And like that,' she said, 'they'll never ever risk anything again. But I find I'm obliged to ask for *your* help once more.'

'I've got to go to the village tomorrow,' he said, 'so I'll have a word with the blacksmith on the way.'

'I can't wait till then for it to be done,' she said. 'When it's all over I'll be so much more at ease for their sakes. I've always been sure that one day I'd find the way of totally protecting them from all ultimate evils and harm.'

'You could be right,' said Timortis. 'I don't know . . . This is going to need every minute of your entire devotion.'

'It's nothing to devote yourself completely to someone you're sure of keeping,' she replied.

'They won't get much exercise,' said Timortis.

'I'm not sure that exercise is all that healthy for them, anyway,' remarked Clementine. 'They're very delicate children.'

She sighed.

'I've got the feeling that I'm very near to the end,' she said. 'It's extraordinary. It's making me feel slightly tipsy.'

'You'll be able to take it easy once it's all over,' he remarked in an ambiguous tone.

'Will I? I'm not sure yet. I love them so much that I've got no more interest in anything for myself.'

'Providing you've got the patience to keep it up . . .'

'Whatever it means,' she concluded, 'it will be heaven after all I've been through already! . . .'

XXVII

14 Jularch

THROUGH THE gaps in the hedges the slow and somnambulistically peaceful animals could be seen munching at the low grass in the fields. On the dry deserted road no signs remained of the previous day's hailstorm. The wind blew the bushes, making their speckled shadows dance in the pale sunshine.

Timortis looked at it all in careful detail—at all these landscapes, seascapes, goatscapes that he would never see again. The day was drawing near when he should take the place that fate had reserved for him.

'Suppose I hadn't taken the cliff path,' he thought. 'The 28th of August. And now the months have all grown so strange and muddled ... Time in the country passes more quickly ... Without landmarks, without milestones ...'

'And what have I assimilated, after all? What have they given to me out of their own free will? Could they ever communicate *anything* to me?'

'Glory Hallelujah died yesterday. And I'm going to take over. With a void at the beginning, I had too heavy, too hard a handicap. Shame, all the same, is the thing that is still the most widespread ...'

'But I had no business trying to plumb their depths. I had no business trying to find out all these things. Why did I want to be like them? Must one necessarily end up with just this, this alone, because one has no prejudices?'

Once again he saw that day when the sphinxwings were dancing in the air. He went over all the steps he had taken along this over-familiar road. They weighed heavily on his legs

235

and he suddenly felt terribly weary. Why take so much time to say farewell to something gone over so often? Why find it so hard to break loose? Why did I stay so long in the house on the cliff? It will have to be left tomorrow to go and live in Glory Hallelujah's gold.

The house. The garden. And beyond them, the cliff—and the sea. Where is Angel now, he wondered. Where did he go on that doubtful contraption which tottered away at the centre of the ocean?

With the golden gates behind him, he went down the path on the cliff till he came to the strand with its damp pebbles, the fresh spiky smell of the sea, and the fringe of fine foam on the shingle.

Nothing was left to show that this was the spot where Angel's departure had taken place. Just a few stones blackened by the blaze of the burning launching path. That's all. His eyes automatically went upwards. And he stood stock still, transfixed.

The three children were running towards the edge of the cliff as fast as they possibly could. Their silhouettes were shrinking because of the distance and the sharp angle of his observation. They were running as if they were going over flat ground, ignoring the rolling stones under their feet, unconscious of the dangerous drop into space, apparently seized by a fit of madness. A single slip and they would fall right over. One trip, and I'll be picking up their broken, blood-spattered corpses at my feet.

The path which they were following was the one used by the Customs and Excise Men and shortly ahead of them was an abrupt drop. None of the three showed any signs whatsoever of thinking of stopping when they came to it. They must have forgotten.

Timortis's nails dug into the palms of his hands. Should he shout? And risk making them fall over? Obviously they couldn't see the drop which was only visible from where he was, below.

236

Too late. Alfa Romeo, who was leading the others, tackled it. Timortis's nails—his whole fists—were completely drained of blood as he closed his eyes and shuddered. The children's heads turned towards him. Saw him. And then, launching themselves into space, they swept round in a hairpin bend, swerved down and landed at his side, babbling, laughing, giggling as gaily as month-old swallows.

'Did you see us, Uncle Tim?' asked Alfa Romeo. 'You won't tell on us, will you?'

'We were playing at pretending we didn't know how to fly,' said Noel.

'Isn't it fun?' said Joel. 'Would you like to join in with us?' It was all clear now.

'Then it *was* you the other day with the birds,' he said.

'Of course,' said Alfa Romeo. 'We saw you too, you know. But we were trying to see how fast we could go—that's why we didn't stop. And you know we haven't told anybody we can fly yet. We're waiting until we can do it really properly like experts so that we can give Mummy a surprise.'

Give Mummy a surprise. And what a surprise she's got in store for you, my lads. This changes everything.

If this is what the situation is, then she just can't. She must be told. She can't be allowed to lock them up under these conditions ... I must do *something*. I must ... I can't allow ... I've still got one day left ... I'm not yet in the boat on the scarlet stream ...

'Go back and get on with your games, boys,' he said. 'I've got to go and see your mother.'

They whizzed off, skimming over the white tongues of the waves, chasing after each other, and then came back to his side, escorting him for part of the way, helping him over the highest and most difficult rocks. In a few moments he was back at the top of the cliff again. With a determined step he hurried off towards the house.

XXVIII

'BUT LOOK,' said Clementine in surprise, 'I just don't understand. Yesterday you agreed with me that it was a good idea. And now here you come telling me that it's absurd.'

'I still agree,' said Timortis. 'Your answer provided them with perfect protection. But one problem still remains. One that you forgot to ask yourself.'

'And what is that?' she asked.

'Well, do they really need all this protection?'

She shrugged her shoulders impatiently.

'It's obvious that they do. I die of worry the whole day long thinking of all the things that might happen to them.'

'Using the word *might*,' stated Timortis, 'is frequently a confession of a lack of power—or of vanity.'

'Don't let's get tangled up in your unnecessary digressions. Try to be slightly normal for once.'

'Then listen to me,' insisted Timortis. 'I'm seriously asking you not to do it.'

'But for what reason?' she asked. 'Tell me what you're talking about.'

'Oh, you wouldn't understand . . .' muttered Timortis.

He hadn't dared to give away their secret to her. He must at least leave them that.

'I think I'm in a better position than anybody else to judge what's good for them.'

'Not quite,' said Timortis. 'They themselves are in a better position than you are.'

'This is absurd,' said Clementine, curtly. 'These children

238

are forever running permanent risks . . . Like all children do, anyway.'

'They know how to look after themselves in ways that you don't,' said Timortis.

'Well,' she said, 'you don't love them like I love them, and you don't understand the things I feel and go through.'

Timortis stayed silent for a moment.

'Of course not,' he said, eventually. 'How could you expect me to love them like that?'

'Only a mother could understand me,' said Clementine.

'But birds die in cages,' said Timortis.

'They live very well in them,' said Clementine. 'It's even the only kind of place where they can be really suitably looked after.'

'Good,' said Timortis. 'I can see that there's nothing more that I can do then.'

He got up.

'See you later then. Although I probably won't be seeing you again.'

'When they've got used to it,' she said, 'perhaps I'll be able to get into the village now and again. But I find your objection all the more difficult to understand since you're going off to lock yourself up in the same kind of way.'

'But I'm not going to lock other people up,' said Timortis.

'Me and my children are one flesh,' said Clementine. 'I love them so much.'

'You've got a funny idea of what the world's all about,' he said.

'I thought the same thing about you. There's nothing funny about my ideas. They're my world.'

'No, you've got it muddled,' said Timortis. 'You want to be their world. And if you look at it from that point of view, then it's extremely destructive.'

He went over to the door and went out of the room. Clementine watched him go.

'I don't think he looks very happy,' she thought. 'He must have missed his mother.'

XXIX

THE THREE golden moons, one for each of them, came down
and landed in front of the window-panes and played at pulling
faces at the three brothers. All three of them, in their night-
shirts, were squeezed into Alfa Romeo's bed. They could see
the moons better from there. At the foot of the bed their
three tame bears were dancing in a ring and singing *The
Lobster's Lullaby*, but very quietly, so as not to wake Clementine. In between Noel and Joel, Alfa Romeo was thinking
hard. Something was hidden in his hands.

'I'm trying to remember the words,' he said to his brothers.
'The ones that begin . . .'

He suddenly stopped.

'I've got it. This is how it goes.'

He put his hands to his mouth, without separating them,
and said a few words in a quiet low voice. Then he put what
he was holding on the eiderdown. A little silver grasshopper.

Instantly the bears ran and sat round it.

'Mind,' said Joel. 'Nobody else can see.'

The bears shifted so that their backs were against the foot
of the bed. And then the grasshopper bowed to them and
began a series of acrobatic tricks. The children were filled with
obvious delight.

But it soon got tired. Blowing them a kiss, it made a very
high leap and didn't come down to land again.

But nobody minded. Alfa Romeo raised his finger.

'I know another trick!' he said, bombastically. 'When we
find some furry fleas, we have to let them nip us three times.'

'What happens then?' asked Noel.

'Then,' said Alfa Romeo, 'we can grow as small as we like.'

'And creep under doors?'

'Under doors, of course,' said Alfa Romeo. 'We can become as tiny as fleas.'

The bears, growing interested too, crept over.

'And if we say the words the other way round, can we grow bigger?' they all asked together.

'No,' said Alfa Romeo. 'Anyway, you're fine the way you are. But I can show you how to grow monkeys' tails, if you like.'

'No fear!' said Joel's bear. 'No thanks!'

Noel's bear scrambled away quickly. The last one thought about it.

'I'll think about it,' he promised.

Noel yawned.

'I'm feeling sleepy. I'm going back to my own bed,' he said.

'So am I,' said Joel.

A few minutes later they were asleep. The only one left awake, Alfa Romeo looked down at his hands and winked. When he winked in a special way he could grow two extra fingers. He'd show his brothers how to do it in the morning.

XXX

THE BLACKSMITH'S apprentice was eleven, and his name was Andy. With his neck and shoulders in the leather harness he was pulling as hard as he could. The dog at his side was pulling as hard as he could too. The blacksmith and his mate were walking silently behind them, giving them a hand when the path was too steep, but flinging fistfuls of curses at Andy with the other one at the same time.

Andy's shoulder hurt, but he was bubbling over with excitement because he was going into the garden belonging to the big house on the cliff. So he pulled harder than ever. The last farm-houses of the village had already been left far behind.

Glory Hallelujah's old barge glided along over the crimson canal. Andy glanced across . . . The old man wasn't on it. It was somebody unusual, dressed in rags like the old man, but with a bright red beard. Motionless, stooping over, he was drifting along with the current, staring into the thick and slippery water. The blacksmith and his mate jeered at him, and then went by, laughing.

The cart was very hard to pull because of the weight of the heavy iron plates. They were massive and thick, with solid square bars toughened by the flames of the forge. It was their fifth journey, and their last. Previously the cart had been emptied in front of the gates and its contents had been taken into the garden by the others. This time Andy was going inside too, so that he could run straight back to the village if the blacksmith needed anything he might have forgotten.

The gritty grey ribbon of the path unravelled ahead of them

as it was trampled over by the child's impatient feet. The wheels squeaked and the cart jogged over the petrified muddy tracks. The weather was grim and overcast—there was neither sunshine nor rain hidden in the dull metallic greyness.

The blacksmith started up a shrill, heartlessly merry whistle. He thrust his hands deep down into his pockets, but made no attempt to hurry.

Andy's heart was beating like mad between the shafts. He wished he was a horse so that he could plod faster.

And he did go faster. His heart almost burst.

At last they reached the turn in the road. The high wall surrounding the house. And the gates.

The cart stopped. Andy was just getting ready to back it through the gates when the blacksmith said 'Stay there and wait,' to him. He was sneering from leer to ear.

'We'll take the stuff inside,' he said. 'You must be worn out.'

He gave Andy a great kick in the guts because he didn't get out of the harness quickly enough. Andy yelped with pain and ran to the wall, with his head in his hands, to hide himself against it. The blacksmith let out a great hairy laugh. He lugged the cart lightly through the gates and slammed them noisily behind him. Andy could hear the sound of the wheels crunching over the gravel, then getting fainter and fainter, until there was no sound at all except the wind rustling in the ivy at the top of the wall. He sniffed, wiped his eyes and sat down. And waited.

. . . .

A sharp kick in the ribs wrenched him from his sleep and he was on his feet again in a flash. Night had slowly been falling. His guv'nor was standing in front of him, looking down at him and laughing.

'I thought you wanted to go in there,' he was saying.

Andy was still half asleep and couldn't get an answer out.

'Go in there and fetch my big hammer. I left it in the room.'

'Where?' asked Andy.

'Get a move on!' barked the blacksmith, raising his hand.

Andy ran in as fast as his legs could carry him. Although he badly wanted to see inside the big garden, he could not stop to look because his feet were making straight for the house. But on the way he got the deep impression of a vast empty space, intimidating without any sunshine. He reached the steps and stopped. He felt scared now. Then, remembering his guv'nor's command, he went on. He had to get the hammer back. He started clambering up the steps.

The light from the living room trickled on to them through the open shutters. The door was ajar. Timidly, Andy knocked.

'Come in!' said a sweet voice.

He went in. He found a tall lady in a beautiful long dress standing there. She looked at him, but did not smile. She had a way of looking at you that made your scalp tighten.

'The guv'nor's forgotten his hammer,' he said, 'and I've come to fetch it for him.'

'I see,' said the lady. 'Hurry up then, sonny.'

When he looked round he saw the three cages. They were at one end of the room and all the other furniture had been taken out of it. Each of them was just large enough to hold a rather small person. Their thick square bars concealed most of what was inside them, but there was something moving there. Inside each of them was a cosy little bed, an armchair and a tiny table. They were lit by an electric light from the outside. As he went over to them to fetch the hammer he caught a glimpse of yellow hair. He searched carefully, slightly embarrassed because he could feel that the lady was watching him. Then he spotted the hammer. As he bent down to pick it up he opened his eyes wide. As his eyes met theirs, he realised that little boys were in the cages. One of them called out for something and the lady opened the door and went in to him, saying words that were so sweet, so sweet, although Andy could not understand them. And then once more he felt the lady's eyes flash into his as she came out, so he hurriedly said 'Goodbye' to her and started walking, his arm nearly dragged out of its socket by the weight of the heavy hammer. When he got to the door, the sound of a voice held him back.

'What's your name?'

'My name's . . .' another voice began to say.

That is all that he heard because, gently yet firmly, he was pushed out. He went down the stone steps. His thoughts were reeling. And when he reached the great golden gates he looked back for the last time. How wonderful it must be to be able to stay all together like that, with somebody to cuddle you and rock you to sleep in warm little cages crammed with love. He set off for the village. The others hadn't bothered to wait for him. The gates slammed behind him with a final resounding clang. A gust of wind had probably caught them. It went on whistling between the bars.

About the Author

During his brief lifetime, Boris Vian (1920-1959) worked in the capacity of novelist, playwright, poet, journalist, actor, scriptwriter, translator, painter, composer, jazz trumpeter, engineer, and mechanic. In 1952, Vian joined the College of 'Pataphysics, a group of writers whose members included Raymond Queneau, Eugène Ionesco, and Jacques Prévert. Also involved in a number of other intellectual and artistic circles, he was close friends with Jean-Paul Sartre and Albert Camus.

As a writer, Vian proved to be quite prolific, publishing over a dozen novels and plays, and translating numerous American detective novels into French, including Raymond Chandler's *The Big Sleep*. Vian's greatest success—and greatest curse—was *J'irai cracher sur vos tombes* (*I Spit on Your Graves*), a witty pastiche of the American thriller genre. Originally published under the name Vernon Sullivan (supposedly an African-American writer) with Vian credited as the translator, the book quickly became a bestseller in France. In 1959, Vian was involved in a project to adapt the novel into a movie, until a series of artistic differences led to his removal from the project. Tragically, Boris Vian attended the movie's premiere, where he reportedly stood up during the opening scenes and yelled, "These guys are supposed to be American? My ass!" just before dying of a heart attack. He was 39 at the time of his death.